Jealous Murder

River View Series, Book Four

Jeanette Taylor Ford

Cover by Dave Slaney

PUBLICATIONS

1

ISBN: 978-1-9993107-2-1

Disclaimer: this is a work of fiction. Although places mentioned in Herefordshire are real, with the exception of the village of Sutton-on-Wye, this book does not reflect or suggest anything untoward in those places, particularly in the case of The Black Swan in Leominster. Apart from the name – picked because of its distinctive look in the town – I have no knowledge of the real owners, staff, layout of the pub or its customers. All those who people the pub in my story are completely fictitious.

Yet again, I must thank my editor, Angela, for her hard work making my work presentable.

And thanks, Dave, for yet another wonderful cover.

Jealousy Is Murder

Prologue

The figure, clad in black from head to toe, crept stealthily into the compact lounge of the small terraced house in Portsmouth. It was hot in the room, as the gas fire was on full blast. A half empty mug sat on the small table beside the sofa, on which sprawled a man in his late twenties, handsome under his pallor and five o'clock shadow. He was fast asleep, his head lolling to one side on a cushion and legs outstretched before him, heels resting on a colourful rug,

The glow from the fire caught on the blade of the knife, honed to lethal sharpness, giving the momentary illusion that it was a beautiful thing. The eyes of the perpetrator held no emotion as they gazed upon their target to make sure the hit would go in exactly the right place. Then, with a slight 'shwooshing' sound, made by the assailant's all-enveloping garment, the knife found its mark with unerring accuracy. The victim's eyes flew open, the mouth moved in a gasp of surprise, then he slumped as death bore him away.

Not stopping to gaze further, the murderer went over the house, treading in plastic-covered shoes, picking up items of value in hands protected by rubber gloves, then left the house by the back door, leaving it open and creaking in the breeze blowing off the English Channel.

Chapter 1
End of May, Eight Years Later
The Olde Village Shoppe, Sutton-on-Wye, Herefordshire.

"Oh, my goodness, Len! You'll never guess who's just been on the phone."

Madge greeted her husband as he came in from making a late delivery.

"Who's that then?" he replied as he dumped his jacket on a chair. She didn't bother to nag him because she know he'd put it away after he'd listened to her.

"Pauline."

"What – our Steve's Pauline?"

"Yes, dear – that Pauline."

"What did she want?"

"She wants to visit us." Madge sat down as if her knees had run out of strength.

"Goodness! When? What have we done to deserve that?"

"Tonight. She wants to stay the weekend. Apparently, she has to go up to Yorkshire for some reason and thought it would be nice to come and see us."

"Blimey! Nice for who? We haven't seen hide nor hair of her for years – how long?"

"Oh, must be at least six – about two years after our Steve..."

Madge dabbed at her eyes and Len patted her shoulder awkwardly.

After a few moments, Madge got up again and gave her husband a quick peck on his cheek.

"I'm going to pop out, love. I need to walk it off or I won't deal with her. Would you shut the shop please?"

"Of course, girl. Off you go, and try not to worry, like." Len knew her well. She didn't often get into a flap but Pauline had that effect on her, and thinking about Steve always upset her.

She took her coat from the back room and let herself out of the shop.

****

Lucy was giving John and little Rosemary their tea when a knock came at her kitchen door. She opened it to find her best customer there.

"Madge! This is a surprise. Come in."

Lucy took in Madge's white face, pulled out a chair for her to sit at the kitchen table and poured her a cup of tea from the large white pot with coloured spots.

"Oh, thank you, my dear," said Madge gratefully and put her hands around the cup as if to warm them.

"Are you okay, Madge? You look rather pale."

"Oh, am I? I suppose I may be, I've just had a bit of a shock. I've been walking to try to calm myself down a bit. I could have called you, but as I was out, I thought I may as well drop by, like."

"Well, I'm always happy to see you. So, is there something I can help you with?"

"Yes please. I'm – we're – having a visitor over the weekend and I wondered if you could bake a couple of extra loaves for me and maybe some posh sort of cake or flan or something? I don't mind what it is, but you know that Saturdays are really busy for me at the shop and I won't have time to bake. I wish she'd given me more notice."

"She?"

"Yes – it's Pauline, my ex-daughter-in-law, my son Stephen's wife."

"Ah," Lucy knew immediately what the problem was. Madge had told her some time ago about her son's untimely and brutal death. It had been attributed to a burglary, as several valuable items had gone missing. There had been a spate of robberies, some with violence, in the area. Stephen was supposed to be out that night with his wife and some friends but he'd stayed

5

at home because he was not feeling well. His wife had returned home very late, to find him dead on the sofa. He'd been killed by a single stab-wound in his heart; the time of death somewhat confused by the heat in the room from the full-on gas fire.

A man had been arrested for the robberies and Stephen's murder. David Ackroyd was now serving a long sentence for the robberies with violence and the murder.

"I never really took to her, you know, Lucy, but she was our son's choice and so we did our best. I always got the feeling that she looked down on us – just being small shop-keepers – you know, like."

Madge sipped her tea, falling silent. Lucy wiped her children's faces and lifted the baby out of the high chair. John took his sister's hand and together they went into the next room. Lucy followed them and saw they were settling down to play with the Duplo and went back to continue her conversation with Madge. She knew her children would be fine playing together; John was a placid little boy with a kind and generous nature – like his father, Lucy thought – and he always knew how to keep Rosemary happy, beyond a child of his years.

"You haven't seen Pauline for ages, have you?" Lucy sat at the table and poured herself a cup of tea.

"Not since that David Whatsit got put away – got to be at least six years. She married again to some rich playboy she met, Mark Norton-Smythe. Sends us a card at Christmas, like, and that's about it. Could have knocked me down with a feather when she rang, like. Can't think why she'd want to visit us."

Lucy picked up the teapot and gestured questioningly. Madge pushed her cup and saucer towards her and Lucy poured. She watched as Madge absently spooned sugar in and stirred her drink.

"Don't get me wrong, Lucy, I don't mind her coming. It might be nice to see her, but..."

"It's brought back the memories."

"Yes. Oh, Lucy, it's so awful to have your child die, let alone in such circumstances. I can't believe that man killed my lad for the sake of a few bits of jewellery."

"It does go beyond understanding."

"He never killed anyone at his other robberies. He did hit a bloke who came upon his burgling his house but he reckoned he only did that out of shock because he thought no-one was there, like. He's always claimed he didn't kill our Steve. And, although I don't much like her, what must it have been like for Pauline, coming home from a night out and finding him dead?"

Lucy nodded. "Must have been a shock."

"I'll say. I did feel for her. They'd only been married about six years and a lot of that time he was at sea, being in the Navy, like. He was home because he'd just left the Navy and was about to start a new job on land."

"They had no children then?"

"Sadly, no, although in the circumstances perhaps it was just as well. They'd decided to wait until he came out of the Navy so he could be a full-time father. Apparently, they'd been hoping that it would happen when he started his new job, but he was taken too soon."

"How sad. Does she have any now?"

"Yes, she has two daughters, although the elder one is a step-daughter from his first marriage."

"At least she's had a happy ending then. What time are you expecting her?"

"About nine, I think." Madge checked her watch and stood up hastily. "Goodness! I've been out much longer than I intended. Len'll think I've got lost. I've to clean up and make the spare bed. Thanks for the tea and the chat, I feel better now, able to cope."

"I'm glad. I'm always here if you need me, you know."

Madge patted Lucy's hand. "You're a good lass and a good friend. It was a great day that brought you to our village."

Lucy smiled. "I couldn't bear to be anywhere else. I'll bring you what you need tomorrow."

The two women hugged and Lucy shut the door behind Madge and went to make sure that Ken's meal would be ready for him when he came home.

****

Madge didn't particularly want to rush home, although she had to, having realised how little time she had to prepare for Pauline's arrival.

She had to admit she wasn't looking forward to this visit, for, although she hadn't actually admitted to Lucy, she wasn't overly sure she liked her daughter-in-law that much. She hoped the visit would go smoothly...

Chapter 2

Pauline arrived around nine forty-five. She looked tired.

"Sorry to be so late. Got stuck on the motorway – an accident. You know what it's like," she said, as she bent to air-kiss Madge.

"Well, at least you're safe, that's the main thing. Would you like something to eat? I made a nice casserole, just in case."

"Oh, no thanks, I'm not hungry. I'm ready for bed, if I'm honest." Pauline stifled a yawn. "Sorry."

"No problem, my dear. Your room's ready. Perhaps you'd like a drink? Coffee? Tea? I've got Horlicks, or hot chocolate. Or perhaps a nightcap?"

"A cup of tea would be just the thing, thank you. I need to call Mark, let him know I've arrived safely. He does worry, poor darling."

"I'm sure. Why don't you go on up and I'll bring your tea when it's ready?"

"You're an angel, I'll do that."

"Do you remember the way?"

"Of course. Thank you. We'll have more time to chat tomorrow evening. Goodnight, Len."

"Night, love. Hope you sleep well."

"I'm sure I shall. I'm half-way there already."

Madge hastened to put the kettle to boil and heard the slight creak as Pauline climbed the stairs. She couldn't help sighing with relief that, for this evening at least, she'd escaped having to entertain their visitor.

****

The shop had been open for two hours when Pauline put in an appearance the following day. She came into the shop, looking like she was dressed for a country garden party, hair immaculate, finger nails so newly painted that Madge could smell it.

"Sorry I'm so late up, Madge. I must have been very tired."

"It's no problem, my dear. You have perhaps been overdoing things lately and needed the sleep?"

"That will be it, I expect. But your bed is so gorgeously soft and cosy that I didn't want to get up – and it was so nice not to have the girls running around and shouting. I could learn to live with that."

Pauline gave a delicate laugh and Madge smiled. "Len will look after the shop for a while and I'll do your breakfast."

"It's alright, don't bother. I don't have much; a cup of coffee and some toast is all I need. I'm sure I can manage that myself."

"Well, I'll come and make sure you can find everything."

In the kitchen, in spite of Pauline's statement that she could manage, she sat at the table and allowed Madge to serve her coffee.

"Are you sure you want toast? I have some wonderful fresh bread here, baked by our own Lucy especially for our shop. It seems a shame to toast it."

"Mmm, looks lovely. I'll just have a slice then."

Madge put butter and strawberry jam on the table and Pauline took a piece of bread, buttered it and spread it with the jam. She examined the lid. "'Aunt Bea's Pantry, Herefordshire.' Not heard of that before."

"It's Lucy's business; she took it over when her aunt died and kept the name. She makes jam and jellies, preserves, chutneys and all sorts with the fruit she grows as well as bread and cakes for me and the nursery cafe."

"Ah, the nursery – the hub of the village! And how is the luscious Kenny?"

Madge watched with a certain amount of distaste as Pauline set down her bread and licked delicately at her finger with its violent red nail. She must have done them again this morning, Madge mused, for she was sure the nails had been pink last night.

"Married to Lucy."

10

"Hmm. She's done alright for herself, whoever she is. Inheriting a business and managing to hook the most eligible bachelor in the village. Must be quite a woman."

"She's a lovely person and she works hard with her business – and a good friend," replied Madge sharply, noting the expression in Pauline's face and not liking it.

"Hit a raw note there, have I, Madge? Perhaps I should meet this enigmatic and resourceful female."

"You should leave her alone. She's a nice girl and a good mother and loves living here. She's helped a lot of folks in the village in various ways; the village is all the better for her being here."

"Is that so? What it is to be so adored! Well, I'll say this for her, she's a great bread and jam maker. That was delicious."

Madge was glad to see the calculating look on Pauline's face had cleared and was now showing only signs of approval for the food. Inwardly, she heaved a sigh of relief and then wondered why, for surely Pauline couldn't create any problems for Lucy? No, she dismissed that thought; Pauline just didn't like the thought that someone could catch Kenny. She remembered how she'd attempted to flirt with him when she'd visited them with Stephen, much to her son's and Kenny's discomfort.

"So, what will you do today? I'm sorry that Saturday is always such a busy day for Len and me. If you'd given us more notice, we might have been able to get someone else in to run the shop today and spend the time with you."

"Oh, don't worry. To tell you the truth, it's a joy for me to be able to have time to myself. Between my family and my business responsibilities, I don't get much 'me' time. My husband often has to go away on business, so I'm on my own with the girls. I'm going to wander around the village and maybe take a drive out into the countryside. Don't worry about me, Ill be fine and I'll probably eat lunch in a pub somewhere. It'll be lovely and I'll spend the evening with you and Len – and part of tomorrow too, before I have to leave."

"Well, if you're sure. I feel terrible that we're not being proper hosts. Would you like anything else to eat? More coffee?"

"I won't have anything else to eat, thank you. The bread and jam was delicious but I have to keep an eye on my weight, Mark likes me to keep trim – he's such a fitness freak. But I will have another cup of coffee please."

Madge had just poured the coffee when a call from Len meant she needed to return to the shop. She started to apologise, but Pauline waved it away with her hand.

"You go. I'll be fine."

Hurrying back to the shop, where several customers waited to be served, Madge couldn't help feeling grateful that they couldn't actually spend the day with Pauline. Yet again, she wondered why she felt that way; the woman hadn't said or done anything particularly wrong but Madge's dislike of her had come back strongly. That evening and the next morning would have to be faced but now Madge was far too busy to worry about it.

Chapter 3

"You could have knocked me over with a feather, Lucy. She arrived back from her day out, said she'd had a phone call from her husband and she had to go home right away. She gathered her things and left – just like that. No explanation as to what had happened or anything. Mind you, I was glad. I can't help it, I just don't like her, can't tell you why."

Lucy stood talking with Madge, having just made her Monday delivery of bread, cakes and pastries to the village shop.

"How odd. She didn't tell you where she'd been, what she'd done all day or anything? Or when her husband called?"

"No, not a thing. I haven't a clue what she did all day. I'd think her husband had only just called her, or she would have come back earlier, wouldn't she?"

"You'd think so. So, she never got to have any of my special cake then? Shall I have it back? You don't need to pay me for it."

"Oh no, dearie, me and Len are really enjoying it. I'm quite good at cakes, you know, but I've never made one like that. What's it called again?"

"Black Forest. Cherry and chocolate. I don't make it often, but you wanted something special for Pauline."

"Yes, well, she missed out, didn't she? Mind you, it's a good thing I don't make it, going by the amount that my Len has snaffled on the quiet, thinking I wouldn't notice!" Madge laughed fondly, "Although how he thinks I really won't notice, I don't know, seeing as there's not much left. I thought this morning that if I want another piece, I'm going to have to hide it from him."

Lucy chuckled along with her. "Looks like I've found the way to Len's heart!"

"You certainly have. Mind you, he's pretty fond of you anyway, as we all are."

"I'm so lucky to have come here. Even after all this time, I still look around at Kenny and the children, our home and this village and think how blessed I am and then I wonder how on earth I thought I was happy, living and working in London – and going out with James – I must have been crazy."

"Ah, but you didn't know about us then, nor had you met your Kenny. Your aunt was a wise woman indeed."

"Yes. I shudder to think I might just have sold the house and stayed in London when I inherited River View if she hadn't made that stipulation in her will. And Dad wouldn't have met Sheila either."

A silence fell between the two women, as they each thought about how Lucy had come to the village and the things that had happened since. Lucy shook herself from her reverie.

"Anyway, I must get on. I'm glad for you that you were let off the hook regarding your visitor. Let's hope she takes another several years before she decides to land on you again."

Madge gave an involuntary shudder. "Oh, indeed! I'm not in a hurry to see her again. Thanks again, dear."

"See you tomorrow."

With a smile and a wave, Lucy left the shop, and glancing back through the window, she saw Madge setting to, arranging the loaves and cakes that she'd just delivered.

Climbing into her little van, decorated with 'Aunt Bea's Pantry' and a design of jars of jam and a delectable selection of cakes, Lucy drove home so Kenny could go to work. She always delivered to the shop early, while Kenny watched the children, then later she would take John to nursery school and take baby Rosemary with her while she delivered to the garden centre's cafe, which didn't open until ten o'clock.

It only took a few minutes to drive back to River View. She let herself in through the kitchen door, where Kenny was seated at the kitchen table with the two children. He stood up to kiss her.

"Hello, Sweetheart. How was Madge this morning? Has she survived her weekend guest?"

Lucy repeated what she'd been told.

"Hmm, odd. Mind you, I never did really like her, you know." Kenny unconsciously repeated Madge's words. "I never

14

liked the way she flirted with me in front of Steve. Fortunately, we knew each other well and he knew he could trust me. So horrible what happened to him."

"Yes, absolutely. She's fallen on her feet though, married to a rich bloke and living the high life."

"I think she regretted marrying Steve; she always gave me the impression that she felt a cut above him and Madge and Len."

"Yes, Madge said something similar. She felt Pauline's attitude. Anyway, needless to say, she was more than happy that Pauline took herself off without having to spend an evening. And Madge and Len celebrated by eating most of that cake I made."

"Goodness, they must have been celebrating to eat all that."

"Apparently, Len loves it and keeps pinching bits when he thinks Madge isn't looking."

The two laughed as Kenny picked up his jacket, kissed the top of his children's heads and Lucy and left.

Lucy sat down and poured herself a cup of tea. Another day was under way at River View.

****

While Lucy and her children were quietly enjoying their breakfast, someone else was sitting at a table with breakfast toast sitting on a plate. However, the toast wasn't being eaten but was left to cool while the person paced the room. Eventually, they went to the lounge, pulled a bottle from a drinks cabinet and knocked back a brandy. As the liquid seared the throat, the glass was put down hard on the side and the person started striding again. Something had to be done now that the bitch had been found. She had to be stopped. But how?

Chapter 4
Near the End of August, Same Year

Charlie huffed on the roof window of the camper van and rubbed it with his hand. Ignoring the dirt on his palm, he peered through the glass, his nose flattened against it. He could barely make out the shape of the trees, dark against the moonlit sky. Nothing moved and there was no sound, only the occasional hoot of a nearby owl. He could well be all alone in a world that held nothing but that owl, although presumably there must be some small creature about to meet his maker, courtesy of the winged night creature that would swoop upon it. His stomach rumbled loudly but he had to ignore it, for there was nothing in the dingy camper left to eat.

Sighing, he flopped back onto his bunk and lay down, pulling the scruffy duvet over himself. Wide eyed in the darkness, he wondered how long it would be before his mother came back - or indeed, if she would be back. Every time she left him, he was never sure if he would see her again. He hated being there alone, in the middle of nowhere, with only the trees and an owl for company. However, he hated even more the times when she brought someone back with her and the smells of something obnoxious would invade his space and often he had to lie in his bunk with his fingers in his ears, trying to ignore the noises and the swaying of the old pile of junk they called home. Then, in the morning, he would awaken to comatose bodies sprawled obscenely on the double bed where his mother slept and would hasten to let himself out of the van and down to the stream until his mother shouted for him. He'd learned from bitter experience that it didn't do to hang around when she had 'a friend' there, for he'd often received abuse and punches, or worse, from the said 'friend'.

He'd fallen asleep by the time the door was wrenched open and a feminine giggle seeped through his unconscious. The sound of a heel banging against the metal step and the slight movement of the van as someone tripped through the doorway jerked him fully awake. He sighed when he heard the deep tones of a male voice swearing as he must have stubbed his toe in the darkness, followed by his mother's giggles and the man's laughter as they fell onto the bed. Charlie peered through the chink when a dim light filtered through the crack and he saw the back of a man's head and heard his voice plainly say, 'Oof! I never expected this. Come here, you brazen woman!' His mother giggled again as her bed creaked under the strain of two people and then there was silence as the boy watched them kissing. He lay down, stuffed the duvet around his ears and prepared for a sleepless night.

****

Sunlight streamed through the window, especially where Charlie had wiped it clean. Eyes squinting against the light, he was surprised to recall there had been no rocking and no smell. Puzzled and confused, he shimmied up his bunk so he could peer, very carefully, through the curtain towards his mother's bed below. As far as he could see, there was only one figure in the bed and it was his mum; he could see her bare arm laying on her pillow above her head as she slept on, the curtains still keeping the worst of the light out.

So, where was the bloke? Charlie peered around the other end. No sign of him. Was he outside, perhaps? Maybe having a smoke?

Quietly, he climbed down from his bed and, after slipping his feet into his tatty trainers, tiptoed to the door. He was a master at knowing how to open it without a sound, having had much practise over the years. Pulling the door closed behind him, he jumped nimbly out and peered around the field. There was no sign of anyone, but he saw tracks where a car had been that had not been there when he went to bed. Realising there was no man to worry about, Charlie relieved himself behind a bush and sat on the step of the van to wait for his mother to wake up.

****

He didn't know how long he sat there on the step; it seemed like a long time. His stomach rumbled loudly. What time was it anyway? He thought he'd take a cup to the stream, at least he could have a drink.

He crept to the van. His mother hadn't moved; her arm was still crooked above her head. She must be really tired, he thought. He'd give her a bit longer, so he took a mug from the miniscule sink and made his way to the stream. The day was warming up now and he was glad, for his clothes were not substantial.

It was lovely by the stream. The rippling water looked clear and inviting as the sunlight danced and glinted on the surface. He washed the mug before he filled it and drank, the water was cool and refreshing. He drank a whole mug full, then filled it again and sat on the grassy bank, enjoying the freshness of the warm air on his face. Now, he could hear more sounds than last night, birds singing in the trees and the distant mooing of cows. The field the other side of the stream had long grass that swayed softly in the gentle breeze that occasionally puffed half-heartedly as if it was too tired to make a real effort. The effect was soporific and Charlie felt his eyelids relaxing and slowly shutting until the mug slipped sideways in his hand, spilling the cold water onto his leg, making him jerk back to full consciousness.

The water had temporarily fooled his stomach into thinking it was being fed, but now he was fully aware that the grumbling was more persistent. Enough was enough; his mother had to wake up and they had to find food. Even though she had money, she was so bad at getting food in. She seemed incapable of planning ahead, it was hand to mouth all the time.

Usually, they never stayed in one place for long. It seemed that she couldn't stand to become familiar with a place. They'd been here longer than usual, though, and he'd been glad. The farmer that owned this land had been happy for them to be there "as long as you don't leave a load o' mess around, like" and the wife was nice. Sometimes she gave him something to eat and she spoke to him kindly.

Charlie made his way back to the camper van. He didn't bother to be quiet this time. He put his mug in the sink and called out, "Mum, Mum, wake up. I'm really hungry." There was no answer, so he drew back one of the curtains at the side of her bed to let light in and crawled onto the bed. He put his hand on her shoulder and shook her.

"Mum! Wake up!"

Something made him stop – why didn't she stir? Usually, if he woke her, she'd moan and turn over. Her face was cold. Panic hit him. He pulled down the cover which was right up to her chin and saw dark bruises around her neck. On the telly he'd seen someone touch a person's neck just underneath the ear to see if there was a pulse. Her cold skin made him shiver and he couldn't feel anything, only her coldness. Then he remembered another film where they'd held a mirror to the mouth to see if the person was alive because it had clouded. He knew she had a small mirror in her bag and fished it out. As he held it by her mouth, he prayed, 'Please Mum, be alive.' However, nothing appeared on the mirror. A cold hand grasped him round his heart. His mum was dead. His dad was gone, now his mum was too. They'd both left him, he was all alone in the world. Tears filled his eyes. "Why, Mum? Why have you left me?"

Scruffy he might be and he hadn't had much schooling, but Charlie was a bright lad. As he sat, crying for his mum, he remembered that male voice he'd heard last night. And what about those livid bruises around his mum's neck? In that moment, he knew his mum hadn't just died; she'd been murdered. That man, whoever he was, must have done it. Had he known the boy was there? If he did, would he come back for him?

19

Fear filled his heart. He scrambled off the bed, and opened his mum's handbag. He found a wad of notes in a tatty purse, some loose change and a photograph. He stared at it for a minute; it was of his mother and dad, taken before he was born. They looked so happy. It was the only photograph she'd had of them together, he had to keep it. It slipped away when he tried tucking it inside his shirt, so he reached an old backpack he'd found that someone had thrown out. He stuffed the photograph, the money, and a few items of clothing along with a small, grubby panda that his dad had given him as a baby into the bag. He grabbed a dirty cagoule off the floor, stuck that in his bag, and left the van, shutting the door behind him.

He made his way to the farmhouse, hoping he might see the farmer's wife. Not wanting her to see his bag, he stowed it behind a hedge not far from the road, then wandered into the farmyard.

"Hello there, young Charlie! What are you doing this fine morning? Where's your mother?"

The woman was standing in her doorway and he went towards her.

"Me mum's still asleep, Missus White, and I've waited ages an' ages. I'm so hungry, cos I never had no tea niever."

"Oh, you poor lad! Come you in and I'll make you something. Your mum must be worn out, poor lass."

Charlie nodded, keeping his eyes cast down so she didn't see his tear. She put out her arm and drew him into the kitchen.

"Sit you there, my lamb. I've just made a pot of tea, would you like some?"

At his nod, she poured him a mug-full, adding milk and sugar. Then she liberally buttered a slice of bread.

"There you go, eat that while you wait, like."

Charlie gobbled up the bread. Soon, the wonderful smell of fried eggs and bacon reached his nostrils and he closed his eyes and indulged in the delicious aroma. In no time, a laden plate was laid before him and he looked at her with tears in his eyes as he thanked her fervently.

"Get on wi' it then, lad, I haven't got all day," she said gruffly, and he grinned at her and tucked in.

Afterwards, he had to admit, he felt stuffed, a feeling that he'd rarely had in his life, certainly in recent years. What his mother did with her money, he didn't know, but it didn't come his way in the form of much food, or clothes.

When he'd done, he really wanted to lie down and sleep, but he had to get away, as far as he could manage.

"Fank you, Missus White. That's the best food I've ever had. It will keep me goin' fer ages an' ages. Me mum'll be pleased."

"Aye, well, you're welcome. Take these." She handed him a bag and when he peeked inside it was full of sandwiches. "For your mum. If you're in any trouble, if you need me, you come to me. Understand?"

Charlie nodded. "Yes, Missus White. Fank you, fank you very much. I gotta go now."

He forced himself to walk because he knew she was watching him from her doorway, but as soon as he knew he was out of her sight, he picked up his bag from the hedge and ran as fast as he could, the old backpack bouncing crazily on his back.

Chapter 5
River View Farmhouse

"John, where have you put your boots?"

Lucy was vexed and not a little harassed. It was the day of the Village Fair and Kenny was already there, making sure that everything was running as it should. She'd been up since five, baking for the cake stall. Kenny had done his best to help, taking care of the children while she worked in the kitchen.

"Don't know, Mummy." John's big, serious eyes gazed at her as his bottom lip trembled slightly. She pushed a stray lock of hair out of her eyes and her heart melted. He was so like her beloved Kenny. And, at four years old, he seemed much too serious for a small child.

A knock sounded at the kitchen door and a voice called out, "Helloo – Lucy – want any help?"

"In here, Rowena," called Lucy and Rowena's mop of blonde hair appeared around the door to the living room. She came in, all smiles.

Rowena was fourteen, and her family had recently moved into the village. They'd stayed for a while in a bungalow that Lucy owned while her brother Harry was in hospital, having been injured in a canoeing accident. Rowena's dad, George, worked for Kenny at the nursery and her mother worked part time in the nursery shop. Rowena and Lucy had become good friends because the young girl often came to help the young mother as she was interested in becoming a chef. But she often helped her with the children too.

"Hello, what's up?"

"Oh, not a big crisis! We can't find one of John's favourite boots so we can go to the fair."

Rowena looked at her friend critically. "You look tired."

"I suppose I am. Rosemary is cutting teeth so we've had broken nights and I've been baking cakes since five this morning. I wish I'd taken Kenny and Sheila's advice and not done so much this year. It's getting harder now I have two children, although

22

Kenny's been a great help. I just seem to be tired all the time at the moment."

"Right. Well, you sit down and get the young lady ready and I'll help John to find his boot. Okay, John?"

Lucy sat with baby Rosemary on her lap, smiling as she listened to Rowena making searching for the boot a game for John. She was thankful to be able to have a few minutes to sit and cuddle her baby, although Rosemary obviously didn't want to be cuddled, for she wriggled to be put down, so Lucy set her on the floor and watched her as she rolled around on the carpet. Lucy knew she should be taking the cakes down to the stall, but somehow, she just couldn't seem to move.

"Here we are! Lost boot found." Rowena and John burst happily back into the room. Lucy started to get up.

"No, you stay there. I'm going to make you a cup of tea – have you had breakfast? You did? Right. I'm still going to make you some tea and you're going to stay there and relax. Then John and I will take a little walk down to the field and arrange to have your cakes fetched by someone – no, don't argue – you're worn out."

Rowena soon produced the tea, being familiar with Lucy's kitchen, insisting again that Lucy relax and Lucy let herself be persuaded – she was very tired. Rosemary had fallen asleep on the floor so Rowena gently picked her up and put her in her cot, took John's hand, and Lucy heard the sound of the back door being closed. She leaned her head back into the softness of the chair, silently blessing her teenage friend, and promptly fell asleep.

Twenty minutes later, she was awoken by voices and reluctantly opened her eyes.

"Dan – and Linda! Oh, it's good to see you."

Linda gave her a kiss on the cheek. Dan gazed across at her, smiling.

"We've come to take the cakes down for you," he said, rubbing his hands together.

"I've come with him to make sure he doesn't eat any on the way" laughed his wife and Lucy giggled. Dan was rather partial to her cakes.

He looked offended. "As if I would! That would be stealing and I'm an Officer of the Law," he said, in his best pompous voice.

Lucy laughed and Linda joined in. Soon, all three of them were laughing. Then, deciding someone better do something, Linda nudged her husband. "Come on, we'd better take the cakes or the fete will be over and all Lucy's hard work will have been for nothing."

With the cakes already packed in trays, it was easy to pop them into the spacious boot of Dan's car. They wouldn't let Lucy help, but ordered her to sit down.

"You stay there until the baby wakes up and then come when you're ready. Don't worry about John, Rowena is doing a great job watching over him. We'll see you later. Now – rest, you deserve it."

The house seemed very quiet after they'd gone and Lucy wandered back to her chair. She thought she didn't feel sleepy any more, but discovered she was wrong, and her eyelids closed very easily.

Half an hour later, Lucy opened her eyes, feeling much refreshed. Almost at the same time, she heard the faint cry of her baby and she got up to fetch her.

"We both feel much better now for our naps, don't we, Rosy-Posy?" she talked to the chuckling child as she changed her nappy and made her ready to go out.

Moments later, the pair of them were off down the lane, Rosemary in her pushchair, delighted to be out in the sunshine. It only took a handful of minutes to reach the field at the bottom of River View Lane where all the fun was going on. Joe's wife, Anna, was seated at the gate taking the entrance fees and she greeted Lucy cheerfully.

The field was full of movement with crowds of people walking around, looking at the colourful stalls, tombolas, lucky dips, bottle tombola, plant stalls and all manner of games to keep everyone busy and happy.

At the end of the field nearest the entrance, two lines of vintage cars were parked on display. Lucy walked over to them.

"Hello Dave, Margaret – oh, and there's Ron too! Hello, hello! So great to see you."

She hugged the burley farmer and his wife and then the elderly bewhiskered man who had come towards her with his arms outstretched.

"Hello there, lass. What do you think of The Collection?" asked Ron, proudly waving his hand to encompass the two rows, as if he was the owner, instead of Dave. The farmer and his wife stood, smiling indulgently.

"They look wonderful, I'm sure there will be lots of interest in them. You can really see them properly here. How have you managed to bring them all, Dave?"

"Well, Margaret and I bring one each and Ron brings one – his pride and joy, the Model T of course. And quite a few workers and friends help me by coming in them with their families. They have mostly gone to enjoy the fete while we keep an eye on the cars," Dave replied.

"I must say you folks put on a brilliant show here, what?" commented Ron, his eyes sweeping the field. "There are more here than I expected for a village."

"Our summer fete is famous," laughed Lucy. "People come from the surrounding villages and other places and even from Hereford itself. In fact, it's becoming more and more popular, as we seem to grow each year. It's hard work, but worth it."

"It's a lovely village," put in Margaret. "A nice place to live."

"It is. I love living here. Everyone is so friendly and of course I love our house. You must visit us, now you know where we are. Give me a bit longer until this madam lets me sleep better and you can have a meal with us."

"I'd like that, wouldn't you, dear?" Margaret turned to her husband.

"Oh yes, I'd like to see more of the village and it would be great to come to you," was the reply from Dave.

"Ron too, of course. Oh look, there's Harry!"

"Yes, he loves to help us at shows."

"Well, I think I should find my son. Hope to see you all again later. Bye for now."

Lucy kept a lookout for Rowena and John and found them at last where John was playing on a huge blown-up bouncy castle. Other children from the village were also playing there. She spotted Flora watching the castle.

"Hello Flora. Is Archie on the bouncy castle?" asked Lucy, smiling. The castle was not a straightforward bouncy castle but a conglomerate of passageways and areas with soft play toys and at one place a ball pool, and at yet another was a slide. Lucy understood Flora's anxious expression as she tried to spot her son amongst all the other children.

"Oh, hiya, Lucy. Yeah, Archie's on there somewhere – 'e loves it, it's already 'is second time on it. But there's so much of it and the bigger kids worry me. They sometimes knock the little kids over when they're runnin' around in there."

"Don't worry, I'm sure he'll be fine. John's in there too."

"Oh goodness, 'e's even smaller than Archie."

"What do you think of our village fete then, Flora?" asked Lucy.

"It's grand, I love it, an' so does Archie. We ain't never 'ad the chance to do fun stuff like this afore."

Lucy nodded slowly, put her arm around the other woman's shoulders and squeezed gently. What she understood of Flora's life before she came to the village was sketchy, but she knew the woman's life had completely turned around over the past few months. She'd been married to a man called Jake, who was a violent bully and the employee of one of the worst men Lucy had ever heard of. The same man who had come close to murdering her best friend, Stephanie. Both men were now dead; Steph was safe and Flora had a new life with her son in the village of Sutton-on-Wye. Flora and Archie lived in the flat above the Wye View Restaurant because Stephanie and her husband Alex had moved into a beautiful house on the edge of the village.

"Hi – hi, Lucy, Flora!"

Lucy turned to see the subject of her thoughts materialise out of the crowd. Stephanie and Alex, her husband, came towards them. Alex was wearing a baby sling and a small head with a mop of dark hair was just visible at the top.

"Ah!" Rowena, Flora and Lucy all crowded around to try to look at the tiny sleeping baby. Alex held the sling out in order to give them a better look.

"We thought it would be easier to have her in the sling than to try to push a pram around here," said Stephanie. "But even as small as she is, she gets heavy, so Alex is giving me a break."

"Oh, she's so sweet. And so tiny! Hard to believe that Rosemary was like that not long ago," said Lucy. "How are you feeling, Steph? What's she like at night?"

"She's pretty good. She wakes up for a feed every three hours and goes straight back to sleep, for which I'm thankful. Alex is very good; he helps where he can but I admit I'm tired."

"You'll get used to it. It gets easier once the night feeds stop."

Stephanie and Alex had called their baby Faith Patricia, the second name after Alex's mum, who had died a few years ago of cancer. The couple had been amazed to find they were going to be parents after ten years of marriage, although they'd been so busy building up their business, the Wye View Restaurant, that they'd not really thought of having a family. Now though, they were thrilled. Even though Alex had wanted a son, he'd fallen instantly in love with the little scrap with the mop of dark hair the minute she'd wrapped her tiny fingers around his. Flora had been a welcome addition to the staff of the restaurant, making it easier for Stephanie to take time off to care for her baby.

The sound of a whistle broke into Lucy's reverie. It was the end of Archie and John's session on the bouncy complex. It took some persuading to coax both little boys off the apparatus and to put their shoes on.

"Shall we go to the refreshment tent?" said Stephanie. "I'm dying for a drink."

"Yeah, let's go get a drink, shall we, John?" said Rowena, taking his hand. "If we're lucky, we might get one of your mummy's yummy cakes, if there's any left."

"Cake!" shouted John, and, letting go of Rowena's hand, he scampered after Archie, already on his way towards the doorway of the huge marquee where they would find Sheila in charge of the tea urn.

Chapter 6

They all hurried after the two little boys, concerned they would get lost in the crowds. But they realised they needn't have worried, for both were standing on tiptoe, eyeing the cakes, with Kenny's mum, Sheila, keeping an eagle eye on them.

"Now, John, you can only have one cake. Too much cake is not good for little tummies," said Sheila, patiently removing his hand getting dangerously near the confectionery.

"I got a big tummy, Gan'ma," said John, lifting his t-shirt to show her. She laughed indulgently.

"So you have. It looks like too many cakes have gone into your tummy already. Ah, here's Mummy. And your mummy too, Archie."

"Which cake would you like, John?" asked Lucy and he pointed to a cupcake with lots of icing on the top. "And what about you, Archie?"

Archie choose another cupcake with chocolaty icing and they all sat around a big table with their drinks and cakes. Baby Rosemary sat on Lucy's knee with a biscuit.

"Look – there's Linda and Dan." Rowena pointed to a couple just coming into the tent. She waved frantically at them, they spotted her and came over.

"Can we join you?"

"Course you can. Pull up those chairs." Lucy pointed to two chairs just made vacant. Dan grabbed the chairs and they sat down.

"Phew, it's hot." Dan wiped his brow with a snowy handkerchief. "What would you like to drink, my love?"

"Oh, a cold drink. You know what I like. And bring me one of those cakes too, will you? I don't mind which one. Lucy made them, so they'll all be scrummy," replied Linda.

Dan went off for the supplies and Linda relaxed in her chair. "I'm glad to sit down for a bit. It's a wonderful fair – I've been longing to be here for one, ever since Rowena told me about them. So, where's Harry? And where's the lovely Kenny?"

"Oh, Harry's with Dave's vintage cars and Kenny will be around somewhere, making sure things are running okay everywhere. George and Netta are manning the plant stall for a while, I believe," replied Lucy. "A few of the nursery people take it in turns to man the stall so they all have time at the fair. Oh look – there are Kenny and Harry now."

Lucy watched as her husband joined Dan at the counter, accompanied by a lad of about seventeen, Rowena's brother, Harry. His accident had brought his family to live in the village and were now so much part of it, it was as if they'd always been here.

Lucy couldn't help her heart thumping a bit faster as she watched her husband coming towards them with a bottle of fizzy drink in his hand. After all the years they'd been married – it was coming up for seven – the sight of him still had that effect on her. Their eyes met and he smiled at her; she knew they were both remembering that first summer fair when she'd escaped with a headache and sat under the weeping willow tree near the river where he'd comforted her and made sure she was alright. Although she'd not changed things straight away, looking back, she acknowledged that was the time when she realised that she wanted a man like Kenny rather than the man she was engaged to then. Sometime later, Kenny proposed to her in that same spot, under the willow tree. Never for one moment had she regretted saying yes.

She loved her life; they lived in the lovely farmhouse, called River View, left to her by her Aunt Bea and she ran the business, 'Aunt Bea's Pantry', started by her aunt. They had two sweet children and her husband adored her. What more could any woman ask? Not only that, but her dad had married Kenny's mum, so she had her dad living practically next door. Kenny's business, 'Baxter's Nurseries', was the centre of the village life, providing employment for many residents and also running the main village events – this village fair, the Bonfire Night display and the Halloween party in the village hall. They also provided the huge Christmas tree on the village green every winter.

When Dan, Kenny and Harry joined them, Flora gave her excuses and left with her son. She was never entirely comfortable in Dan's presence, after all, she'd had to face trial and Dan had been the investigating officer in charge. Archie ran off in front of her, oblivious to his mother's feelings.

"I don't think poor Flora will ever feel right around you, Dan," remarked Stephanie. "I can understand it though."

He nodded. "How is she with you?"

"Well, she was apprehensive for a while but I think she's pretty much okay now. We couldn't do without her, she's been a great help since I had Faith. She can turn her hand to just about anything. She doesn't mind what she does, she's always willing."

Dan nodded again. Flora had, after all, saved his sergeant's life.

The conversation flowed gently around the group while they enjoyed their refreshments. They complimented Lucy on the cakes and she accepted their remarks graciously.

A mobile phone rang. It was Dan's. He looked at it and groaned.

"Cooke. Okay, I'll be there shortly." He put the phone in his pocket and put his hand on his wife Linda's. "I'm sorry love, I have to go."

"Oh Dan – can't someone else go?"

"No. I'm the DI on call, remember?"

Linda looked around the group. "That's the reason we travel in different cars. Alright love. I'll see you when I see you."

He bent to kiss her, said 'Sorry' again, waved goodbye to his friends and made his way out of the marquee.

His long-suffering wife waved her glass around in the air. "Story of my life," she said and laughed. Lucy couldn't help but feel sorry for her; even on a Bank Holiday the pair couldn't guarantee having an undisturbed day out together.

Chapter 7

It took Dan about half an hour to reach the village of Moreton-on-Lugg from the village of Sutton-on-Wye. Following the directions he'd been given, he drove through the village and spotted a uniformed policeman standing by a large gate. He rolled down his window to show the officer his ID, then realised it was PC Atkins, who opened the gate to let him through.

"Where am I headed?"

"Just down there, Sir," Atkins pointed across the expanse of field. "But you'll have to drive around the edge of the cornfield, and then through another gateway. You'll see from there."

Grateful that there had been no rain for a long time and he wouldn't be trawling his car through a lot of mud, Dan thanked him and set off, driving carefully to protect his precious vehicle from the worst of the ruts. Dust rose from the ground and he sighed, knowing he'd have to put the car through the car wash at some point. Dan could put up with some dirt, but this was over the top.

Finally reaching the other gate as indicated by Atkins, he was glad to see his sergeant, Graham Grant, talking with a tall, stockily-built man. Other uniformed police officers were busy putting up blue incident ropes. A classic green and white Volkswagen camper van stood beyond them, close to a hedge.

Dan climbed from his car, slamming the door behind him and paced over to the men.

"Right, what do we have?"

"Glad to see you, Boss," replied DS Grant. "This is Mr Tom White, he's the owner of this farm. There is a dead young woman in the van."

Dan shook hands with the farmer. "Did you discover the body, Mr White?"

"Yes, about an hour ago. Called the police straight away, like."

"Better have a look. I'll want to talk with you again in a while, if that's alright? You're looking rather shaky. Is your house nearby? Perhaps you should go with this officer and we'll come to see you there? No need for you to stay here."

"Thank you, I will. I felt alright at first, you know? I'm not usually squeamish, like, but the smell was bad."

Dan grimaced; that didn't sound good. Sounded like the body had been there a while.

"Understandable, sir, and shock takes a while to set in. I don't suppose you're always finding dead people on your land." he joked feebly.

The farmer gave a ghost of a smile, and said, "You'll have a job, there's one heck of a mess in there."

"Oh?"

"Looks like someone was intent on pulling the place apart, like. Anyway, I'll be away to the house."

Donning a protective gown and gloves, Dan grimaced at Grant, who was also ready.

"Right, I suppose we'd better look."

Feeling somewhat reluctant, the two men made their way to the camper and climbed inside. The smell hit them immediately and Dan resisted the urge to gag. It was quiet, still and dim at the bed end because Charlie had only pulled back the one curtain and the window wasn't clean.

It was hard to see properly, but the foot of the bed was nearest to them. Dan realised at once that they couldn't take a proper look without crawling on the bed.

"Can't do it. Need a torch. Can't see a blinking thing and we can't climb on the bed."

"Try this, Sir." Grant handed his boss his mobile phone, with a small torchlight shining from its end. Dan shone it on the figure in the bed. Now, they could see more clearly, especially where the covers had been pulled from her neck.

"Look like bruises around the neck to you, Grant?"

"Yes, Boss."

"Definitely a suspicious death. I did think it might be drugs but now I'm not so sure. Have you called Forensics?"

"Yes. They should be here soon."

"Good. Let's get out of here."

Thankful to be out in the fresh air, Dan looked around carefully. Spotting the tyre marks Charlie had seen, he hunched down.

"Look at this, Grant. Another vehicle has been here."

Grant eyed the marks doubtfully. They were very faint, dust having been blown over them in places.

"Could be the farmer's, Sir."

"We'll ask him. Ah, here's the team now."

Dr Stan Wilson, the pathologist, alighted from his Land Rover and pulled on white overalls. He was a strange sight; you'd be forgiven if you mistook him for a farmer in his beat-up Land Rover, and wearing his tweed suit. His face had a ruddy look that made you think he led an outdoor life, instead of being cocooned in his scrubbed and clinical lair where he dissected cadavers for the police, searching for clues to lead to murderers. His Herefordshire burr would mislead you even further. However, Dan knew he was the best.

"Hmm, DI Cooke! Another body in a field? Are you specialising in them, like?"

Dan smiled, experiencing a flashback to the time Farmer Price had found a skeleton buried in a field belonging to Lucy Baxter. Goodness – how long ago was that – and Stan was still teasing him about it?

"Not a seventy-year-old one this time, Stan. This one has all her flesh on her, although rotting away rapidly in this heat, I shouldn't wonder."

"In the van?"

"Yes."

"Hmm, love that van! It's a classic, you know. There are modern ones about now but the old ones were great."

Dan and Grant waited for the pathologist to come out of the van. It didn't take long.

"Hmm. Difficult position, and such a mess. I can't get near her."

"Any idea of time of death?"

"Can't be accurate, like, until I get her on my slab. Given the heat, an educated guess would say about four or five days but I can't be more specific now, I'm afraid. Poor girl, she's only young, like, early thirties, perhaps?"

"Yeah, we thought that, didn't we, Grant?" Dan responded and Grant nodded his agreement. "Well, she's all yours now, Stan."

"Thank you, most kind."

Dan and Grant left Stan and the team to get on with their jobs.

"Shall we go find the farmer? Do you know where the farmhouse is, Grant?"

"Yes, it's up that way." Grant pointed to the right.

"Okay, I need to get my car out of here. Do you have your car?"

"No, I came out with uniform."

"Come with me then. Let's go and hear what the farmer has to say."

Chapter 8

Dan and Grant were let in the farmhouse by the police officer who had escorted Farmer White back for his cup of tea.

"Thank you, erm...?"

"Riley, Sir."

"New, aren't you, Riley?"

"Yes, Sir. I transferred here about a month ago."

"Good to meet you, Riley. Now, where's Mr White?"

"In here, Sir. Mrs White is there too."

They were shown into a large room, a typical country kitchen with bunches of herbs hanging on the wall by the range and a huge table in the middle of the room. A middle-aged woman, her hair in a bun, her ample figure swathed in a large wrap-around pinafore and looking like she'd stepped straight out of the nineteen-fifties was in the process of wielding a large teapot, refilling mugs on the table. She looked up as they came in.

"I'm Detective Inspector Cooke, and this is Detective Sergeant Grant," said Dan. "Are you Mrs White?"

"Oh, yes I am, dearie," she answered. "Would you gentlemen care for a cup of tea? I was just pouring."

"Yes, please, that would be very nice. Grant?"

"Yes, thank you, Mrs White."

Dan waited while she poured the tea and then cradled his mug in his hands as if they were cold. He realised with surprise that they were, even though the day was warm. He cleared his throat.

"Mr. White, can you tell me how you found the body? What made you go there? Did you know the van was parked there?"

"The van has been there most of the summer, Inspector. The young woman asked if she could stay here for a while, like, and we said she could, provided that she didn't leave any rubbish around."

"So, you knew the woman?"

36

"Well, only insofar as we knew she was there, like. We didn't actually *know* her, if you see what I mean?"

"I do, sir. Did you know her name?"

"She told us she was called Mandy. She said she travels around a lot because she doesn't really have a home, but this was such a lovely place, would we mind if she stayed here a while because she was fed up with moving on? We didn't see why not, because we don't use that piece of ground really. The river often floods it in the winter but in the summer it's a pleasant spot. She seemed like a nice girl and young Charlie's a good kid."

"Charlie?"

"Yes. She has a son called Charlie. I think he's about twelve, although he doesn't look it because he's so thin, like. He liked to help my wife feed the chickens and he'd sometimes do odd jobs for me, like. I think he was a lonely kid, we felt sorry for him, didn't we, Bets?"

"Yes, love, we did. He was always willing, like. And if I got the chance, I'd feed him. I know he never had enough food. I don't know how they lived really, you know."

"So, where's Charlie now?"

"Well, that's what was worrying me. I'd see him most days, like. But I haven't seen him for, oh – a few days now. I was concerned he might be ill and so I sent Tom down to the van to see if things were alright and if we could help, like. But he found – he found..."

Her hand to her mouth, she gave a little sob. Her husband rose from his chair to put his arms around her.

"I found the van just as you saw it, Mr Cooke, and there's no sign of young Charlie."

"Okay, take your time, Mrs White. Why don't you have a cup of tea? You've been busy dishing it out to everyone else."

Tom White made his wife sit down and pushed a mug of tea in front of her and then stood beside her, his arm across her shoulder.

"Can you tell me about the last time you saw Charlie?" asked Dan, gently.

"Yes, it was – where are we now? Monday? It would be Thursday morning. He came here and he said his mum was still asleep and he was really hungry. So, I brought him in and gave him a good breakfast, eggs, bacon and beans with a chunk of my home-made bread and a mug of tea. He said – oh!"

"What, Mrs White?"

"He said she'd been asleep for ages and ages and he was hungry because he'd never had anything to eat the previous afternoon either. He also said my food would keep him going for ages and ages. I never thought anything of it at the time. You don't think his poor mother was already dead then and he hadn't realised?"

"If he is twelve, I should say that he did realise, Mrs. White. It rather sounds to me like he came to you for food before he ran off, because he knew he wouldn't get anything to eat again for a while."

"He couldn't have killed her, could he?" Betsy White looked at Dan, her eyes wide with questioning.

"Now, now, then Bets, don't take on. I don't think it's likely, do you? He's such a thin, weak little lad – how could he do in a grown woman? And why would he kill her anyway? She was the only person he had."

"Oh yes, Tom, you're right. I'm being silly. I know he loved her. I saw how they were together. No, he couldn't have killed her."

Tom patted her shoulder, then looked at the two detectives.

"I really should get back to my work, I'm sorry. Is there anything else that you need from me?"

"Just one thing. Do you ever drive a vehicle to that area? We saw tyre marks there."

"No, I never drive there. No reason to. If I need to go there for anything, I walk."

"Okay, thank you. Officer Riley here will take statements from you and your wife, sir. Then you can get back to the farm. Oh, one more thing, if we send a police artist here, do you think you could help us get likenesses of the dead woman and her son? If we can circulate pictures of them, we might be able to find out more about them and hopefully someone will spot the boy."

"Of course, we'll do anything we can to help," agreed Betsy White.

"I was just thinking. You'll need to take the van away, won't you?" Farmer White's brow was creased with concern.

"Yes, that would be the usual procedure. Why, is there a problem about that?"

"It's just that you'll need to bring a large vehicle to bring it off, won't you? I'm concerned about my crop. I don't harvest the corn cobs until November, like, and a large vehicle would need plenty of space."

"Hmm, yes, I see the problem. I'll have a word at HQ about it. Would you be happy for it to remain where it is until after your harvest? I'm sure the forensic team will gather all they need from it in situ, after all, it wasn't a crash or road accident. I'll see what I can do."

"Thank you, I'm grateful; I did think it would be a problem."

"Well, we'll leave you in peace now, and thank you for all your help."

The two detectives made their way back to the camper van and, as forensics had all they needed, they made a thorough search of it. They discovered where the boy slept, just under the raised roof and they bagged up a few items to take back with them. There really wasn't much to find, but at least they now knew what the woman's name was – Amanda Jones.

On the drive back to Hereford, Dan and Grant discussed the situation.

"Obviously, the boy has run away," observed Grant. "I wonder why."

"Maybe he thinks he's in danger."

"Yes," Grant nodded slowly, "That would make sense. But why would he think that?"

"Perhaps he thinks the killer might come after him. Perhaps feels the killer may have seen him or something like that."

"Because he was in the van when it happened. Yes, that would make sense. But where would he have been and not been seen in a van that small?"

"I don't know, Grant. Although he obviously slept in the roof and it would probably have been dark when his mother and whoever killed her returned. Perhaps the murderer simply didn't notice the roof section. One thing I do know is, we not only have a murdered woman on our hands, we also have to find a lost boy who probably doesn't want to be found – damn!"

Chapter 9

Charlie wandered aimlessly along the road. He had no idea where he was and he was tired. Although he'd hated living in the camper van, he thought longingly of his bunk there. It was more comfortable than the places he'd spent the past four nights. The first night he'd slept in a barn on some old sacking. The second one he'd slept on a river bank. It had been a dry night and the sound of the river had been comforting. He wondered if it was the same small river that had run through Farmer White's fields. Upon that thought, he'd decided to follow it but eventually he couldn't get through the hedges and was afraid to be caught on private land.

The third night he had spent in someone's summer house, after creeping into their garden late one night, afraid of being caught or an alarm going off. However, nothing happened and he'd been able to get into the summer house, where he'd found a couple of sun lounger chairs and cushions. At first, it had seemed comfortable, but as the night wore on, he found himself more disturbed and waited for first light wakefully. As soon as the dawn chorus started, he moved quickly, trying to put everything back how he'd found it, and crept away as rapidly as he could.

Last night had been the worst. Having decided that being on someone's property was dangerous, he'd bunked down for the night under a hedgerow. The road seemed quiet, so he felt reasonably safe, but the ground was hard, the hedge was prickly and it had rained. Now, damp, tired and miserable, he plodded along and came to some shops, although many of them seemed to be closed. There weren't many people about, so he sat on a seat. His stomach rumbled loudly. He hoped there would be a shop where he could buy something to eat as he still had his mother's money.

As he sat there, bone weary and hungry, he noticed someone going into a shop further along the road. He decided to go and take a look to see what sort of shop it was. It turned out to be a newsagent. He picked up a packet of ready-made sandwiches, a packet of biscuits and a bottle of fizzy pop. The Indian man at the checkout smiled at him in a friendly way.

"Good day, young man. You're out and about early. What are you going to do on this Bank Holiday?"

"I don't know yet." Charlie gave the man a tentative smile and hurried out the door. He went back to his seat and undid the sandwiches, stuffing the first one into his mouth hungrily. The next he ate more slowly and drank his pop. It was Bank Holiday Monday then. That's why there's not many people about.

As he sat eating, one or two people came into view. One man, walking a very woolly dog went into the shop, the dog waiting patiently outside. Moments later, he reappeared carrying a newspaper and the pair walked towards Charlie was sitting. The dog stopped to sniff at something and the man said, "Come on, Charlie, I've got to get to work."

Charlie's head shot up. "Eh? Did you say something, Mister?"

"I was just talking to my dog, Charlie," said the man in his soft Herefordshire burr.

"Oh, I thought you were talking to me. My name's Charlie too."

"Is it now? It's a good name. I've not seen you before, like. Are you new around here?"

"I think I'm lost."

"What do you mean you're lost?"

Charlie shrugged. "I don't know where I am." He stroked the dog's head as it fawned around him.

"You're in Leominster. (He pronounced it 'Lemster') Where did you think you were?"

"Don't know."

"Where do you want to be?"

"Hereford."

"How come you're in Leominster then?"

"Mum put me on a bus but I think it must have been a wrong bus because it came here." Charlie had to make something up quickly. "I was going to my gran's in Hereford. Now I don't know what to do."

The man thought for a few moments.

"Tell you what. I need to go to work very shortly. I work in Hereford, like. I could take you there. Would you trust me to do that? I have to take Charlie home and get my car. What do you think? I'm going to Hereford anyway."

"Oh, would you, Mister? I'd be ever so grateful and so will my nan be. I bet she's really worried."

"I expect she is. Don't you have a mobile phone? Most kids seem to have them these days."

"I broke it and Mum said she couldn't afford to buy me another one."

"Right. If you haven't turned up at your nan's, your mum will be worried too. You wait over there," the man pointed, "and I'll be along to pick you up shortly. Alright?"

"Yeah, that's great. Fanks, Mister."

"No problem. Come on, Charlie-boy, now we really have to move."

Charlie watched the man and dog turn a corner and out of sight and then wandered over to where the man had told him to wait. He drank the rest of his drink and put the bottle in a litter-bin by a bus stop, along with the sandwich carton and a chocolate biscuit wrapper. Because of Farmer White's insistence that he and his mother left no rubbish on his land, Charlie was always careful about putting rubbish into a bin.

He didn't have long to wait, only about fifteen minutes. A car drew up beside him and Charlie bent down to see the man who had been walking his dog. He got in and off they went.

"I'm Bill, by the way, and I work not far from the hospital. Will that be any good to you? If you need to get out anywhere before that, just tell me."

"No, that'll be great," replied Charlie, who hadn't any idea where he was going anyway. "My nan lives quite near there. I'll be able to find my way."

"So, where do you live?"

"Oh, we just moved, I'm not really sure what the place is called. My mum wanted me out of the way so she could get the house straight. That's why she sent me to my Nan's. Nan'll know how to take me back."

"I see. It's a good thing I found you then, isn't it? I expect your nan will let your mum know that you're safe?"

"Yeah, she'll do that. She'll probably smack me one round the lug fer getting' lost." Charlie laughed and Bill grinned.

"She sounds like my mother. She'd clout you first and ask questions after. Heart of gold though, do anything for anyone."

"Yeah. Is she still around?" Charlie wanted to keep the conversation away from him. He didn't want to have to make up any more stories.

"No, she died a few years back. Miss her still. No one can ever replace your mother, no matter how old you are."

"No." Charlie lapsed into silence, having been reminded of what had happened to his mum only a few days ago. How was he going to manage without her? What was he thinking of to run away? Only, he feared being put into care nearly as much as he feared the man who had killed his mother.

Chapter 10

Once Charlie had been dropped off by Bill and the car had driven away, he had no idea what to do next. He wandered along the road towards the town centre. There were people about but not as many as he imagined there would be if it hadn't been a Bank Holiday.

At any other time, he might have appreciated the beauty of the town – if young boys think of such things – but he didn't take much notice of his surroundings. His sole purpose was to try to stay away from people's notice but also to find somewhere he might lay his head that night. He wandered around the old black and white house in the middle of the town centre and wished it was possible he could sleep there but it was a museum and they would make sure it was empty of all visitors before they closed.

He found a fish and chip shop, bought sausage and chips and sat on a seat to eat them. They were wonderful, being the first real food he'd had since he'd run away, apart from that morning's sandwiches. Until he'd reached the shop in Leominster, he'd survived on blackberries and other things he'd found in the country, although the apples weren't really ripe enough yet. On the day he'd nicked a couple of apples off a tree, he'd experienced terrible tummy ache. That was another thing; he knew he smelt. He needed to bathe somehow and to find clean clothes, at least underpants. It was not good to have to 'go' under bushes and not have means to clean himself afterwards. He hated it, at least there was always water in the van, even though he had to collect it himself.

Water – he needed a source of water, he couldn't keep buying it Surely there would be a fountain or tap somewhere where he could refill a bottle?

Then he came across a supermarket that was open – oh yeah! Charlie found some boys' underpants and a pair of jogger bottoms which were reduced, so he had more than enough money for them. He'd intended looking in a charity shop but of course there weren't any open on a bank holiday. He also bought a bar of soap and a two-litre bottle of water, which only cost twenty-nine pence – now that was a price he could afford!

Joyfully, he paid for his shopping and stowed them away in his old backpack. The bottle of water made it heavy, but he didn't mind because it would keep him going at least until tomorrow and then he'd be able to buy another one.

The checkout lady was smiley and friendly so he asked her if there was a swimming baths in the town.

"Oh yes, dearie, go out of here and over the bridge. Just ask anyone, they'll tell you if you can't spot it, like."

"Fanks."

Charlie set off with purpose. It was a bit scary walking over the bridge because it was a wide, four lane road. There were pavements, so it was safe. The bridge spanned a river and the boy stopped in the middle to gaze at the rippling water, a church's large square tower rising on the left side and a grassy area on the opposite bank. It looked lovely, and for the first time, Charlie appreciated Hereford. Another bridge, obviously very old, was before him, picturesque with its arches. Obviously, the one he was walking across had been built to accommodate the demands of modern traffic, since it was obvious the old bridge had been built many years before cars had been invented.

He carried on walking and came to a roundabout. He looked around and to his left he saw a sign to the leisure centre. He crossed over the road and followed the path to the large square building. After paying the entrance money, he collected his arm band intending only to have a shower, but the pull of the baths, plus the fact he'd paid, enticed him to swim. However, he had no swimming trunks, so he shut himself in a shower cubicle and enjoyed a long shower, soaping his hair and body and loving the feel of coming clean. Hopefully it would last, and he would find somewhere to sleep where he wouldn't get so dirty and, if he stayed around here, he could use the toilets in the supermarkets. Now, all he had to do was find somewhere to sleep.

Charlie had an enjoyable day on Bishop's Meadow, walking around, seeing everything. He walked along the river and across Victoria Bridge and looked around the Castle Green, all the time seeking somewhere he might lay his head that night but also enjoying the sights. It was a lovely place.

The trouble was, the park was such a public place and he suspected that people would be there until late in the evening because it was a pretty place to walk with all the lights alongside the river and eating places overlooking it. So, he decided to walk along the other way, under the old bridge and the new bridge that he'd come over that morning. Eventually, he came to some fields where he was able to climb over the gate and there might be somewhere he could sleep without being discovered.

There was a distinct nip on a breeze that night and Charlie found it hard to sleep, even though he wrapped himself up in all his clothes. The grass felt damp underneath him and so he made his way slowly back along the river path towards the bridges and the park, guided the street lights across the bridge. The river flowed darkly beside him, so he kept to the side of the path furthest away from the water, just in case. A runaway he might be, but he didn't want to be a drowned runaway.

Settling down in a back entrance to the leisure centre, he was glad of the shelter from the wind, although he wasn't much warmer. He sat there on the unrelenting concrete, unable to sleep. Tomorrow, he would go around the charity shops to look for a warm coat and maybe a sleeping bag or even just a blanket. He needed something.

But as he sat there, trying desperately to sleep in the hard and uninviting place, for the first time, Charlie wondered if he would survive a winter living outside. Perhaps being in care would be a better option? At least he would have something warm to sleep in at night. But there was still the problem of that man being after him. Disturbed and cold though he was, eventually, he fell into a light and troubled doze.

In his asleep/awake mode, Charlie thought back to his last day with his mother. It had started earlier than usual, for although his mum had as usual gone out for the evening, she was not back late – and she had obviously not been inebriated, which was also different. She was up and about in good time and had been in good spirits. They didn't have a lot in the van to eat, but she promised that the following day they would go out shopping.

"Good fortune is coming our way at last, Charlie," she'd told him as they ate beans on toast for their lunch (they never seemed to have breakfast). "I've met this amazing bloke. 'E were luv'ly, and 'e took me out fer a meal in some place in the country an' we talked an' talked. I'm goin' ter meet 'im agin ternite. 'E 'as this posh car and 'e ses 'e 'as a nice 'ouse an' 'e wants ter tek me there at the weekend when 'e goes 'ome from 'is 'oliday wot 'e's on now. 'E ses 'e feels we 'as a connection and 'e 'as a job fer me and I ken give up the van an' live in. 'E's given me lotsa money already. 'An advancement, 'e said, ter git some nice clothes."

She waved a wad of money at the boy, who had never seen so much in his life.

"I'm goin' ter wait an' see wot the place is like, then tomorra we'll have a spending spree." She'd ruffled his hair and they'd grinned at each other. They'd spent the afternoon paddling in the stream and sunning themselves on the grass until she'd said it was time she got ready. He'd sat outside the van on the steps, listening to her humming happily to herself while she'd dolled herself up. Then she'd skipped out the door, taken his face in her hands and kissed him.

"Be a good boy."

"Yes, Mum. But I'm hungry, isn't there anything to eat?"

"I told you, we're going shopping tomorra!" she'd snapped. "You can last out til then. I gotta get the bus or I'll be late meeting Des."

And with that, she'd hurried away with Charlie staring glumly after her.

Chapter 11

The morning brought Dan to the station early. A briefing meeting was held soon after nine o'clock when all the team were in. As soon as the Super came in, Dan went to report the situation.

"Although we have to find the murderer of this young woman, what really concerns me is the boy."

"I agree, Dan. We need to hold a press conference about him. Do we have a description of the lad?"

"Yes, Sir. Unfortunately, there is no picture of him but the farmer's wife gave us a good idea of what he looks like. I'm afraid for his safety. If the killer finds him before we do, he will turn up dead, but apart from that, living rough is no life for a young boy, even though he's pretty used to rough living, he won't be used to sleeping just anywhere. I don't know if he has any money either so he'll be reduced to stealing, poor lad."

"Yes, we must find him, top priority. I'll get onto that. Let me know how your investigations go."

"I will. Thank you, Sir. The team will be in now, ready for briefing."

In the briefing room, Dan put up pictures of the dead woman and her van in situ.

"This is Amanda Jones, we have found her driving licence. Julie, I want you to find out everything you can about her, where she came from, her family, everything."

"Yes, Gov."

"Grant, I want you to organise uniform in a house to house in the village of Moreton-on-Lugg and outwards. I realise it's a long shot, but someone might have seen something. I have permission to use uniform in this. When you've done that, I want you to go out with me. We're going to go around Hereford to see if anyone has seen this woman in the town."

"Yes, Boss."

"Right then, thank you everyone."

Dan sat at his desk when the others had dispersed to carry out his instructions. He was deep in thought when Grant returned.

"Penny for 'em, Boss?" Grant has always called Dan 'Boss', rather than the more accepted term of 'Gov'.

Dan rose from his seat. "Nothing really, Grant. It's just that it puzzles me – why should this young woman, who appears to be not at all the usual sort, have been the victim of a killer? She keeps herself to herself, living quietly in her van, taking care of her son. By all accounts she hasn't been in the county for long – so why would someone kill her?"

"Was it theft? Did she disturb someone in her van?"

"Hmm, unlikely – what on earth could she have that anyone wanted? She obviously didn't have much. In any case, she was in bed."

"Could she have been running away from someone?"

"She could, I suppose." Dan pulled up his shoulders. "No point in speculating right now, not until we have some answers from pathology and hopefully some background to her life, if Julie can find anything. Right, let's go and question the good citizens of Hereford."

As they were about to leave, Dan's phone rang. He answered it and briefly responded, "Yes, that's fine. I'll be there."

"Press conference at four, Grant. We're putting out an appeal to the public for the boy."

"That's good, Boss. I don't like the thought of that lad living out there."

"Especially as it's chilly at night now. The days aren't so bad as yet. But I got the feeling the lad doesn't have much. That duvet on his mattress was pretty nasty."

"Yes," replied Grant, wrinkling his nose at the remembrance of the stuffy and smelly camper van that had been the boy's home. "The farmer's wife said he was thin and small for his age, not much meat on him to keep warm."

"No. Right, we'll do the rounds of the pubs, see if any of the landlords remember Amanda."

****

It was a thankless task, as the pub hunt didn't reveal much. One landlord thought he'd remembered seeing her but she seemed to be with a group of people rather than on her own or with anyone specific. Dan left his card with him in case he should remember anything else that might be useful.

After a fruitless search, Grant said thoughtfully, "Do you think I should see if my – erm – contacts know anything? If she was into drugs, someone would have come across her."

"Good thinking. Yes, it's worth a try."

"I'll get onto it."

"Meet back at the station. I have to go there now for the press conference."

"Okay, Boss. See you later. I'm thinking it might have been better to go into the pubs in the evening, to spread the picture around. The punters might have seen her or been with her."

"Yes, you're right. We might just have to do that. I have to get back now. See you."

Grant fished in his pocket for his second phone and began to dial.

****

The press conference went well. Dan put out a statement describing the dead woman and her son and appealed for any information anyone might have. It was especially important for the boy to be found because the concern for his safety was paramount.

Reporters tried to ask questions but Dan patiently told them that he had no more information to give them at that time. They had to be content with that for now.

Chapter 12

Charlie awoke from his troubled slumber with a groan; every part of him hurt. He had no idea what the time was but it seemed early. What could he do with himself that day? After he'd gone through his memories during the night, today he was sad and listless. He drew out of the doorway, not wanting anyone on their way to work to find him there. He took himself off to the wooded area at the edge of the park where he relieved himself. The unrelenting cold of the concrete had seemed to seep into his bones and even moving didn't warm him. There was no one about; he was all alone in this big park, with not even a dog walker, it was so very early. But he couldn't face sitting in that doorway any more.

He crossed the empty car park, headed towards the road and came to the large, wide bridge that he'd come over yesterday. There was barely any traffic now. He stopped in the middle of the bridge to look over the wall at the river. *It was a nice river,* he thought, *much wider than the little one their van had been near.* He missed that small river. It seemed friendly and homely somehow. He'd spent many hours each morning by the side of it, waiting for his mother to get up. It had been his friend. This river was too busy to be his friend. The square tower of a church loomed to his left, the main body of it hidden behind buildings, and he decided to take a look. Following the road over the bridge, he turned right and there, at the end of the road in front of him, was the church, and it was very big. When he reached the green in front of it, he read that it was Hereford Cathedral. At that time in the morning, of course, it was closed, but Charlie couldn't help admiring it. Although a country boy at heart, he loved old buildings, especially churches. There was something about them that made him feel safe somehow, although he couldn't have explained why. He sat on a bench on the green at the side of the cathedral and waited for the world to wake up. Gradually, people appeared and the traffic built up. His stomach rumbled loudly and it drove him towards the town in search of something to eat.

In the centre of the city, he spied an open archway that turned out to be an indoor market. He wandered around it and saw few of the vegetable stalls were in the process of preparing for the day's trading but most of them weren't open yet so he decided not to stay. Once outside, he recognised where he was and headed down Eign Gate towards the Tesco he'd been in the previous day. However, that wasn't open either, so he walked on, down the underpass, keeping his head low as people came towards him. He wandered on up the road and saw a huge Sainsbury store. People were going towards it so he thought he'd have a look around. He felt conspicuous in the big store; he could feel curious eyes on him, so he bought a packet of sandwiches and hurried out again.

As he sat on a wall eating his food, he thought about what he should do. Although he wanted to stay in the town, on the other hand maybe he should go to the country where he might find barns or similar to sleep in at nights. He couldn't face another night sleeping in a doorway, especially as it was getting colder. And he missed his mum. He knew nobody in this place, no one cared about him, he had no friends, no family. When his money ran out, how would he survive? If he'd stayed at the farm, Missus White would have looked after him, he was sure. But he had no idea where the Whites' farm was or in what direction it was. Frightened, his sense of loss and being lost suddenly overwhelmed him and the tears started to fall again.

"Cry baby!"

A jeering voice brought Charlie's head up swiftly and he swiped the tears off his face with his wrist. A group of boys about his own age, wearing a school uniform, were laughing at him. He slid off the wall and put up his fists. Two of them prised his bag off his back. He fell on them, trying to fight them off.

"Hey, you kids! Leave him alone! Get off him, Gerry Parker – I'll tell your mum! And you, Aaron!"

The boy called Gerry gave Charlie a push and the other boy dropped the bag. The group sloped off, leaving Charlie on the ground. He scrambled to his feet, picking up his bag on the way.

"You alright, kid?"

"Yeah...fanks."

Charlie looked at the girl. She looked about fifteen and was attractive with bright blonde, curly hair and blue eyes. She wore the same uniform as the boys.

"Never seen you before. Are you from around here?" she asked, her eyes narrowing slightly, as if trying to remember.

"Er, no. I gotta go. Fanks for yer 'elp, Miss."

With that, he took to his heels and didn't stop, even though he heard her call 'Hey, stop!'

He ran back into the underpass towards the town. He had to find a coat, then he would leave this place.

Chapter 13

Mary Brown had just opened the St. Michael's Hospice Charity shop that she managed when a small figure came in. She noticed how he stood near the place where the heating blew in, then wandered around the clothes, looking carefully. Seemingly aware of her, he was trying to keep out of her eyeline.

She was only too aware that people stole, even from charity shops. Where was his mother? Surely he wasn't on his own? He put on a coat and zipped it, putting up the hood. He looked so thin, and she sensed he had a sadness about him that made her wonder as he took the coat off again and approached her counter with it.

The price label said it was five pounds ninety-five pence and she noticed him looking carefully in his bag and counting money.

"That will be three pounds, please, young man," she said, smiling pleasantly.

"But the label ses five pounds ninety-five, Miss," he said.

"So it does, but it's now on sale. I haven't had time to change the price yet," Mary replied. She was rewarded by a wide smile that completely changed his face. What an attractive little fellow he was, she thought.

"Oh, Fanks ever so, Missus," he said, and handed over the three coins.

"You're welcome. Would you like a bag?"

"Is it okay if I wear it now?"

"Of course it is. It's yours. Let me just take the label off for you."

Taking a pair of scissors from out of a small drawer, she deftly snipped the thread holding the price and popped it into a bin. He slipped the coat back on and gave her another bright smile. She watched him through the window as he went out of the shop, and headed towards the underpass. It was only a short encounter, but somehow there was something about him that stayed with her throughout the day, even though her shop became busy later on.

****

Charlie had intended to go back into the town, but thought better of it, so headed back the way he'd come, along the road with the big Sainsburys. However, he didn't go there again but kept walking. He wondered where those kids went to school and shuddered when he remembered the bullies. It made him think of the golden-haired girl who'd seen them off. He wished she was his big sister – he'd have liked to have a sister like her. He felt ashamed now that he'd run away from her when she'd been kind, but he was always afraid that he might be caught and taken to the police. He had to avoid that at all costs. There seemed to be far too many eyes and ears in the town, not to mention too many police-people wandering about for his liking. It had to be easier in the country, didn't it?

He had no idea how long it would take him to get to the country, or in what direction he was going; he just followed his feet. The further away from the bustle of town he got, the better he liked it. Hopefully, somehow, he would find the refuge he needed where his feet took him.

At a roundabout with a big monument in the middle, a cross on a plinth, he saw shops set back from the road and went across the road to take a look. There was a newsagent that also sold sweets and other things so he bought some biscuits and chocolate bars to keep him going. He squirrelled them away in his bag, along with another bottle of water from the Co-op next door. Across the road, there was a vegetable shop where he bought a couple of apples. His money was diminishing, so he needed to be careful.

Beside the road that headed back towards the city, there were four leading off the roundabout. Which should he take? He crossed back to the pavement he'd been on when he reached the roundabout and stood with his eyes closed, asking God, if there was a God, which way he should go. Turning around and round on the spot, he opened his eyes. The road straight ahead was called Kings Acre Road. That was the way to go, so he set off. It was a lovely road with trees either side, and grassy edges to the pavements. Although the trees would soon be turning colour and shedding their leaves, at the moment they were still decked out in their summer finery.

The sun warmed him as he walked and eventually he took off his coat and tied it around his waist. Eventually, he came to a fork in the road but decided to carry on straight. He could see fields in the gaps between the houses and knew that he was near the country.

Most other boys of his age might be worried about being alone in the country, but not Charlie. The grass, the trees, the birds and the open skies were his friends. His heart lifted, and he walked on.

****

Mary Brown wasn't the only one who had the boy on her mind throughout the day. Gloria Wigginton found the memory of Charlie's tear-stained face kept intruding upon her as she tried to apply her mind to mathematics and science during her school day.

Gloria had had a hard life, being the daughter of an alcoholic prostitute. She'd had to more or less bring herself up, found herself looking after her mother. Night after night she was left alone in the house while her mother went in pursuit of her 'business'. She'd long since hardened herself to the shame that her mother was one of the best-known characters in the Hereford night-life. If the kids at school had once taunted her because of her mother, they knew better now. No one messed with Gloria, not that she'd ever used violence. She had simply developed a demeanour that showed everyone that she was above anything they might throw at her, so they gave up on her and found other victims. In fact, she was something of a heroine since the time when she'd been kidnapped by a London gang on the orders of their Boss, the notorious Lucian Avery. She and Rowena Thompson, who had also been kidnapped, had become firm friends.

The two girls had become inseparable. Before the kidnapping, Gloria would have slit her own wrists rather than let another girl – or boy – anywhere near her house, for she was ashamed of the place she lived in. But Rowena had made it plain that she didn't care what Gloria's house was like, she just liked being with her friend. Gloria would also spend time at Rowena's house and they did their homework together. Rowena's mum or dad would take Gloria home later. As long as her breakfast and other meals were there for her, Gloria's mum Ruby didn't much bother about where her daughter was.

Because she'd had such a life, Gloria had looked into Charlie's face and seen what other folks might not see – a child who'd had a tough life but was close to breaking point. She kept wondering what had happened in his life that made the misery show through the defiant look. As she ran around the track that afternoon, she let her mind dwell on him. In the end, she had to shake the memory of that tear-stained face away. She couldn't do anything for him as she didn't know who he was or where he came from and would probably never see him again.

Chapter 14

That evening, Bill Williams was relaxing before retiring to bed, half listening to the late-night news when the name 'Charlie' suddenly came through his consciousness.

"Eh? What was that about a Charlie, Bev?" He patted his dog, who had sat up on hearing his name. "Good boy, Charlie."

"It's a lad that's gone missing," replied his wife. "His mum's been found dead and he's run away."

"Can you rewind it please, love? I want to hear it properly."

Bev rewound it to the beginning of the report. Bill saw a detective, whose name appeared beneath as he spoke: 'Detective Inspector Dan Cooke'.

'A woman was found dead yesterday morning in a Volkswagen Caravanette on land on a farm between Moreton-on-Lugg and Marden. She had been dead for around four days and appears to have been murdered. We have identified her as Amanda Jones. She is described as in her mid to late twenties, five feet three inches tall, with long blond hair, blue eyes and spoke with a south-county accent. If anyone knows, or think they know, anything about this woman, please contact the Hereford police or their local police, who will pass the information to us.

The woman has a son, name of Charlie, who is described as twelve years old but thin and small for his age, and he also has blond hair and blue eyes. When last seen, he was wearing grey jogger bottoms, a blue t-shirt and black trainers. It is thought he has a thin, light grey hooded top. He is missing and concern is growing for his safety. If anyone has any information that could help us locate Charlie, please get in touch. The number to call is on your screens below. Thank you.'

A pencil drawing of the boy was on the screen, next to a driving licence photo of the dead woman.

"My goodness, Bev, I think that lad I gave a lift to yesterday was that boy. He said his name was Charlie. The drawing isn't exactly right, but it's near enough."

"You'll have to tell the police," Bev told him.

"I'm going to call them now, before I forget."

Bill tapped out the number that had been on the screen and spoke briefly into it.

"They want me to see Inspector Cooke. I said I'd go in on my way to work tomorrow."

****

Mary Brown made it a habit to watch the late news before retiring to bed. She was always too busy to watch it earlier. Having made her Horlicks, she returned to her sitting room just as it was beginning. The local news item about the boy and his mother caught her attention. The picture of the boy was so like the lad that had been in her shop first thing that morning. It wasn't exactly right, obviously it had been drawn from someone's description of him, but it was pretty close. She also seemed to remember that 'her' lad had been wearing dark blue jogger bottoms, because she remembered thinking how well his new coat, which was also dark blue, went with the rest of his clothes. He was certainly wearing a grey hoodie. Could it be the same child? What if she'd made a mistake and it wasn't him, she'd feel silly about wasting police time? Although, he'd had money, what if he'd been able to buy new jogger bottoms? And, although he hadn't said much, she was almost sure she'd detected a southern-county accent.

"What do you think, Meisha?"

Her beautiful black Labrador looked back at her steadily, then she put her right front paw out to her. It seemed that she was telling her she was right. Mary decided to call the police in the morning. If she was wrong, then she was wrong, but if she was right, she would have helped, wouldn't she?

Mary didn't always sleep very well, and the thought that the lad with the sweet face might be trying to sleep out in the cold played on her mind. He was out there somewhere, knowing his mum was dead and there was no one to care for him. Years ago, Mary had worked in a children's home and she thought about the children she'd cared for there. No child should be trying to live out on the streets, it just wasn't right.

****

There he was, thinking he'd committed the perfect murder and it seemed he'd made a terrible mistake. She'd never said she had the kid there – why hadn't she? Although he'd assumed she'd left the boy with someone else, obviously she hadn't, so where the heck had the boy been that night? There had been no sign of him in the van, there wasn't room. He couldn't believe it when he saw how she lived and had almost backed out when she opened the door. It was a shambles and he shuddered when he thought of it. It smelt dirty and, although he couldn't see in the dim light, he was sure it had been. There was no way he could have lain in that bed, even if he'd wanted to bed her, which he didn't. The shudder came again as he thought about what he could have lain on, what he might have caught.

He was sorry though, for he couldn't help liking her and had seriously considered walking away and reporting that he hadn't been able to do it, for whatever reason, he'd make something up, then realised he had to do it, come what may. How soft her hair was, but he'd been careful not to touch it too much, just in case. In spite of her obvious lifestyle, there was something almost childlike about her; he remembered how she'd revelled in his 'loving care' of her. She'd dozed most of the time in his car as he drove her to the farm but had managed to direct him to her van and let him in. As he'd picked her up, she trembled and he'd laid her carefully in her bed and said 'There now, just have this little drink as a nightcap and I'll join you.' Like a trusting child she'd drunk it. He'd watched her sink deeper into sleep and then he'd pulled down the covers slightly (after putting on his gloves), put his hands around her slim neck and squeezed. She never made a sound and afterwards he'd pulled the covers up around her neck. He'd done his best to search the van but there were so few places to hide anything and she had nothing in her bag, except for the money he'd given her. Eventually, he'd had to give up the search and crept out of the van, taking the glass with him.

The brandy in the bulbous glass sparkled in the light of the flame-effect gas fire which was on because the evenings were turning chilly. He took a sip, savouring the feeling of it slipping down his throat and glanced at the window and the garden beyond. Seeing the outside made him think of the boy again – hm, yes, he needed to find the boy, for he might know something, where she would have hidden it. Although his heart sank at the thought of possibly having to kill a child. There's also the girl's uncle's house, he'd have to find a way of getting in there to search – and the cottage. He thinks no one knows he goes there, but he's so wrong! Perhaps I'll wait until the kid gets found and I'll be able to get at him then, although I really needed to search that van more thoroughly. Forensics will have taken it away, dammit! Perhaps I'll sort out the uncle first.

****

"Here we have the driving licence picture of Amanda Jones and the artist's impression of the boy Charlie. Also, we have the camper-van licence number. DC Coombs is looking into information about Amanda. Have you found anything yet, Julie?"

"No, Sir. There's not much of a trail. I can't find her birth or where she came from. I think she may have changed her name at some point."

"Keep digging, please."

"Yes, Sir."

"Grant, ask Johnson to do a search on the camper's number plate and find out who has owned it. It may lead us to someone who's known her or at least had contact with her."

"Will do, Boss."

The phone rang. Dan picked it up. "Cooke." He listened then responded. "Good, tell them I'll be down very shortly."

"The desk Sergeant says a Mr Williams is here. He thinks he's seen Charlie. Grant, come with me. We'll wind this up for now. Julie, would you get onto Johnson for me please as I want Grant with me."

"Of course, Sir."

"Mr. Williams? Please, come this way."

Dan indicated a room off reception, that Dan privately thought of as 'the soft interview room'. It was semi-informal, with soft-seated chairs but still had a shiny wooden desk. "Would you like a drink, Mr Williams?"

"No thank you, I've just had breakfast and am on my way to work. This won't take long, will it?"

"No, of course it won't." Dan smiled at the man, who was, he estimated, in his late fifties or early sixties but had a pleasant face that made him appear almost youthful. The dimples that appeared when he smiled gave him a cheeky look. Dan liked him and instinctively felt this was a good man.

"If you would just give your full name and address to my sergeant here, we can begin."

Grant rapidly wrote down the information and then sat ready to take notes.

"Thank you for coming in. If you'd tell us, in your own words, how you met the boy we believe is Charlie Jones."

Bill told the detectives exactly how he'd met Charlie and how he'd brought him into Hereford and dropped him off near the hospital.

Dan showed him the artist's picture. "Do you believe this to be that boy?"

"Yes, I do, although it's not exactly right, but very close. To be honest, although I offered to give him a lift, I thought he might not be there when I went back. I was a bit reticent really because you hear all sorts of things and I didn't want to get accused of anything. But he was there and so I took him. He definitely had a Devon-type accent. I'm ninety-nine percent sure it was him."

Dan stood up. "Thank you. That's been a big help. At least we now know he's around the city somewhere."

He led the way out, and as they were shaking hands in the foyer, a woman pushed her way through the outside door. Dan's eyes slid to her, recognising her face but not able to place her.

As Bill walked out, she came up to Dan. "Mr Cooke, I'm Mary Brown. I work in the Hospice Shop in Eign Gate."

Dan's frown cleared. "Of course, I remember you now. How are you?"

"I'm well, thank you. I came to see you because I think I saw the missing boy."

"Ah! Walk this way. Would you care for a coffee or tea?"

"That would be very nice. Coffee, please."

"Can you organise three coffees for us please, Bob?" Dan addressed the desk sergeant.

Once back in the soft interview room, Dan indicated for Mary to sit and he and Sergeant Grant sat the other side. Mary gave her name and address and then proceeded to tell them about the boy who came into the shop.

While she was speaking, the coffees arrived and Dan sipped gingerly at his.

"I was a little doubtful about coming in because my boy wasn't wearing grey jogger bottoms, Mr Cooke, he was wearing blue ones that looked new. Once he'd bought the coat from my shop, he looked quite smart. But the picture you put up on the broadcast looked so like him. I think he had some money, perhaps he'd just bought the jogger bottoms."

Dan nodded. "By all accounts, the boy never had much. If he found money his mother had stashed away, he might well have gone on a spending spree. We never found any at all in their home."

Mary nodded. "That's likely, I'd say. I'd also say he was being very careful with whatever money he had. He only bought a warm coat. But that's not going to be enough to keep him warm at nights. And the money he has will run out eventually. How will he live then?"

'*How indeed?*' thought Dan. Out loud, he said, "We're very grateful to you for coming in. We'll update the description of his clothes on the news tonight. That's very helpful."

"You may or may not know that I worked with children in our local children's home years ago," said Mary. "I've always cared about children and I can't help worrying about that young lad. I do hope you find him soon, Mr Cooke."

"So do I, Mrs Brown, so do I."

Chapter 15

Several reports of possible sightings of Charlie filtered through during the course of the day. The telephonists were skilled at weeding out the ones that weren't relevant, but they'd selected a few that were: a Tesco worker who reckoned she sold a pair of jogger bottoms to a boy, along with underpants and food and water, another from a receptionist at the swimming baths who swore he'd gone in there, a stallholder in the Butter Market thought he'd seen the boy and, even more interesting, a shop worker at the Co-op at Whitecross was sure the boy had been in the shop buying biscuits and sweets and, to back up that statement, the woman who ran the fruit and vegetable shop at Whitecross said he'd bought some apples off her. She particularly remembered it because he'd only bought two apples, although he'd looked longingly at other things, and he'd counted out his small change carefully.

By the afternoon, the team had a pretty good picture of Charlie's movements. Dan gave the team a briefing.

"Going by the timings on all the statements, it seems that, after he'd been brought into Hereford by Mr Williams, Charlie had wandered through the city and came to Tesco. He found his way over the bridge to the leisure centre where it seems he probably had a shower and changed his trousers and probably put on clean underwear. The staff at the leisure centre found a pair of pants in the bin in the changing rooms. They are now at forensics. He probably stayed in Hereford somewhere, probably in the vicinity of Bishop's Meadow on Monday night, then early on Tuesday, bought himself a warm coat from the Hospice Shop. Going by the statements from our Co-op lady, Sharon Fisher, and Mrs Dawkins in the grocery shop, Charlie looked to be heading out of town again. He probably feels safer in the country. The question is, which way did he go after that? Did he go up Three Elms Road and out towards Canon Pyon, or up the Kings Acre Road? Or did he wander along the Yazor Road towards the racecourse – in which case he could still be in the city.

We need to be vigilant; I'll ask uniform to keep an eye out for him in the city, especially in the Roman Road area. One would hope he won't wander off towards Dinmoor and find himself back in Leominster, where Mr Williams found him."

"Sir, Johnson has traced the camper-van back to someone called Simon Denton, lives in Hooe, Plymouth," said Julie Collins.

"Really? Is he the one that sold Mandy the camper?"

"According to records, he still owns it, Sir."

"Does he indeed? Interesting. Could she have stolen it?"

"No reports of it being stolen, Sir."

"Hmm. Any luck tracing more of Mandy's life?"

"Not a thing, sir. Except, on closer investigation, it seems the driving licence is a forgery."

"A forgery? Goodness me – now why would a young woman need a forged driving licence?"

"To hide her real identity, I'd say, Sir."

"You're right, Julie, can't be any other reason. So, the big questions are, who was she really and who was she hiding from?"

****

While Dan and his team were thinking around the questions that had arisen about his mother, Charlie was on the lookout for somewhere to spend the night. The Kings Acre Road wouldn't offer him what he needed. Not seeing the need to hurry, he wandered past houses of different kinds and a place with mobile bungalows all set out in streets. At the entrance to Huntington Lane he considered if he should go that way, but in the end, he decided to stay on his chosen route. When he needed a rest, he sat on the grass verge, his back to the road, and ate a couple of biscuits and had a drink of his water. It was a warm and sunny day so he sat on his coat and enjoyed the warmth, thinking of the dog called Charlie that he'd met on Monday and he wished he had a dog to keep him company. He was lonely, and missed his mum. She might not have been the kind of mother he would have liked; she wasn't motherly and she hadn't cooked lovely cakes or dinners like he dreamed about, and he had definitely suffered at the hands of her men friends, but she was his mum and he did love her.

At times like this, he remembered when they'd lived in a house and slept in a proper bed. In those days, when he was little, his mum had been a happy person and they'd had fun together. He remembered a man who he was sure was his dad. He only stayed with them sometimes and when he did, his mum was really happy and the three of them loved being together. Although now, Charlie sometimes wondered if that time was actually real. Was it wishful thinking? Did he want a dad so badly that he'd dreamed him? He had a photo of his mum and a man who she said was his dad, so he knew the man was real, so where was he now?

His mum had nice friends who would take them out for treats and they'd have ice-cream and play in parks. He vaguely remembered a sort of park nearby with grassy slopes and trees – and the sea, he was sure there had been sea. But he hadn't a clue where that was, for they had been wandering around the country in the camper-van for years, going from place to place, sometimes with other travelling people, sometimes alone. He could never make up his mind whether he preferred being alone with her or being with other travellers. Other travelling kids had bullied him and on several occasions he'd been cuffed by the men or slapped by women. Most times though they'd been great, friendly and caring and they'd looked after him. It seemed to him that, as soon as they got settled and he started to make friends, his mum would decide it was time to leave and off they'd go.

Charlie sighed a heavy sigh. Even though he hated living in the camper-van, he'd give anything to go back and live there again with his mum. But she was gone and he was on the run, with nowhere to hide – and worse, no one to love him.

Chapter 16

"You won't find him in, luv."

Dan turned to look up at the bedroom window in the house next door to the one he and Grant were standing outside. A woman was leaning out, her hair in curlers and a cigarette hanging onto her lower lip. It made Dan think she'd strayed off the old set of Coronation Street; she reminded him of Florrie Lindley. (Not that he was old enough to have seen them first time round but he'd seen bits of old episodes of the soap.)

"Is this Mr Simon Denton's residence?" asked Dan.

"Yes. Hang on a mo, I'll come down." The head disappeared and the window slammed shut.

Dan looked at Grant, who had his collar turned up and his hands shoved in his pockets. It seemed a pleasant day, but the wind that whipped off the English Channel was somewhat cutting.

A few minutes later, the woman's door of opened and she came out. She'd whipped out the curlers and was not wearing the suspected floral overall but a shirt and jeans with a blue quilted body warmer over her shirt.

"Police, are yer?"

"Uh, yes."

"Thought so. I can smell them a b***** mile off. I don't want to be seen talking to yer, yer'd better come in." Without waiting to see if they would, she went back into her house.

Dan and Grant shrugged at each other and went back along Mr Denton's short path and up next door's garden and into the house, where the door shut behind them. They followed the woman into a room at the back. It had a table surrounded by four chairs and sideboard. The window overlooked a small but neat back garden.

They each sat on a dining room chair.

"I'd just brewed a pot, would yer like some tea?" asked the woman. "I allus 'ave one about now."

"That would be nice, thank you."

The woman left but returned quickly with a tray laden with three mugs, a large blue teapot and milk in a jug. Dumping the tray on the table, she went out again and returned with a plate of chocolate digestive biscuits, which Dan saw Grant eyeing enthusiastically. He smiled to himself, knowing Grant's weakness for chocolate biscuits, especially the ones before him.

Finally, after she'd poured the tea, she settled at the table with them. Dan cleared his throat.

"This is very nice of you, Mrs – erm?"

"Clara Gleeson."

"Mrs Gleeson." Dan nodded. I'm Detective Inspector Daniel Cooke and this is Detective Sergeant Grant."

"Oh, do call me Clara, everyone does."

"Clara," agreed Dan. "So, is Mr Denton at work?"

"Oh, bless you – no, he don't work. At least, he's a writer, so I suppose that's work. He's away, he travels a lot, especially during the summer. I keep an eye on his house for 'im. What d'ya want 'im for? I'm sure 'e aint done noffink, 'e ent that type."

"Oh no, I'm sure he isn't," Dan hastened to assure her. "We did hope he might be able to help us with our enquiries. How long have you known Mr Denton?"

"Oh, years an' years. We've lived next door to each other, gotta be nearly twenty years."

"That's a long time. Do you know him well?"

"Well enough." Clara narrowed her eyes a moment and then nonchalantly helped herself to a biscuit and bit into it. "You don't live next door to someone fer that long without getting ter know them. 'e were good ter me wen my old man got sent down."

"Ah." So, Clara's husband was a guest of Her Majesty. No wonder she didn't want to be seen talking with the police.

"Mind you," she went on, "the cops did me a favour. Nasty begger, my old man. It were a relief when he got banged up – serving a long sentence too; I 'ope 'e never gets out. Life is better without 'im."

"Right. Now, perhaps you can tell us a bit about Mr Denton."

"What's all this about?" she said, rising from her chair. "I ain't goin ter help you git Simon inter trouble."

"It's okay, Clara, Simon isn't in trouble at all. Do you remember him having a camper-van?"

"Oh, of course. It's beautiful, all bright and shiny. 'Ere, nothin's 'appened to 'im, 'as it?" Clara looked alarmed.

"No, no, not at all. So, he has a camper-van now, does he? It's a big, modern one?"

"Yes, that's right, although he's 'ad it a few years now."

"Did he ever have an old Volkswagen one?"

"Yes, 'e did. 'Ad it fer years an' years. 'E loved that old van. But h'e decided 'e needed more comfort, so 'e bought the one 'e 'as now."

Dan nodded understandingly. "Yes, I can imagine. Do you know what he did with the old van? Did he sell it?"

The woman nibbled her biscuit thoughtfully. "No, I don't. I assumed 'e'd sold it."

"Grant, will you show Clara the pictures?"

Grant opened his phone and showed Clara the photo of Mandy.

"Clara, do you know the woman in this photograph?"

She screwed up her eyes and looked for a long time. "There's something about her that seems familiar, but I can't say for sure."

Grant brought up another picture. "Or this boy?"

Immediately, Clara shook her head. "Nope, never seen 'im before."

"Well, thank you, you've been very helpful. I think that's all we can do for now. Here's my card; when Mr Denton comes home, would you give him the card and ask him to call me please?"

She took the card and walked with them to the door. Once outside, she said, "Um, the woman you showed me the picture of – who is she?"

"That's what we are trying to find out."

"Can I ask why?"

71

"Well, since you ask so nicely, it's because she is dead."

"Dead?"

"Yes, someone has killed her. Good day to you, Mrs Gleeson."

And with that, Dan strode away and Grant hurried to open the gate for him.

Once in the car, Dan drove away without speaking. After a few moments, Grant said; "She was lying, Boss."

"I know."

"So, what do we do now?"

"Do? We look for somewhere to eat, what else?"

****

Dan and Grant had almost finished their meal at The Ship when Dan's phone rang. It said 'unknown' but he winked at Grant as he answered. "Detective Inspector Cooke. Yes, Mrs Gleeson, we're still in the area. We'll come back to you shortly."

"Right, object achieved Grant – she's had time to think. Let's go."

Clara opened the door immediately at the knock.

"I'm sorry, Mr Cooke, but I didn't know what to say earlier."

"So, what do you have to tell us? You did know the woman, didn't you?"

She hung her head and nodded.

"Yes, and the boy too."

Dan led the way back to where they'd sat previously.

"Sit down, Clara, and tell us what you know."

"Well, I don't know that much actually. I do know that she is Simon's niece and the boy is her son, although I haven't seen him for a few years. He was quite small the last time I saw him, but the drawing does look like the little boy grown up, if you get me?"

72

Dan nodded. "So, she is related to Simon? Is Mandy Jones her real name?"

"No. Her real name is Mollie Denton; she is Simon's brother's daughter. But 'er parents both died in a plane crash and so she came to live with Simon when she was about ten. Lovely child, she was."

Dan watched the sad look on her face and knew she was probably thinking about the child that had been Mollie.

"You must have known her quite well as she lived next door to you?"

"Yes, I did know her well. She lived with Simon until she was oh, about eighteen or nineteen. She were a clever girl and had a good job, so she found herself a flat in town. She worked for a shipping company or sommat, I was never quite sure where exactly. She were very happy, had a nice boyfriend, a sailor, he were, so 'e wasn't there all the time. There's a lot o' them around 'ere because it's a naval port, see? Then she 'ad 'er baby, Charlie."

"She had a boyfriend, you say? Do you know who he was? Did you ever see him?"

"No, I didn't. Whenever 'e was home, she didn't come round. She used to say that she had to spend all her time with 'im when 'e was there 'cos 'e was allus so short o' time to be 'ome. She used ter come round 'ere ter see us when 'e was at sea."

"Did she ever tell you his name or where he came from?"

Clara screwed up her face, thinking.

"I never knew 'is name. Mollie never once mentioned it. Charlie used to call him 'Daddy' o' course. She never really talked about 'im, yer know? But something must 'ave gone wrong, 'cos they broke up when Charlie were small, about three or four, I think he was. Simon asked her to come back and live 'ere but she wouldn't at first. She were changed though, it was as if the light had gone out o' 'er after they broke up. Simon were worried about the kid – and ter be honest, so was I. We were glad when she decided to come back 'ere after all."

"So, she and Charlie came back to live here with Simon? How long did they stay?"

Clara wrinkled her face as she tried to think. "Oh, I'm not sure. Around a year, maybe. Hard to be sure, time goes by so quickly. I know Charlie never went to school, although he did go to nursery."

"Then what happened?"

The woman got up and started to pace around the limited space. She was obviously agitated. "Sommat happened – Simon would never tell me what. Although he did tell me that he'd let her have his precious Volkswagen camper-van and she just took off in it with the boy and I never saw them again."

"Never? They never came back here at all?"

"Nope. Not that I ever saw anyway. And now she's dead, so I'll never see her again. I loved that girl, Mr Cooke – and the little lad. Simon never got married and was alone so we were sort of like parents to her and grandparents to the boy. I missed them like crazy and so did Simon. I think that's why he goes away a lot. He'll be so upset when he finds out she's dead. And what about Charlie? Where is 'e, who's looking after 'im?"

"We don't know. I'm sorry to have to tell you that he's missing. Apparently, he ran away when he realised his mother was dead and we've not been able to find him as yet. We are making every effort to do so."

"Missing? 'E's out there somewhere, all alone, knowin' 'is mum's dead? Poor little chap."

"Indeed."

"Did you say someone killed her?"

"Yes."

"Poor, poor girl – and poor Charlie. I tried to call Simon after you left but his phone was off. 'E does that when 'es working. It could be days afore he gets back ter me. I wanted ter ask him whether I should tell you anyfing. But I couldn't get 'im and our girl is dead so I decided I should 'elp yer. I'm sorry fer messin' yer about, Mr Cooke."

"Don't worry, we had a feeling you would change your mind. So, you have no idea where Mr. Denton could be?"

She shook her head. "No. 'E could be anywhere – in this country or abroad. 'E goes ter all sorts o' places – research fer 'is books, yer know."

"Yes. Is there anything else you can tell us that you think could be helpful?"

"Not really. But one thing I can tell yer is this: whatever made Mollie up an' leave 'as ter be serious, cos Simon, 'e loved that old camper-van like a child and 'e would never 'ave let 'er 'ave it if it hadn't bin badly needed. Something serious, Mr Cooke, and that's why Simon wouldn't even talk ter me about it, he said the less I knew, the better it was fer me. I didn't argue because I could see 'e was frightened an' so was she."

Chapter 17

Dan and Grant agreed it had been worth taking the long drive down to Plymouth. Now they knew Mandy's real name and where she'd come from and that she had a relative in Plymouth. They hoped Simon Denton would get in touch with them soon; perhaps he could give them more information.

"So, Simon Denton gave Mollie his van and continued to pay the road tax on it since she left with it. What could have caused her to leave so suddenly, I wonder?"

"Could it have anything to do with the mysterious boyfriend? Perhaps he was going to fight for the boy?" mused Grant.

"It's possible. Seems somewhat drastic though. Why not stay at home and fight it? I'm sure the courts would have decided in her favour as she'd always had the boy and they had a good home with her uncle."

"Does seem somewhat extreme."

Dan got on the phone. "Hello, Julie? I want you to look up a birth registration for me. Charlie Denton, about twelve years ago, born in the Plymouth area. Yes, that's our Charlie. Mother's name, Mollie Denton. If there's a father's name, I need to know. Also, can you find out where Mollie Denton was living then? Ask Johnson to track where the camper-van has been since it left Plymouth. Call me back if either of you have any information. Thanks."

"Boss, should we go to a library and search the newspapers? Maybe something happened that involved Mollie Denton eight years ago."

"That's an idea. Find the library, Grant, and let's hope it's still open."

The librarian in Plymstock was very helpful.

"The back newspapers are online now, sirs. If you type in the year, it will bring up all the area's newspapers for that time. It's rather tedious, but better than trawling through a lot of old and dusty papers."

They agreed it was and went to one of the library's computers and followed the instructions.

An hour or so later, having searched the papers from the year Charlie was born, they were sore of eyes and fed up. Dan got up and stretched his back, groaning slightly.

The librarian smiled at them. "No luck?"

"Doesn't seem so."

"Were you looking for anything in particular? I've lived here all my life, I might know something."

"We were looking for anything that might have involved a young woman named Mollie Denton. She lived in Hooe, though, so you probably wouldn't have known her."

"Mollie Denton? As a matter of fact, I did know a Mollie Denton. We went to the same secondary school and later she lived in a flat not far from where I live."

Dan and Grant looked at each other incredulously.

"Goodness, that's a real surprise! Of all the people we could have met and we find someone who actually knew Mollie. Did your Mollie have a child called Charlie?"

"Yes."

"It looks like it is our Mollie Denton. Are you free to help us, Miss...?"

"It's Mrs actually, Mrs Marie Dale – and my husband's name is Jim!" she giggled. "I got a lot of teasing about that from the older members of my family."

Dan and Grant looked at each other and then at her with questioning looks.

"Jim Dale – Mrs Dale's Diary – the old radio programme...?"

"Oh yes! I remember my mother used to listen to that," laughed Dan.

"Look, I have to close as it's six o'clock. Why don't you take a seat in the foyer and I'll join you shortly? I have a few minutes to spare as my daughter is at her friend's house doing homework today."

They watched as the few people who remained in the library walked past on the way out. While they waited, Dan called Julie to tell her not to worry about the address of Mollie's place. Then they followed the librarian out and she locked the door.

"Can we give you a lift home?"

"It's only a short distance, I always walk. That's one of the reasons why I like this job, although how long I'll have it for, your guess is as good as mine!" she sighed. "It seems libraries are being closed all over the place – local authorities and their cutbacks."

The drive back to her house was indeed short. Her home was a semi with a neat front garden. When they got out of the car, Marie waved her hand towards a block of flats further down the road. "Mollie used to live in one of those."

Marie unlocked the door and invited them in. "My husband and daughter will be home soon, so do you mind if I get the meal ready while we talk? I'll make us a drink too, would you like tea or coffee?"

They sat at the table in the spacious kitchen, while Marie bustled around, spooning coffee into mugs in readiness for the kettle to boil and gathering vegetables to chop. "I hope you don't mind instant, we don't have a coffee maker."

"That's fine. When you've drunk coffee from the machine at the station, just about anything else is like nectar." Grant laughed cheerfully.

She put their mugs before them, and said, "So, what would you like to know about Mollie? I haven't seen her in ages, is she alright? She's not in trouble, is she?"

"I'm sorry to have to tell you that Mollie is dead, Mrs Dale."

"Dead? Oh no! What happened? Did she have an accident?"

"I'm afraid someone killed her. That's why we are here trying to find out about her. You see, she had a false driving licence under the name of Mandy Jones. It wasn't until we came here and talked to her uncle's neighbour that we found out her real name."

"Oh, how strange. Mollie always seemed so happy. She adored her little boy, Charlie."

"So you knew Charlie?"

"Yes." Her hands flew to her cheeks. "Charlie! Is he okay? Where is he?"

"Well, he's alive, but he's run away. We're hoping he will soon be found, it's not easy for a twelve-year-old boy to live on the streets."

"No. Oh, I do hope he's found soon. I'm sure his Uncle Simon will have him back and look after him. Simon is so nice. I haven't seen him for years though, not since Mollie left here."

"Did you see much of Mollie when she lived here?"

"Oh yes, I saw her a lot. We were friends, you see, and my daughter, Emma, is only a little older than Charlie, so we used to take them to the park or they'd come here and the children would play while we chatted. It was nice and I missed her when she went away."

"Did you ever meet her boyfriend, Charlie's father?"

"Well...I saw him once or twice, but I never really met him. If I saw them out together, she would just wave and carry on. I used to think it was odd but she once said to me that she didn't see him often so she wanted to keep him to herself. I had to accept that explanation, I suppose."

"Did she tell you his name?"

"No – oh hang on, yes. I heard her once refer to him as Steve. Yes, that's right, Steve. What his other name was, I don't have a clue."

"What was he like?"

"Handsome! Dead good looking – perhaps that's why she never introduced us." Marie giggled and tossed her dark curls. Attractive, with her dark hair and her make-up perfect, she had a good figure too, Dan mused. Yes, that could be the reason, a little jealous protection of 'her' property from her pretty friend?

79

"Now I come to think of it..." Marie said, thoughtfully, as she paused in her chopping. "He seemed to be here so little. When he was here, he didn't seem to stay long. I used to comment to her about it but she always said it was because he had so little shore leave. But I know other sailors who are able to stay much longer with their families. When they have shore leave they are often home for weeks."

"Maybe he was married already and that's why he never stayed long..." Grant said slowly.

Dan stared at him. "Grant, I think you may have hit the nail on the head. He was married; she was his bit on the side and Charlie was probably an accident."

Marie resumed her meal preparation. "Mollie never behaved as though Charlie was an accident. She adored him. And on the few occasions I saw them together, the boyfriend always looked happy. He'd carry Charlie on his shoulders and play with him in the park. Whoever he was, he loved Charlie and he seemed to love Mollie. I saw the way he looked at her and there was no mistaking it."

"So...Mollie had a sailor boyfriend who came as often as he could to see her and his son. A happy little family. Then he stopped coming. I wonder why?"

"Perhaps the wife found out," remarked Grant.

"That would seem to be the obvious conclusion," agreed Dan. He stood up. "Well, Mrs Dale, I think that's all for now, unless you can think of anything else about Mollie that might be helpful?"

Marie looked up from the oven.

"I don't think I can."

"Well, if you do think of anything, would you please call me on this number? I'll leave my card on the table here. Thank you for your help."

"You're welcome, although it wasn't much. I do hope you find young Charlie very soon. I'd really like to know. Would it be too much to ask, because I know I shall worry about him now that I know what's happened?"

"Yes. Give Grant your phone number and we'll be happy to let you know."

Grant scribbled the number she reeled off and then folded his notebook away in his pocket.

"We'll see ourselves out, Mrs Dale, we don't want you to spoil the food. We'll be in touch."

Once outside, Dan and Grant conferred.

"We need to find Charlie's father as a matter of urgency. I feel he holds the key to this mystery."

Chapter 18

Charlie tried to avoid shops for the past couple of days, trying to exist on apples and other fruit he found in gardens or farms, always careful not to be seen. He found blackberries in hedgerows and, to his shame, stole bread from a kitchen when a door stood open, only taking one slice, tempting as it was to take more. Water was a problem too. Although only a boy, he could not continue to exist like this. Lucky so far; he'd found a barn with bales of straw to sleep in for three nights, but it was getting colder and soon there wouldn't be any fruit around to find. In any case, his stomach told him that a diet of only fruit was not good enough; he was constantly hungry and his bowel movements were loose, adding to his general discomfort. He knew he smelled, and longed for a bath or a shower. Once again, he thought of the van, at least there he could wash, and in warm water if he heated the tiny kettle. And Missus White was always willing to fill his stomach.

He was weary, hungry and completely fed up but he had to move on because the farmer who owned the barn had found him and shouted at him. Finding the strength to run, he'd fled until he was out of sight. He continued to plod on, not knowing where he was going. He eventually came into a pretty village, with a pond and a green next to it, and benches to sit on. On the opposite side was a village hall, also surrounded by grass. Along the top part were buildings that housed a village shop and, further to the left, a restaurant. The shop drew him and he pressed his nose to the window, to see shelves stacked with tins of food, magazines, sweets and biscuits and all kinds of things. Perhaps at least he could get some water there; he was desperate for water. Should he? Although it might give him away, his need for something other than fruit drove him inside. With closed eyes, he breathed in the smell of fresh bread that wafted towards him from a shelf. There were loaves of the usual sliced bread, but also large loaves, which he knew were called bloomers, and small rolls, some round, some finger-shaped. They looked wonderful and Charlie wanted to taste all of them!

"Hello there, young man. Can I help you with anything?"

Charlie spun round to see a cheery-faced woman in a pink overall, standing behind a counter. He didn't know what to say, but as he was trying to think, he spotted some pies in a glass-top display box. His mouth began to water.

"Please, miss, how much are the pies?"

"Well, they are one pound fifty, but you can have one for a pound if you like."

A pound? Charlie's smile became wide. "Oh, yes please!"

"Would you like it warmed? They are lovely warmed."

Speechless, he nodded, and watched her while she took a pair of tongs, put a pie on a glass plate and took it through a doorway behind her. Moments later, he heard the sound of a microwave.

While he waited, he looked around the shop, and picked up a big bottle of water. It was more expensive than the one he'd bought at Tesco, but he needed it. He also collected a packet of biscuits and brought them to the counter, at the same time as she brought in his pie. She popped it in a thick cardboard box with a plastic knife and fork.

"There you go, young man."

"Oh, fank you, Missis."

He was aware of her eyes on him as he counted out the money onto the counter. She gathered them up. "That's just right. Mind how you go now."

Charlie went to sit on a bench on the green. He had a feeling the shopkeeper might split on him, but he was longing to get his teeth into the pie. It smelt divine and he was already salivating in anticipation.

The pie was as good as it looked, the meat was tender, the gravy rich and delicious and he felt it was the best pie he'd ever eaten. He swigged some of the bottled water, and then stuffed the bottle and the packet of biscuits in his backpack. He didn't really want to move on, for he liked this village, but he had to, because he had a feeling that the woman had recognised him. Indecision came upon him again – would it really be so bad to be found and go into care? Visions of a warm bed and regular food swam before him, weakening his resolve. Should he just let himself be caught? But no, the habit of running was in him and so he gave in to it again. Just a bit longer...

Madge had, indeed, recognised the boy. The sight of his poor, ravaged face with the dark, sunken eyes had stabbed at her kind heart. And she caught the smell of him as he moved. Poor little fellow. What must it be like for him, knowing his mum was dead and having to live outside? The artist's drawing of was close, but Madge fancied his face was even thinner now, and no wonder. She could just see him, sitting on the seat, and knew the pie hadn't lasted long, for he must have been starving. Hopefully, Lucy's pie will keep him going for a bit. Lucy only used the best ingredients in her pies, no scraped-up scraps with gristle in her products! And the pastry was light and delicious.

Madge made the phone call. Much to her frustration, when she came back, the boy was gone.

Less than an hour later, Dan and Grant walked into Madge's shop.

"Oh, Inspector Cooke. I'm so sorry, but the boy's gone. He was sitting over there eating a pie, but when I came back from calling you, he'd gone."

"He can't have gone far in such a short time. We'll spread out and look around the village."

"If you find him, please be careful with him, he's so thin and looks ill, poor little fellow."

Dan put a hand on her shoulder. "Don't worry, Mrs Harrison, we'll look after him. We desperately need to find him, for he can't live out in the open alone for much longer. I have other officers with me and we'll make a search of the village. We're grateful to you for calling us so promptly, this is the closest we've got to him so far."

As they went outside another police car pulled to a stop behind their car. Besides themselves, there were four uniformed police officers in the marked vehicle and Julie Coombs and PC Johnson were in Grant's car.

Dan gave them their instructions and the other six went off in different directions.

"Grant, we'll go up to River View."

Grinning, Grant started up the car and very shortly, they were pulling up outside the old black and white farmhouse belonging to Lucy and Ken Baxter.

Lucy looked surprised when she opened the door.

"Dan! Oh, hello, Sergeant Grant. This is a surprise – can I help you? Is there a problem? No one has unearthed any more dead bodies in one of my fields, have they?"

Dan grinned at her. "No. Not that we've heard anyway. However, we've had a call to say that our missing lad has been seen in the village. Have you seen him at all?"

Lucy frowned. "No, of course I haven't. I would have called you. How long since he was seen?"

"Less than an hour. He went into the shop. Do you mind if we look around your property?"

"Not at all. Help yourselves, you know the way around. I'll make you a drink while you look. I do hope you find him."

As they set off to search, Lucy shut the door behind them. They could hear Clarry barking inside the house and looked at each other, smiling.

"Time to say hello to Clarry later, Grant. Now, which way shall we go first?"

****

It was some time later when they returned to the house. Lucy's grounds were extensive but the trees were shedding their leaves, making it easier to search. They went through the walled garden into the grounds of Sutton Court to see two uniforms making a similar search there, so they returned to their own area. After searching all the grounds, they looked in the barn and then up the steps to the old hay loft above, but as it was locked with the key on the outside, they didn't bother to go in.

"You never found anything then?" asked Lucy, as she poured their tea and laid out an inviting-looking lemon sponge cake in front of them.

"Not a sign. I think he must have gone the other way, or further out. We'll make a search of Little Sutton and Long Sutton. He can't have gone far. We can warn householders and farmers to keep a special eye open for him or any signs he might have been there. This cake is superb, Lucy."

"Glad you like it. Oh, there's Rosemary, she's woken from her nap and I'll have to fetch John from nursery shortly."

"We'll not keep you, Lucy. We're grateful for the tea and cake. You'll keep your eyes peeled for the lad, won't you? I really want to find him, to know he's safe. He might be able to help us too, he might have seen something."

"Of course I will. Goodbye, you two and good luck."

Lucy shut the door immediately behind the two men and they heard her call, "Alright, Rosemary, Mummy's coming!"

****

From his position crouched behind the barn wall, Charlie watched the two men drive away and sighed with relief. Thank goodness they hadn't brought dogs or he wouldn't have stood a chance. The dog inside the house knew he was there. Charlie wondered what sort it was. By the sound of its bark, he guessed it was a small one. He hoped if he met it, it wouldn't be vicious, he'd had experiences with small, nasty dogs.

Over the years, Charlie had become adept at dodging people looking for him, well aware that fists would be used should his hunters come upon him. It had been easy at this place – there were so many nooks and crannies, walls, trees and bushes to shrink into that it had been a doddle to not be seen by the two detectives. Although they wore normal clothes, they looked like police and Charlie was not about to take any chances. At one point, they'd passed so close to him that he'd been able to see them clearly and he had to admit to himself that they had pleasant faces, the sort of faces you could trust, he'd thought, and for a moment he had been tempted to give himself up. But his fear took over and he didn't. The next thing he had to decide, should he move on, or stay around here for a while?

Chapter 19

"John, have you eaten one of those bread rolls I put to cool?"

"No, Mummy." John looked up, his big brown eyes wide and innocent. Lucy could indeed see no signs of bread around his face, or crumbs on the floor. She frowned.

"I was sure there were sixteen rolls, but now there are only fifteen. How strange, I must be losing it. Too many things on my mind I expect. Now, my darling, you sit at the table and eat your breakfast while I get Rosemary's food."

"Yes Mummy." John sat obediently at the table and started to eat his puffed rice. Lucy popped the baby into the high chair and set a bowl of baby cereal in front of her and gave her a spoon. Lucy also had a spoon and between the two of them, Rosemary somehow managed to get fed, although the contents of the baby's spoon more often than not ended up elsewhere. Mealtimes were usually messy affairs. Lucy removed the bowl and gave her a finger of toast and Rosemary happily chewed it while her mother provided John with his toast.

When the two children had eaten, Lucy gave John a face cloth and smiled as she watched her serious son clean his face and then get down from his chair. He'd always been a neat and tidy child, even when he was Rosemary's age; fastidiously eating his food so he never made his face or surrounding areas very mucky. *'Not like his sister'*, thought Lucy, looking at her daughter's face, which was now liberally smeared with butter and Marmite. She deftly cleaned the baby's face and hands with another face cloth and lifted her from the chair.

Once Rosemary had been stuffed into her coat and into the push chair, and John was ready, Lucy donned her coat and the three of them set off to take John to nursery with Clarry daintily walking beside them, panting happily at the prospect of a walk. As they stepped out of the house, the little dog barked.

"What's the matter, Clarry? There's no one there. Come on, we need to get going," persuaded Lucy, giving the lead a little tug. The small dog that looked a bit like a walking hearthrug soon gave up and walked along with them.

****

Charlie, looking through a window that, surprisingly, was not as dirty as the camper-van window had been, had a few nasty moments when the little white dog had barked, her nose pointing in the direction of the upper barn window. His heart in his mouth, he shrank back away from the window and shivered in fear. The dog stopped barking and he risked another peek at the window and was relieved to see the small group going down the drive.

Although feeling guilty for stealing it, he sat back and relished the still-warm crusty roll. He'd taken the opportunity while the family were upstairs. The dog had barked from another part of the house but doors must have been shut, for she didn't appear. He'd crept quietly into the kitchen, leaving the door open, grabbed the roll and fled, running up the stone steps to the upper barn, shutting the door behind him.

He had discovered the barn the previous evening, after spotting the man, who was obviously the husband of the lady who lived there and the children's father. Even before the kitchen door closed, the little boy had run up to the man, arms open wide to receive his hug. The sight of that joyful moment invoked a distant memory, of a man, who Charlie knew was his father, and how, as a little boy, he would run into his arms in the same way as he'd just seen.

As he shrank back behind the wall at the end of the barn, he let his mind drift back to those days. The memory of it was strong and clear as if it had only happened recently, even though he could only have been three or four. He remembered riding on his dad's shoulders and them playing together in a park, or with his toys at home, wherever that home was. The picture of his father's face was becoming blurred, although he remembered the man's eyes and the way they sort of softened when he looked at him and his mother. How he'd been safe with this man and how happy his mum always was when he was there. In spite of trying to be brave, tears ran down his cheeks at the great sense of loss – loss not only of his mum and the man but also the sense of belonging. There had been another man, an older one, who they'd lived with for a while and he'd also had a sense of security and safeness. Suddenly, it had all changed and he was living in that van with only his mum and a succession of different places and people had become their lives. A tear trickled down his cheek. He'd once had safety, security and love, he was sure of it. But now, there was no one – he belonged nowhere, no-one loved him and nobody cared.

Once it was almost dark, he moved. The door at the top of the stone steps had a key in the lock so he went to see if it had somewhere he could sleep. As he moved stealthily up the steps, he heard the dog bark and shrank back against the stonework, keeping as still as a statue and held his breath. There was no movement from the house, so eventually he opened the door and crept into the room beyond, took the key out of the lock, and shut the door. Solid shapes loomed darkly in the fading light but he was able to explore, using his hands, carefully feeling around them. They were mostly chairs and other household items that had obviously been discarded. Hopefully, there would be a bed. There wasn't a bed, but there was an old mattress. He couldn't believe his luck. Old blankets covered things so he carefully removed them to use on his makeshift bed.

Charlie was well pleased with his accommodation. He had a bed with covers in a room that gave protection from the elements, almost as good, if not better, than the camper-van. His stomach rumbled loudly so he scrabbled in his bag for the biscuits, ate three and drank some water. Then he lay down on his bed and fell asleep.

In the morning, he awoke to sunlight streaming in through one of the small windows. With no idea of the time, he continued to lay in his bed, because, for once, he was cosy and warm. He liked it here and decided to try to stay. Hopefully, the family never went up there so he could keep his bed.

Eventually, hunger and the need to empty his bladder drove him from his comfy cocoon and he emerged carefully from the loft barn. There was no sign of life in the house but he could smell something delicious. He ran swiftly to the kitchen window and peeped through the glass. The room was empty, but he could see a whole load of bread rolls cooling on racks on the worktop. His mouth watered and he made up his mind quickly. Taking a big risk, he'd opened the door quietly and crept inside, grabbed a roll and fled.

Having watched the family leaving the premises, he left the barn again and wondered what to do. With his precious backpack, just in case, he decided to take a look around the village, although he'd have to be careful not to be seen, especially by the woman in the shop. As he was about to leave, he had a sudden thought. He had no idea how much the roll would cost but he put his hand in his money bag and drew out three ten-pence pieces and laid them on the kitchen doorstep. Then he headed towards the river path that he'd discovered the previous day.

Chapter 20

Dan's team watched with concerned eyes as he paced the incident room. They knew he was frustrated; indeed, they all were.

The pictures of Charlie and his mother seemed to look down on Dan and mock him.

"This case is going nowhere!" Dan ran his fingers through his hair fretfully as he stopped to look at the incident board. "I thought we were making progress when we found the real identity of Molly Denton and met people who had known her. We have a description of the boyfriend, who was obviously Charlie's father, but he's not named on the birth certificate and no one seems to know who he is. And we can't find Charlie – how inefficient are we that we can't find a small boy?"

"We have the tyre-print, Boss, that was by the camper-van. It was from a SUV."

"Was it indeed?" Dan looked at Grant. "Interesting. Right, Judy, I'd like you and Johnson to look into who owns a SUV in this area. Grant, we're going back out to take another look at that camper-van."

Grant was startled. "We are? But we've already searched it."

"I know. But I have a feeling..."

"Right, I'll fetch the car." Grant knew about his boss's 'feelings' so didn't question further. When his sergeant had left the room, Dan said, "I know it's not very interesting, Judy, but if you find anything, take Johnson and go interview the owners. You have a good nose, you'll sense if any of them are suspect."

Judy sat up straighter after receiving the compliment and immediately set to on her computer. Dan gave a small smile and nod and left.

When they arrived at the camper-van, Dan walked around the outside slowly, then he opened the door and they went inside. It looked a mess as it had been examined thoroughly by Forensics and then by the two of them afterwards.

"Help me move this bed, Grant."

In spite of their efforts, there was nothing to be found. Dan sat on the seat that had formed part of the bed. They hadn't bothered to put it back together.

"Search the front, Grant. I'm going back outside."

Dan again circled the van, very slowly. He could hear Grant scrabbling about in the cab. He laid down on the grass and peered underneath.

"Bingo!"

"Eh? Ouch!" Grant appeared, rubbing his head ruefully. "Did you have to make me jump like that, Boss? What have you found?"

Dan had a slim black package in his hands.

"This was under the van. It's magnetic." He opened it up and drew out the contents. Inside were photographs, a bank book and letters. He put them all back inside the package. "Lock it up, Grant. Let's go."

Once in the car, Dan said. "I'd like to just pop in on the Whites. They might have seen that SUV."

Grant nodded and headed out of the field.

Farmer White had just come in for a cup of tea, so it was perfect timing. They shook hands and followed him into the kitchen. Without asking, his smiling wife poured a mug of tea out for them and pushed a large piece of fruit cake into their hands.

"Have you found Charlie yet?"

"I regret to say we haven't, Mrs White. There was a sighting yesterday but he vanished again. At least we know he's still alive."

"Well, that's something, I suppose. He's determined, isn't he?" She said, with admiration in her voice. "Although I can't help worrying about him."

Dan nodded. "Yes, we're worried too. I think most of the county are looking out for him."

"What can we help you with, Inspector?" The farmer looked at his watch. "As I'll be needing to get back to my work, like."

"Of course. Sorry. We were wondering if you saw any vehicles parked in the lane, before Mandy's death, at any time over the period that the two were living in your field?"

The husband and wife looked at each other briefly, faces screwed in thought.

"Can't say as I did, no," said Farmer White.

"No large cars, such as an SUV?"

"No." The two shook their heads.

"Might any of your workers have seen something? Are there any around?"

"Hmm, well, Billy and Greg are both working in the far fields. I could ask them, save you going to them? I could call you if they'd seen anything."

"That would be useful, thank you. As soon as you can, please?"

"I'll be going over to them in a bit."

"Thanks. Well, we'd best be off. If you do recall anything, do call us."

"Will do." They shook hands and headed for the door.

"I've just remembered," Mrs White said suddenly. The men stopped and looked at her. "I once saw a car in that lane, parked up, like. It was one of those really posh sports car-type things with an open top. I don't know what sort, I'm really bad at knowing cars. It was beautiful, red, with a black interior. I was just coming home from a trip into Hereford and so I had to pass it. I remember wondering what on earth it was doing there, parked up in the middle of nowhere, like."

"When was this?"

"Oh, ages ago, back in April or May, can't quite recall now. I go into town most Saturdays, you see, they tend to merge in the memory – you know how it is, like"

"I do indeed," responded Dan gravely. "If you saw the car again, would you know if it was the same one?"

"Yes, I think so."

"Would you keep a look out, in case?"

"Of course I will."

"Although I can't see how it can help us, as it was at least four months ago. Well, thank you both again. We'll let you know when we find Charlie."

"Oh, that poor lamb; I wish he'd stayed here, I'd have looked after him, like."

"I know you would have, Mrs White, and I wish he'd stayed too. It's bad enough looking for a murderer, without worrying about a missing boy as well."

"What do you think about that sports car sighting, Grant?"

The two detectives were in the car on the way back to Hereford.

"I dunno at this point, Boss. I can't see how it can be connected. Seems a random place to be parked up though."

"Hmm. I wonder if there are any public footpaths there, could the car owner have been walking?" Dan mused.

"I don't think there are, Boss. I'm sure the Whites would have said if walkers come to that area. It would have to be across their land, I would have thought. But I got the impression it's unusual for vehicles to be parked there."

"My thoughts exactly. I have a sneaking suspicion that it's part of this, but I can't quite get my head around it yet."

"Could it have been someone come to see Mollie and the boy, perhaps?"

"That's a possibility, although I'm not sure how she would know the kind of person that would have such a flash car." Dan gave a deep sigh. "Step on it, Grant, I'm in dire need of a caffeine shot."

****

Clara Gleeson had just returned from a trip to the shops when she saw a man walk up the path to her door.

"Yes?" she asked, as she dumped her shopping bags on the ground and stared at him suspiciously. He was good looking, she thought, eyeing his dark suit and handsome regular features,

95

blue eyes and dark brown hair brushed neatly in a somewhat old-fashioned style for a young man.

"Mrs Gleeson? The name's Smith." He held up a police ID. "I've been sent from Hereford. We're concerned about Mr Denton because we've not been able to track him down. Do you have a photograph of him, or know where we can get one from his house? It would help us so we can send it through our systems all over the country and the world, if necessary. Have you heard from him at all?"

"No, I haven't."

"Hmm, worrying. You'd have thought he would have seen the news about his niece."

"You don't think something could have happened to him too?"

"We hope not. Can you help us with a picture?"

"I have a key to his house. I'm pretty sure he has one in his study, the one he uses for his books. In fact, can't you just lift a picture off the internet? He's pretty well known, you know."

"No, I didn't know. Don't have much time for reading; too many criminals to chase!" He flashed his teeth at her.

"Yes, quite. I'll fetch the key." Clara picked up her shopping, and went in, shutting the door behind her. She didn't want him seeing where she kept Simon's key. She left her bags on the kitchen table, took the key out of a pot on her mantle-piece then went back where the policeman was still waiting.

"I'm sorry but I can't let you into Simon's house. You don't have a warrant, do you?"

He shook his head. "That's okay, I'll wait out here."

It wasn't long before she returned with a framed photo in her hand. He took a picture of it with his phone.

"Thank you. I can send this to my boss. That's very helpful of you, Mrs Gleeson. You can take the photo back to where it belongs now."

She watched him stride down the path and out into the street beyond. She heard the sound of a car door being shut and an engine start. A silver car went by and the driver waved her a salute. She didn't wave back, but turned to return to Simon's house.

As she walked through the silent house, picture in hand, the walls seemed to close around her. Placing the photograph back on the desk, which was now covered in a thin film of dust, she gazed at the face smiling back at her.

"I hope nothing's happened to you too, Simon. Come back safely, please."

The face just went on smiling and she sighed and left the house, back to her own friendly home. But she was far from happy.

Chapter 21

Grant fetched some decent coffee and supplies to fortify them once they had returned to Headquarters. While he waited, Dan sat at his desk, donned rubber gloves and drew out the package from the van. There were several letters, Charlie's birth certificate and details of a bank account.

He looked up as his sergeant arrived with two coffees and another large package that revealed two large Costa rolls, filled with chicken and salad. Just what they needed. They set to with gusto, refreshed. Dan now felt he could think straight.

"She had a bank account, Grant. I'd like you to look into that in a while. Let's see what else is in here."

"These aren't going to be much help, by the look of it. They're love letters from the boyfriend, dated several years back. But you never know, you take those three and I'll read these three. See if they reveal anything useful."

The men read in silence, handling the old letters carefully with gloved hands. Dan saw his sergeant's ears were turning bright red as he perused the letters.

"Phew! These are a bit spicy, Boss. He really had the hots for her – and so inventive about what he'd like to do to her."

Dan smiled. "Just keep at it, Grant. Try to contain yourself."

He had to admit that Grant was right. These were almost too hot to handle. *'Who needs porn magazines?'* he thought, as he discarded the first letter and braced himself to read the next one.

"Look at this, Boss," Grant held out his second letter to Dan. "It says 'I'll be over to see you in a week's time. Be ready for me – I can't wait to see you and young Charlie again but you know I have to spend time at home so I'll only be able to stay two nights this time. I've got to be careful as I have an idea 'She Who Won't Be Named' is getting suspicious. Then I might not be able to see you again for quite a while; I need to keep her sweet. But

I'll sort it out and we can be together always. I'm going to tell her this time, I promise. I want to always be there for you and Charlie and you know that my place is really with you, to be with you every night.'

"Hmm, slight contradiction there, I think. On the one hand he's talking about keeping the wife sweet so he won't be able to see Molly for a while, and on the other, he's telling her that he's going to sort it out with his wife to be with them full time," mused Dan. "Typical two-timing adulterer; playing the both to keep them sweet. Going by these letters, I'd say Molly does things with him that the wife wouldn't do."

"Frankly, I'm not surprised, Boss. I'd never expect my beloved to do this kind of thing, she'd be shocked. Mind you, some interesting concepts here..." He caught sight of Dan's expression and laughed. "Just kidding."

"Good. Read that last letter."

Silence reigned again. Dan put his last letter down with a sigh. "There's nothing here to help us, I'm afraid. Nothing more in yours?"

"No Boss, although he does say that he wishes his parents could see Charlie because they'd love him and that he's aggrieved because his wife absolutely refuses to have a child so he has no regrets about leaving her. He wants to be a full-time dad."

"Well, something obviously went wrong somewhere, didn't it? Take these to Forensics, there might be something they can lift off them to help us, although I don't hold out much hope, frankly. The only thing is they are all signed, 'your Steve' or variations on that, so it backs up what Mrs Dale told us about his name, not that it helps us much. I need you to get onto that bank account, maybe that will tell us something."

After Grant had left with the packet of letters, Dan sat back in his chair and ran his hands through his hair. They were up against a blank wall alright. The highly sexual contents of the letters from Mollie's lover floated unbidden into his mind. He shook his head – flip, it had been like reading pure porn. It was going to take a lot of doing to eliminate the pictures conjured up in his head. He'd once read that once you'd seen or read porn, it never leaves you but comes back to disturb you at any time throughout life. He hoped that wasn't true. He had more important things to think about.

As he sat there, he looked at the log to do with the case, sorting through everything that had been done so far, he came across the report of the visits to the pubs in Hereford, which had been less than useful. He reached for his phone.

"Hello, Judy? How are the investigations going with the SUVs? Where are you? Listen, leave that for now. You and Johnson go to Moreton-on-Lugg and ask at the pubs and work towards Leominster. Do you have the picture of Molly? Good. Thank you."

When Grant returned, Dan told him what he'd asked of Julie and Johnson. "It only just occurred to me that it's possible she might have gone to Leominster instead of Hereford – and maybe even a pub nearer to where she was staying. We shouldn't have confined our enquiries to the city; she could have met this bloke anywhere."

"Yes. Good thinking. I should have thought of that too. This case feels rather like pulling teeth, Boss."

"It does, Grant. I've put in the application for a warrant so we can look at Molly's bank account. I'm not sure there's anything else we can do on this. Let's work on those shop robberies. Where did we get to on that? Mind you, I'm having a hard time concentrating on anything else while that boy is still out there."

****

The boy that Dan was so concerned about had had a pleasant day, all things considered. While wandering alongside the river, he'd found a seat under a weeping willow tree and had sat there for quite a while, watching the water and nibbling on his biscuits and wishing he had something more substantial to put in his stomach. Still, it was nice there; he loved the movement of the willow as the fronds swayed gently in the soft breeze, their tips just brushing the water here and there. It was a very pleasant day for September and he hoped the weather would stay like it as it seemed he would be living outside for a long time.

Just as he was beginning to feel sorry for himself again, a black Labrador lumbered up to him. He was obviously quite an old dog, as he had a broad back and white hairs around his muzzle. It came sedately towards the boy, tail wagging slowly, and sat next to him, leaning against Charlie's legs and looking up at him adoringly, as if they'd always been pals. Charlie stroked the animal, loving the way it pressed itself to him. They sat like that for a few minutes, communing with each other, until Charlie heard a man's voice call, 'Butch! Butch, where are you, lad?' At the sound of his master's voice, the dog pricked his ears, then put a paw on Charlie's knee, as if bidding him farewell. Charlie put his arms around the dog's neck and whispered "Don't give me away, Butch." The dog gave him a brief lick and left. Charlie heard the man say, "Oh there you are, Boy. What were you doing?" The boy slid off the seat, ready to run if the man came, but nothing happened, so he sat back again, relieved.

The encounter with the dog had taken his mind off his troubles so he decided to explore more of the path along the river. He was sure the man would have long gone by now. When he climbed the steps, the path was indeed clear. He followed it along and came to a gate and found himself in a large concreted space with a couple of large barn-like buildings in front of him. There were lines of trees, shrubs and other plants on display benches that people were looking at. Behind him, alongside the gate, a house stretched away from him and beyond that was a garden and another huge building, mainly of glass. What was it, should he go back?

He decided to investigate the glass building so walked along a pathway between a row of trees in pots and hurried towards the garden. There were lots of people around, especially inside the building. It was like a shop inside with doors leading out and people were coming out to look around the garden and the plants on display in the concreted area. He realised it was a garden centre. He'd go in and pretend to be looking around – it would help to pass the time and hopefully he'd get warm.

Charlie was entranced at all the wonderful things for sale; not only plants but all kinds of gardening equipment, garden furniture and so on but also ornaments, perfumed candles, greeting cards, hats, scarves and even clothes. An enticing smell captured his attention and Charlie followed his nose to a cafe area. He went up to the counter and looked at all the wonderful cakes and pastries under the glass.

"Can I help you, sonny?"

"Oh – er, yes please. Can I 'ave a 'am roll please and a cake?"

"You may indeed. Are you alone?"

"Me mum's over there somewhere. I were hungry so she said I could come and get sommat."

"Right. One ham roll coming up. Which cake would you like?"

She handed him a plate with the roll and another with the cake.

"Would you like a drink?"

"Oh, er, no fanks. Me mum didn't gi' me enuf fer a drink."

Aware of her eyes on him, he took his plates to a small table with two chairs. He hoped she hadn't recognised him, or he wouldn't be able to come here again. Trying desperately not to wolf it down, he ate his food. It tasted delicious, just like the roll he'd nicked earlier. He jumped when the woman came to his table and put a mug of tea in front of him.

"There you are, love. On the house." She smiled kindly at him.

"Coo, fanks, missis." He wrapped his hands around the mug, loving the warmth that seeped into his fingers. He hadn't realised how cold he'd become sitting on the seat under the willow. The woman was watching him and it made him nervous. Did she know who he was? Would she snitch on him? He ate his cake quickly with thoughts of getting away, but the tea was hot and he didn't want to leave it. As he sat sipping from the mug, the woman was by his side again. She held out a paper bag to him.

"For later," she said, and winked at him. Tears prickled his eyes and he blinked rapidly a few times. She leaned forward and whispered: "Don't split on me," and walked away. Charlie finished his drink and hastened away. He turned once, to see that she was busy with customers and didn't look in his direction.

Chapter 22

Although she was busy with the customers, Netta watched the boy leave – she was troubled, for she'd known at once who he was. Madge had reported him in the village the previous day and so it was no secret that he was here. Shocked at how thin he was, much more so than the artist's drawing, she wondered where he'd slept that night. More to the point, what should she do? He obviously didn't want to be found and had managed to give the police the slip yet again. Thank goodness he was safe; one thing she knew about the village was that no harm would come to him there. But a lad that age shouldn't be all alone and living rough. Why was he so determined not to be found? Was he afraid of being taken into care? Or did he have a deeper reason? She couldn't believe that he had anything to do with the death of his mother, so maybe he was running away from her killer? But surely he'd know he would be safe with the police? Or perhaps he didn't believe he would be.

One thing for sure was that she was run off her feet. She didn't normally serve in the café, she only helped when they became really busy. But Claire, who usually served in the café was off sick, and she'd been asked to fill in until Claire returned to work. She was happy to do so, for she enjoyed working there, it was different to working in the main garden centre, more personal. She hadn't been able to resist giving Charlie the food for later; she couldn't bear to see him obviously so hungry. Strangely, he had money, although probably not much, since he hadn't bought a drink. He was obviously used to doing without much food but she realised that he hadn't been able to resist it once he'd smelled it. Lucy's baking was so good, Netta could well understand how difficult it was to turn away from it.

She resolved that she would talk with George about it later at home.

Not long before Netta was about the close the cafe, Sheila came to her with a message.

"I've just had a phone call from Rowena's school, Netta. She's had an accident during her P.E. Lesson. She's fallen and twisted her ankle. They are taking her to the hospital and want you to meet them there."

"Oh no!"

"Don't worry, you get off, I'll close the cafe. Give us a call later to let us know how she is."

"Would you tell George for me, please. Tell him I'm call him later. I have to run home and get the car."

"Joe will take you in one of the vans, won't you Joe?" Sheila turned to the man who happened to walking past.

"What's that?"

"Can you pop Netta home, please, Joe, as she needs to get to the hospital in Hereford. Young Rowena's had an accident at school."

"Of course. I've got the keys to the van already. Come with me, Netta, I'll soon have you home."

"Thanks, Joe, I'm very grateful."

It only took a few minutes to arrive at Netta's house in Caroline Close. She thanked Joe and ran up the path to her car. Even as Joe pulled away in the van, Netta was easing the car out of the drive.

As she drove to the hospital, she was transported back to the time when they'd rushed to Harry's bedside after his canoeing accident a couple of years ago, and again after George had been shot. She sincerely hoped that Rowena wasn't going to be seriously injured like her two menfolk had been. Third time lucky? She really hoped so.

When Netta had arrived and located Rowena in the Accident and Emergency Department of County Hospital, she found that her daughter was still waiting to be seen. The school nurse, who had accompanied the girl to the hospital explained what had happened and left her in her mother's care.

It was a long afternoon and evening, typical of A & E in any hospital, but eventually they'd been able to leave, having been assured that only a small bone in the side of Rowena's foot had a hairline crack. She had her foot bandaged in plaster of Paris, issued with a pair of crutches and they were able to leave the hospital.

It was late when the famished pair reached home to eat the meals that had been cooked by George. Netta had called her husband to tell him the results of the X-rays so he knew it would be more useful to prepare food than to rush to the hospital.

Netta was so tired that after she'd helped Rowena to bed, she fell into her own bed as soon as she could and the runaway boy was lost from her thoughts.

****

"Archie, why are you looking out of the window when you should be getting into bed?" Flora looked into her son's bedroom, ready to kiss him goodnight.

"I'm watching the boy," he said, and she came to the window to see what he was talking about. She peered into the street just outside the Wyeview Restaurant.

"There's no-one there, lad," she said.

"'E's gone now, but 'e were there. Whose boy is 'e?"

"I don't know, I didn't see him. What was he like?"

"'E's a big boy, not as big as you though," was the reply. "'E was talkin' ter me when I was in the garden. I gave him an apple 'cos 'e said 'e was 'ungry."

"That was nice of you. But he's not there now. I need you to get into bed because I 'as ter go downstairs to work. Be a good lad."

Archie ran to his bed and climbed in quickly. Flora kissed him. "Night, love. I'll try to pop up again later, see you're okay. Alright?"

"Yes, Mummy." The little boy clutched his teddy, put his thumb in his mouth and was almost asleep before his mother left the room. She glanced back at him fondly. She was so grateful that she had such a good boy who went to bed so she could go down to work in the restaurant.

106

When she was gone, Archie got out of bed, put on his slippers and dressing gown and padded into the kitchen of the flat. Taking some bread from the bread bin, he made a crude sandwich with cream cheese, took a banana out of the fruit bowl and put them in a bag. Then he went to the smallest bedroom because it faced to the side of the building. A figure in a hooded top stood near the opposite wall, watching the window. Archie had to stand on the bed to open the small window at the top and stand on tip-toe but managed to open it and shoved the bag out of the window. The boy ran and caught it and gave a wave, which Archie returned and let the window drop down. Unable to hook the arm back, he left it, climbed off the bed and crept back to his own bedroom after peering around to make sure his mother wasn't around. Then he got back into his own bed, tucked his teddy in with him and fell asleep.

****

Charlie had eaten quite well that day, what with the visit to the cafe that morning and the roll that Netta had given him, now he had a sandwich and a banana. Although the sandwich looked a bit rough round the edges, after all it had been made by a small boy, the bread seemed fresh, so Charlie decided that the bag of goodies thrown from the window was to be his breakfast.

He made his way back along the river path and to the grounds of the house with the upper barn that was to be his home for a while. The family in the house were still up and about and he couldn't run the risk of being caught going into the barn. Fortunately, there were lots of nooks and crannies where a boy could hide in this wonderful garden. He loved the grounds and wished he could see it in the summer when all the leaves would be on the trees and the ground would be yielding the vegetables and fruit that he was sure were grown there.

It was getting late when he was startled by the appearance of a woolly white ball on legs which came up to him and made a fuss of him. It climbed onto his lap as he sat on the stone seat in the walled garden and leaned into him as the larger dog had done

107

under the willow, only this dog was cuddling his chest. It aimed a lick at his face and he drew back from it, but cuddled the dog, stroking and talking softly.

"Clarry! Clarry! Come on girl, where are you?"

The little dog leaped off his lap, gave him a glance that seemed apologetic and scooted away quickly. Charlie sat as still as he could, yet again hoping the dog wasn't going to give him away. But it seemed she wasn't going to, for she heard the female voice say, "Oh, there you are! Have you done your business? Good girl. Come on let's go in."

Charlie waited a while and then risked creeping out of the walled garden and into the main garden. The lights were on upstairs in the house, so the boy hastened towards the barn, thinking thankfully of his bed waiting for him.

Chapter 23

"Boss!" Julie Coombs had picked up Grant's habit of calling the D.I. thus. "We've had some luck in Leominster. Apparently, Mollie used to frequent a pub called The Black Swan. The landlord recognised her picture. According to him, she met some pretty doubtful characters there and went off with them."

"Right, that's great. Grant, let's go and see if we can get a take on anyone she might have been with. Good work, guys."

The Black Swan was in the heart of Leominster and was obviously quite old. The white walls and black window frames and doors made it stand out.

It was likely that Mollie would have stayed in one or other of the bars so they would look there first. Inside, it was done in 'olde worlde' charm with beams and a large inglenook fireplace.

The cheerful-looking landlord greeted them pleasantly.

"I've been expecting you, Detective Inspector. Come in and take a seat. Would you care for a drink?"

"An orange juice would be nice, thank you, Mr er.."

"Carter. Jim Carter. And this is my wife, Kate."

A pleasant woman with blonde hair came towards them and smiled.

"Mrs Carter," Dan nodded to her. "I'm sorry to trouble you both when you're about to get busy but anything you can tell us about this young woman would be useful."

"Kate saw her more than me, didn't you, love?"

"Yeah. She usually came into this bar; she liked to sit near the fireplace – at that table there." Kate pointed to a small table near the window.

"Did you ever have a conversation with her?"

"We-ell, when she first came in here, I mentioned that I hadn't seen her before and she said she'd only just come to this area. She was very pretty and attracted a lot of male attention. I often worried about her because I know some of the blokes who come in here and they're not very – well, shall I say that I was concerned when she went off with one or more of them? I suspect

109

they deal with drugs, you know. Jim and I do our best to make sure nothing like that goes on in here, but what folks do outside, we have no control over." She shrugged and looked at them in a way that was begging them to understand that she had nothing to do with drugs.

"Are any of these men here now?" Dan cast his eyes around the room. There were a group of chaps drinking and laughing together round a table and a man and woman talking quietly, heads close together at another table. It was early yet.

"No, they don't come in until later, usually."

"Did she come in here a lot?"

"Oh yes, several nights a week, but always on Fridays and Saturday nights. Sundays she didn't come because she said there wasn't a bus."

"Did she ever tell you where she lived?"

"No, she just said she lived in the country, on a farm. I thought she said she was working there for the summer, although I could be wrong about that."

Dan and Grant looked at each other; they were thinking the same thing – poor Charlie, what a life that kid must have had. No wonder he seemed okay living nowhere, as he was used to being alone and looking out for himself.

"I think we'll take our drinks and stay for a while. If any of her friends comes in, perhaps you'd give us a nod?"

"Sure. But hang on, what's this all about? What's she done?"

"Don't you see the news, Mrs Carter? Mandy got herself killed."

The woman paled visibly as her hand flew to her mouth. "Oh! She's been – murdered?"

"Yes. That's why we're trying to find out about her."

"I'm sure no one who comes in here would have done it. Some of them are a bit rough, but they're not murderers."

"Let us be the judges of that. We'll take our drinks and sit over there. Actually, I'd like something to eat, wouldn't you, Grant?"

"Absolutely, Boss."

They ordered pie and chips and carried their drinks to an empty table. Used to playing the waiting game, they might as well take the opportunity to eat while they were at it. It could be a long evening.

A couple of hours later, the bars were full. When Dan went to get a refill of drinks, the barmaid, a young woman with a large bust and a jolly smile served him. Instead, she leaned across the bar, treating Dan to a close view of her cleavage, which he tried not to look at, and whispered that the two blokes in the corner near the door were two that he'd need to speak to, winked and then left to serve someone else.

Dan gave a side nod to Grant, who immediately left his seat and they walked over to the two men.

"Good evening, gentlemen," said Dan, showing them his I.D. "We were wondering if you could help us. We're looking for anyone who might have seen, or known this girl."

Grant held up his phone to show the picture of Mandy. The men examined it closely.

"Oh yeah, we did see 'er in 'ere sometimes, like, didn't we, Mick?" The first one, a small, weedy-looking man of around forty, had bushy hair and a nose that was somewhat too long for his thin face. He reminded Dan of a weasel or a rat. Grant wrote down his name, Sean Gunnel, and his mate, Mick Smith.

"Yeah. Mandy Sommat. Great girl, lots of fun, yer know wot I mean, like?" The other man gave a smiling wink. Well built, with sandy hair which was long and untidy,he wore a black t-shirt and scruffy jeans and his muscular arms were covered in tattoos. "Saw her often. Lives in a camper on a farm. Great place to hang. Why? What's she done? I ain't done nuthin."

"So you went to her van, then?"

"Yeah, so what? She often had blokes there. Like I said, she's a real good-time girl, like. Where is she?" the bloke peered around and stumbled a bit.

"She's dead, Mick."

"Wha? She can't be! I was bankin' on her ternight..."

"What for? What were you banking on her for, Mick?"

Mick stood up and the chair fell backwards. "Nothin'!" he shouted. "Nothin', the silly bitch." He swung around and Grant just managed to deflect the blow aimed at him.

"Okay, okay, that's enough, Mick!" the landlord appeared and man-handled Mick to the door. "Enough for tonight. Go and cool off. Are you arresting him, Mr Cooke?"

"Not this time. You've had a lucky escape, Mick. What you just did was an arrestable offence, assaulting a police officer. Watch your step, or next time I'll have you."

They were all outside the pub.

"Come on, mate," said Sean, "let's go."

"Before you go, Mr Gunnel. Did you ever go to Mandy's van?"

The weasel-like man dropped his eyes. "Yeah, a few times. Don't tell the wife, she'll kill me."

"You've got both their addresses, Grant?"

"Yes Boss."

"Good. You can take him home now, Mr Gunnel."

The two staggered down the street, looking ridiculous, one tall and burly, the other slight and short but both unsteady on their feet, although the little man was doing his best to hold up his friend.

"Hmm. Not getting a good picture of Mollie, are we? Obviously, she had no high morals. Poor Charlie. Let's go home."

Just as they were about to get into their car, a figure detached itself from the shadows and walked towards them. It was a man, hardly more than a boy really, in the typical uniform of anonymity, black jeans and black hoodie.

"You the coppers asking 'bout Mandy?"

"Yes. You know something? Who are you?"

"Can we talk in the car?" The man looked around nervously.

In answer, Grant opened the back door and the young man slipped inside and Dan after him.

"Can we go somewhere else?"

112

"Drive, Grant, just take us out of town."

Grant headed away from the town centre and into a cul-de-sac of pleasant new-builds. He stopped by the side of the road and cut the engine.

"Right. What do you have to tell us? What's your name?"

"Eddie, just call me Eddie."

In the lad's eyes Dan saw unmistakable signs of substance abuse. He sighed quietly.

"Okay, Eddie, what's all this about?"

"There's folks who wouldn't like it if they knew I'd talked with you. But I liked Mandy, she was always nice to me. I went to her van a few times an' we talked, yer know, like."

"Another visitor to her van. Did you see anyone else around while you were there?"

"I met the kid, if that's what yer mean. Charlie. He's a great kid. I'm sorry someone did for Mandy."

"Can you tell us anything? Did you see her with anyone?"

"She was always with someone. It's how she got money, see? How she paid for her habits – yer know?" Eddie put his head down, so Dan couldn't see his eyes. The detective sighed again; he did know.

"You're saying she was an addict? And a prostitute?"

"Yeah, that's what I'm sayin'. But fings were okay, you know? She came here and picked up a bloke, someone who would give her a lift home, cos the buses don' run back from here to where she lived so she 'ad to have someone tek her home and his payment would be waitin' back there and they'd go and enjoy theirselves. Sometimes there would be a group of us and we'd sleep on the grass outside, like. We did that when we were sure it wouldn't rain, you know? But it did rain sometimes and we'd get wet, like."

"I get the picture," said Dan, drily. No doubt they wouldn't have a clue until they woke up. He thought again about Charlie and what he'd had to live with. He'd like to bet that Farmer White and his wife hadn't a notion what had gone on in their field. "So, why do you need to talk with us?"

The lad looked around nervously and ran his tongue around his lips. "Because I saw *him*, that's why."

"Him? Who's that?"

"Well, it was a stranger, see? I've never seen him before, and I know pretty well all the people around here, either by name or sight and I knew all the blokes as went wi' Mandy. But I saw her with this bloke just the once, like."

"Can you remember when you saw him?"

"Yeah, I think it was the week before the August Bank holiday weekend, the Tuesday or the Wednesday, I'm not sure which."

"Did he come into the pub?"

"Yeah, he was in the restaurant, then came through and chatted to us and Mandy. Then the next night he came for Mandy – yeah, that's right, he ate in the restaurant on the Tuesday, then came for her on the Wednesday."

"Did he meet her in the pub?"

"No, outside. He gave Sean a message to take to her an' she came out. I was just leaving, see, and I saw them. I was curious, so I hid, like I was just now, in the car park, like, and I saw her get into his car."

Dan noticed Grant's eyes in the rear-view mirror, one eyebrow raised in interest.

"I don't suppose you know what sort of car it was, Eddie?"

"Not sure really. It was big. I thought it was a SUV."

Chapter 24

Dan and Grant looked at each other, eyebrows raised further. This sounded like their man!

"Did you get the registration number, by any chance?"

"No, sorry, I didn't. I only got a glimpse, see? It was black and looked new, that's all I can tell you."

"Can you describe him? Did you see him clearly?"

"Not really. He was of average height, about the same as Mick, I'd say, bit taller than me. I couldn't see him properly because of the distance. But there was something about him that shouted 'rich', if ya know what I mean, like?"

"How so?"

"Well, he wore a dark suit, class, which you don't usually see in here, we're mostly casual, even in the restaurant, like. He had dark hair and I thought a bit of designer stubble, although it was hard to see at the distance, like. Expensive shades. You know the kind of thing. I bet, if you asked the waitresses in the restaurant, one of them would be able to give you a better description because they would have served him."

"Good thought, Eddie, we'll do that. Can we drop you anywhere?"

"Nah, I'll get out here. I just didn't want Mick an' them to see me talkin' to ya. They wouldn't like it, you know?"

'I bet,' thought Dan, knowingly. Out loud he said, "You've been very helpful. Here's my card if you happen to think of anything else you think would be useful."

The lad took the card, stuck it in his pocket, and climbed out of the car. Moments later, he'd disappeared down an alleyway.

"Right, Grant," said Dan, as he moved to the front seat, "let's go back to The Black Swan and see if we can get any info out of the waitresses."

Grateful that the restaurant had a separate entrance, they entered and went straight up to the bar where customers ordered food. A young man was manning the till. Dan showed his I.D.

In answer to the questions, the young man said "I wasn't on that night, I don't do Tuesdays. But Elly and Sue would have been. That's Elly over there and that's Sue coming through with food."

"Thanks."

The waitress looked middle aged but attractive in a buxom sort of way. One got the impression of a froth of curly blonde hair with dark roots and a carefully made up face. Her uniform struggled around her bust and hips and she had shapely legs, her feet in flat shoes.

Dan waited until Sue had served the food and drew her to one side, discreetly showing her his I.D. She looked alarmed but he hastened to reassure her. Upon hearing what he wanted, she said, "Oh yes – I certainly remember him. He stood out – oh my – he was gorgeous, reminded me of George Clooney, except he had really dark brown hair and designer stubble. His suit looked really expensive and I saw he was wearing gold cufflinks and had a Rolex watch on. I was sorry when he left, I kept itching to take him somewhere." She giggled, and said,

"But I wouldn't have, you know, I'm married! But he was so tasty."

"And you haven't seen him again since that night?"

"No, more's the pity. We don't get a lot of class in here." She sighed.

"You've been really helpful, Sue. Would you be willing to help a police artist to draw a likeness of this man?"

"Yes, sure. I'll have my kid with me as it's Saturday tomorrow. I can't get to Hereford."

"We'll arrange it so you can do it at the branch here in Leominster. Give Grant here your details, and we'll let you know when."

"Mmm, he can have my details any time." She turned to Grant, and ran her tongue suggestively round her lips. His face reddened and she winked and laughed. "Just kidding, luv."

Dan smiled at his sergeant's embarrassment. "We'll be in touch, Sue."

On the way to the car, he said,

"C'mon, let's get you home to your beautiful misses, who is ten times more inviting than our Sue! We've done enough for one night. I'm for my hot chocolate, and to remind my Linda who I am."

****

When Charlie woke up, his head ached and he was freezing. He couldn't bear to leave the warmth of his bed, although he'd have to get up at some point to relieve himself. He hadn't really investigated the whole loft barn; there was a doorway which led into another 'room'. Drifting back to sleep, he heard Clarry bark and managed to haul himself out of bed to look out of the window in time to see the young mother pushing a pushchair down the drive, a little boy by her side and Clarry on a lead trotting along on her other side.

With his coat drawn around him, he let himself out of the barn, treading carefully down the stone steps because he felt dizzy. If only he could use a proper bathroom. He hurriedly relieved himself behind the wall, feeling guilty because he'd normally go somewhere well away from any buildings. Knowing the family were out of the way, he decided to take a look in the enclosed area underneath his barn.

All sorts of things were in there; gardening tools, broken household items and some plastic buckets. One would come in useful instead of going outside. He wished he had toilet paper but there was nothing like that out there. Once he'd filled his bottle from the outside tap, he took his bucket and bottle back up to the barn, put on all the clothes he had in an effort to get warmer, then

117

crawled back into his makeshift bed and lay there shivering and longing for his mum. His head ached abominably and he hardly knew what to do. The light shining through the dirty windows hurt his eyes but no matter which way he turned, he couldn't shut it out because there were windows on both sides of the barn. In the end, he put his head under the covers. Eventually, he sunk into a troubled sleep.

****

The waitress, Sue, met with the police artist and the picture was sent to Dan by mid-day. The team gazed at the picture of the unknown man, which had joined those of Mollie and Charlie on the wall.

"The questions we have to ask are these: why would a man as attractive and rich as this guy appeared to be need to pick up someone like Mollie? Was it by chance or by design? Is he a maniac who just likes killing women or had he particularly targeted her? If so, why?"

"There's something about this that doesn't smell right, Boss, but at the moment I can't say why," mused Grant.

"I agree with you, Grant. If this man is a maniac killer, why haven't we heard about any others? Maybe there have been others, women who have been killed for seemingly no reason. I want you to do a search, please, Julie."

Julie managed to subdue the sigh that threatened. "Yes, Boss."

"Before that, we need to think these things through. He met her on the Tuesday night and killed her the next night. He must have impressed her that first night. Maybe he promised her something she couldn't resist? Apart from sex and possibly drugs?

"Well, if he was rich and handsome, that might have been enough for her to hang onto him," remarked Julie. "I'm sure if a

118

good-looking and rich man wanted me to be around, I'd make sure I was."

Dan laughed. "But only if he lets you continue to be a cop. I'm sure you're right, Julie, perhaps she didn't need any other incentive."

"I was wondering what Eddie said about how 'he' sent a message with Sean. How did he know she'd be willing to come out to him? Had he seen her before? If so, how? I'm sure the people in The Black Swan would have noticed him if he'd been there before – you can bet your life Sue would have."

"Yes. I'd say he knew about her before that night. I'd say he went looking for her. Was he the reason why she was running away? If so, why did she go with him so willingly?"

"Perhaps she was tired of running? Maybe she thought she might change his mind about whatever it was?" mused Grant.

"Boss – what if he was after her but she didn't know it? What if he was working for someone else?"

Dan looked at Julie's excited face thoughtfully.

"You could have a very valid point there, Julie. When you look at it from that point of view, it makes sense; he knew where she'd be and how to entice her away. It wasn't a case of seeing her and fancying her; he already knew about her and what he was going to do."

"A hit-man," Grant breathed. "Poor kid."

"Right." Dan was galvanised into action. "Grant, we're going back to Leominster to check if the guy had been there before. Julie, please do that search I mentioned. We'll meet back here later and see what we've gleaned. And Grant, we have to see our Mr. Gunnels again, we have his address, don't we?"

"Yes, Boss."

"Let's go! See you later, Julie."

As they sped towards Leominster, Dan thought hard. If this guy was a hit man, who had hired him, and what was so bad about Mollie that someone was willing to pay a lot of money (for hit men always charged large sums, didn't they?) to have her annihilated?

119

Chapter 25

When they returned to The Black Swan, the Landlord looked at the photofit of the man that had taken off with Mollie.

"Hmm, not sure that I did see him. Kate, take a look at this."

Kate examined the picture.

"Oh yes, he's been in here. He was asking questions about various people, including Mandy."

"Did you see him talking to her?"

"I think I did, not sure. If he did, I certainly never saw them properly together – you know – they didn't leave together. In fact, if I remember rightly, he left quite early."

"Can you remember when that was, Mrs Carter?"

"Now I come to think of it, it was the day before the last time Mandy was in here – on a Tuesday evening. She usually came Tuesdays. Yes, it was that Tuesday before the Bank Holiday weekend because we'd had a delivery in earlier in that day, ready for a busy weekend."

Well satisfied, Dan thanked her and they left to seek out Sean Gunnel. He lived in a flat in a rather seedy area. A woman answered the door to his knock. She was a well-built woman with arms like a wrestler's. Upon seeing them, she folded her arms. "Yes?" she said, without bothering to remove the cigarette stuck to her bottom lip.

"We'd like to have a word with Sean, if he's in, please?"

"Is 'e in trouble, the little sh**? I'll gi' 'im what for."

'Anyone would think she was talking about a son, not her husband,' thought Dan. "No, Mrs Gunnel, he's not in any trouble. I spoke to him last night about something and I just need some clarification."

"Sean! Get 'ere! The pigs want a word wi' yer."

The two men inwardly cringed at the bellow the woman gave. Sean appeared, wearing a vest and his trousers held up by braces. He looked askance at Dan and Grant, and said sullenly, "What do you two want now?"

Dan looked at the woman standing behind Sean. She reminded him of a bouncer from a night club, so determined was she to find out what was going on. He decided to play it softly; he didn't want to get the man into trouble with his wife, he looked like he had enough trouble anyway. So what if he visited ladies of the night and took drugs? That wasn't what he was interested in right now.

"Mr Gunnel, I'd like to ask you a couple more questions. Would it be alright to come in?"

The man stood to one side. The fine hairs on the back of Dan's head stood up as he passed the woman, who, with a grim look, had also stood to one side, arms still crossed and glaring at the three men before her. Dan sent up a silent word of thanks for his lovely wife Linda. They went into a room that was surprisingly homely-looking, with squashy settee and armchairs and an occasional table covered by a lacy cloth. A large television dominated the room but thankfully it wasn't on. The four of them sat down.

"Mr Gunnel, could you cast your mind back to that last time Mandy Jones was in the pub, please. Did you take a message from a man to her?"

Sean looked uncomfortable and opened his mouth to speak.

"Well, answer the man!" demanded Mrs Gunnel. "Who is this Mandy Jones?"

"Oh, just someone who goes to the Black Swan. I don't know her all that well, my dear."

'Hmm, not much,' thought Dan.

"Humph – I bet. I can well imagine what sort she is, if you know her," snorted the woman. "Well, did you take a message to her?"

"Oh, um, yes I did. This bloke stopped us – me and Mick, like, just as we were going in. He asked me to tell Mandy to go out to him. Said she was expecting him."

"And in your opinion, was she expecting him?"

"Oh yes. When I gave her the message, she upped and left straight away, like."

"Can you tell me what the man was like?"

"I only saw him briefly – yer know? Good looking, smarmy type. Don't see them sort around here much."

Dan nodded at Grant, who showed him the picture. "Is this him?"

Sean squinted at Grant's phone. "Yes, I think so."

"Had you seen him before that night?"

"Oh – ar. The night before, he'd had a meal in the restaurant, then came through to the bar. He chatted with the barmaid, then came over to talk to us. I noticed 'e kept eyeing up Mandy and she noticed. When he left, she followed him out."

"Oh, did she? And was that it, did she leave with him?"

"No, but she came back in looking very pleased with 'erself and told us she was going ter see 'im the next night – that's why she was expecting 'im, like, an' why I told 'er 'e was waiting fer her, like."

"I see. She didn't happen to mention his name, did she?"

"Um, yeah. I think she called 'im Den, no, Des – that's right, Des. 'Is name was Desmond – a right ponsey name, I reckon."

Grant scribbled furiously in his notebook. Dan got up from the sofa. "Well, thank you, Mr. Gunnel, you've been very helpful."

The two detectives bade the couple goodbye. As they walked away from the door, they heard Sean being berated very loudly by his overbearing wife.

"Poor bloke," remarked Grant as he unlocked the door to the car. "With a wife like that, I'm not surprised he spends most of his life down the pub and socialising with women like Mandy."

"Yes, well, maybe she wasn't always like that, maybe his lifestyle has driven her to it," replied Dan, who liked to reserve judgement. "Maybe he's getting his just desserts."

"Yeah, perhaps you're right, Boss. Talking of desserts, I'm starving."

****

Once back at Headquarters, Grant went in search of food and Dan found Julie.

"It's back to chasing up the SUV, I'm afraid, Julie. Don't confine the search to private owners, look at vehicle hire firms as well. Start in Hereford and work outwards. It has to be black and new looking."

"Okay, Boss, I'll do that. Do we have any more information about the man?"

"Not really; only that he sought her out, chatted her up and then took her out the next night, the night before he killed her. He hasn't been seen since. Not that we expected that he'd still be around, especially if it was planned. The car is the only clue we have – oh, and Mandy called him Desmond. I don't suppose that's his real name, but it might give us some sort of lead."

Julie nodded and opened her computer. Grant arrived with coffee and sandwiches and they ate. Dan sighed; it seemed they had very little to go on.

Chapter 26

Simon Denton slumped in his chair, away from his laptop, which rested on the table. He had done well with the book but for some reason, the past few days had been very difficult to concentrate. The words just wouldn't come and he often found his mind wandering away from his task.

Making a snap decision, he fetched his coat, hat and gloves and let himself out of the front door to go for some fresh air. He walked briskly down the rough path that led through what passed for a front garden but was actually more like part of the terrain that surrounded the cottage. It was only a short walk to the side of Loch Ericht and this was a wonderful place to partake of fresh air.

Simon stood by the loch and breathed in deeply, at the same time gazing at the blue-green water and the mountains. It was a glorious sight and one he never tired of. He'd found the remote cottage a few years ago and in spite of its ramshackle appearance, had known immediately that this was a place where he could take himself out of the world and write. It had provided him with an endless supply of ideas and plots for his books and he felt at peace there too, while working with his muse. The cottage had its own electricity generator and he cooked with calor gas. The nearest place to buy food and other supplies was Dalwhinnie. Not that he needed much in the way of supplies really, for he ate simply and always kept a supply of warm clothes at the cottage.

Over the years he'd gradually done DIY and improved the cottage to suit his needs. It was homely and comfortable in a masculine sort of way. He loved it and often contemplated whether he should live there permanently, but although he loved the remoteness and peacefulness, he admitted that he really didn't like the idea of being snowed up and completely cut off from the world. So, like a bird, he flew south for the winter, back to Plymouth which didn't have such a drastic climate. He had no television, only a radio which he listened to infrequently, and his phone was useless here, for there was never a signal.

When he'd bought the cottage, he never told anyone about it, not even his neighbour, Clara. It was true that he had a nice camper-van and did take it abroad when he needed to research, but mostly he came here, keeping up the appearance that he could be 'going anywhere.' He'd realised that, once he'd let Mollie have his precious VW camper, his enthusiasm for camping out gradually waned. Once the cottage had called to him, he knew he preferred to be here. After all, it had everything he wanted; stunning scenery, water, and peace away from people. Of late, he'd thought about getting a dog, aware that it was a lonely life, but as yet he'd done nothing about it.

The sky darkened ominously as grey clouds gathered over the loch. The wind became stronger and he drew the collar of his coat closer around him. A few large spots of rain persuaded him to retrace his steps back to the cottage, walking much faster than when he'd gone out. It was raining full-pelt by the time he reached his door, and he stepped inside hurriedly and had to use his whole body to push it shut against the wind.

In the kitchen, he hung his coat on the back of a chair to dry and put the kettle on to boil. He made his coffee and took it through to the sitting-room-cum-study and set the mug on a small table. Choosing a CD from the shelf, he put it into the small CD player and relaxed into his favourite armchair as the music swelled into the room.

The rain pelted against the window and he felt the cottage shudder as the wind gave it all it had, the noise in the chimney in competition with Greig's Piano Concerto. Yes, although he loved it there, Simon had to admit he was lonely. He'd cut himself off from much of humanity, except Clara, for too long. Although he could never stop writing, he realised he was missing out on some of the other important things in life.

That brought his thoughts around to Mollie and Charlie. How were they and where? He hadn't heard from her for a few months and he realised that was why he was restless. It wasn't

125

like her to go so long without sending him a message. She was the only one besides himself who knew about this cottage, although she'd never seen it, for she would write to him. She was another reason why he still kept his house in Plymouth – he always hoped that one day Mollie and Charlie would come home.

His current manuscript was almost finished and was, thankfully, ahead of his deadline. He should stay and finish it, but his restlessness of the past few days made him realise that he would not do so by staying any longer. For once, the wonderful surroundings were not giving him the peace he needed to work. No, Mollie was in his head and he couldn't shake the thoughts away. Something was urging him to find her. He would return home and then put investigations into action; he had many contacts across the country, people who he could trust to put feelers out for him.

As the wind and rain howled outside, Simon was content with the decision he'd made. Tomorrow he would set off on the long drive home and from there he would find his niece and great-nephew. It was time they came back – surely the danger was over now?

Chapter 27

The following day, Simon prepared to leave the cottage. The weather had turned very chilly after yesterday's heavy rain but he only wore a light jacket as he would be warm enough in the van. He put a bag of food in his camper-van; fresh stuff that he couldn't leave behind and also food for the journey. There was a camp-site around half-way where he would stay the night, because it was a long drive from Scotland to Plymouth and he had no real reason to hurry.

As he was making his way back to the house, he heard a car coming along the road. It was rare that a vehicle came this way, so he was curious and watched approach. Even more curiously, it stopped by his gate and a man, dressed in warm casual clothes, and a knitted beanie pulled well down over his ears, climbed out. The face underneath showed the dark shadow of an unshaven chin but it didn't disguise the good looks of the man. He walked through the open gateway and came up to Simon.

"Are you Simon Denton?"

"Yes, who's asking?"

The answer he received was a swinging fist to his head and everything went black.

When he came to, he was lying on the ground, one leg folded beneath him at an awkward angle. He tried pulling himself up and was aware of excruciating pain in his right arm and his left leg was probably broken too. Through the fog of pain, he fumbled around with his left hand until he was able to draw his mobile phone from his right jacket pocket. It wasn't switched on, but when it did, he saw 'no signal'. Groaning aloud, he sank back on the ground and prayed either for help or for death to come quickly.

****

It seemed that God answered his prayers, if narrowly. Several hours later, a group of walkers with a dog came near his house. When the dog, a black and white border collie, ran ahead of its owners, they whistled and it rushed back to them, making it obvious he wanted them to come and look at what he'd found.

A woman saw Simon first and exclaimed, "Oh look! That man has fallen or is ill."

The group of ten walkers gathered around the figure on the ground.

"Stand back, everyone, let me take a look."

A tall, silver-haired man knelt beside Simon to examine him. Adam Renton was a doctor. He soon assessed the situation.

"Hyperthermia setting in," he muttered, "Head wound, broken arm and leg."

"The cottage door is open, I'll see if there's anything we can wrap him in," said a woman.

She hurried into the house and soon reappeared with a duvet and a pillow.

"Thanks, Rose," said Adam, and tucked the duvet around the inert figure. "Can you go back and collect as many towels or t-towels you can find, or anything that I can use for splints, please?"

"I'm concerned, Adam, it looks like someone has searched the house, for all the drawers and cupboards are open and things have been thrown on the floor."

"Oh goodness. You'll need to touch as little as possible, only what we need. Make haste, my dear."

"I'll help," said the woman who first saw Simon and she and Rose hastened back to see what they could find. They returned with several towels and a couple of wooden spoons.

"Brilliant," said Adam, and set to work, using the spoons to splint the leg, tying it with strips of towelling which he shredded with a knife. He used another couple of towels to splint the arm, using one rolled hard to prevent movement. Simon moaned at the doctor moving his limbs but never seemed to regain consciousness. "He needs to be airlifted."

"I've been trying to phone, but there's no signal up here," said another man, waving his phone at Adam.

"Hmm, we have to do something, or this man is going to die. He's been out here for some time, I think."

The man with the phone said, "Can't we put him in there," he nodded to the camper-van, "and take him to hospital or at least to the nearest village that might have a phone where we can call for help?"

"Good idea, Scott." Adam felt in Simon's pockets and drew out some keys. "Looks like the van and house keys. We'll lock his house and take the van. Can one of you drive it if I stay in the back with him?"

"I can drive it," said Scott. "I hired one similar once, for a holiday. It won't be insured for me though." He looked doubtful.

"We can't worry about that now. If we don't do it, this man will die."

"You and Scott go ahead and the rest of us will walk and meet you at Dalwhinnie," said Rose.

Adam, Scott and the three other men in the party lifted Simon carefully, supporting his bad leg and arm as much as they were able and somehow, they managed to lay him on the floor of the camper-van. It would have been better if they could have laid him on the long seat but Adam decided that they'd moved him enough. He stayed inside with the sick man and Scott climbed into the driver's seat.

The group stood back as Scott slowly drove across the bumpy ground onto the road where he was able to drive properly. It didn't take long to cover the few miles to the village. They stopped the van outside the pub and Scott went in to ask the landlord if he could use his phone.

The landlord came out and knocked on the van door and asked what was going on. Adam explained swiftly and the landlord looked at the unconscious man.

"Goodness! That's Simon. How did this happen to him?"

"We've no idea, but from his injuries, I'd say he'd been attacked."

"Attacked? Who'd want to attack him? Poor lad."

"You know him?"

"Och, yes, that's Simon Denton, the writer. He owns yon cottage and comes here to write. Been coming here for years. We don't see much o' him, but we allus knows when he's here."

Scott came out of the pub. "They're on their way, Adam."

"Thank goodness! I've been keeping him warm; I'm going to shut this door again now to try to keep out the cold. You go in and have a beer. The others will be a while yet."

The paramedics arrived about twenty minutes later and not too long after, the helicopter arrived. Between them they got Simon out of the van and safely into the helicopter.

Adam heaved a sigh of relief and, after giving the keys of the van to the landlord, who assured him he'd keep it safe until Simon was ready for it again, he joined Scott and partook of a very welcome beer.

Chapter 28

It was late in the evening the day after Charlie had begun to feel ill, and Lucy opened the door for Clarry to do her last 'business' for the day outside. The little dog ran off and she shut the door hurriedly against a chilly blast. She was tired but had to be up early the next morning as usual, to make the bread for the shop.

The baby Rosemary had been somewhat fractious lately; she was cutting a tooth. Kenny had been very good at getting up in the night to help soothe the little one so Lucy could sleep on. Sometimes she wondered how much longer she'd be able to keep up all the baking that she did; with two small children it was much harder to keep up with everything. John had been such a good little boy that Lucy had managed easily, but Rosemary didn't have John's placid nature and was more demanding than her big brother.

"You get off to bed, my love," Kenny said, as he kissed her. "I'll get Clarry in and lock up."

Lucy wearily made her way up the stairs. When she reached her bedroom, she heard barking. What on earth could be upsetting Clarry at this time of night? She looked out of the window but there was little to be seen as it was dark, but she could still hear the dog. Then she shrugged, oh well, Kenny will deal with whatever it was.

*****

Kenny opened the kitchen door and called, "Clarry! Clarry, come."

A few moments later, the little dog appeared but instead of coming in as she usually did, she danced away, returned and barked at Kenny, then away again. After taking a few steps into the garden, she looked back at him.

"You want to show me something, Girl?" he asked.

131

"Woof!" Clarry danced away again and then stopped to look back.

Kenny took the hint, and, grabbing his fleece off the hook on the door and a torch from the window-sill, he followed the little dog into the garden. He could see her clearly because she was white. She went up the steps to the barn door and scrabbled on it, whining. Kenny was puzzled. He stood at the bottom of the steps and called again.

"What's the matter, Clarry? There's nothing in there."

"Woof," said Clarry, and scrabbled again on the door. Kenny went up the steps and Clarry stood, panting as he reached it.

"There's nothing in there, look, it's locked."

He lifted the latch and pushed and much to his surprise, the door opened. Clarry rushed inside.

"Clarry! Where are you?" Kenny switched on the torch and shone it around the barn. The slither of light picked out the white ball that was Clarry, nosing around a pile of blankets on the floor. As he drew nearer, he saw that it wasn't just a pile of blankets, there was someone under them.

Kenny drew in a sharp breath; the smell around the mound told its own story. He eased down the top of the blanket, to see the face of a boy, pale and with closed eyes.

"My goodness, what do we have here? Move over, Clarry, let the dog see the rabbit." Kenny put his hand on the boy's head. In spite of the pallor, the head was hot. Kenny gathered up the boy, blankets and all and, with Clarry dancing around his feet, carried him down the steps, treading carefully, across the garden to the house and into the lounge, where he laid him on the sofa.

He went to the bottom of the stairs and called softly; "Lucy, Lucy, are you awake? I need you down here."

A few minutes later, Lucy's head appeared around the bend in the stairs. "What's up, love?"

"Come and see what Clarry's found."

Lucy's head disappeared and she reappeared moments later, still doing up her dressing gown and followed him into the lounge.

"Oh, goodness! I think that must be Charlie."

"Yes, and he's very sick. We'll need a doctor."

"And inform Dan Cooke. I'll call him, I have his number in my phone."

She rapidly did the phoning, then turned to Kenny. "He's coming and bringing the police doctor with him. Do you think I should make up the spare bed?"

"Hmm, he looks bad, love. I think he may have to go to hospital."

Lucy fetched a bowl of warm water and a face cloth and gently washed the boy's face. His eyes flickered but didn't open. His lips were cracked and dry and it was obvious his breathing was bad, for they could hear the crackle in his chest.

"Poor lamb," said Lucy, as she smoothed the hair from his forehead.

Clarry stood by the side of the sofa, watching the still figure intently. Lucy stroked her.

"Good dog, Clarry. I think we've got him just in time."

Clarry wagged her tail and wiggled around Lucy but then went back to watching Charlie. Kenny went to the kitchen to put the kettle on; it was possible that the detective and the doctor might need a drink. He brought one for Lucy and himself and they sat waiting in silence. When Clarry gave a short bark, they heard a car pull up outside. Kenny went to open the door.

Dan was followed in by a man who he introduced as Dr. Falkirk, who nodded to the young couple. Kenny showed them into the lounge and the doctor immediately examined the lad.

"Where did you find him, Ken?" asked Dan, as they watched the doctor examine the boy.

"He was in the upper barn. Clarry knew – she barked and scrabbled at the door until I went in and found him."

"So, Clarry's a heroine again? What a good little girl she is," said Dan, as he bent down to fuss the little dog, who fawned around him, wiggling in her pleasure.

"Inspector, this lad needs to go to hospital, he's very poorly. How long was he in that barn?"

"We don't know, doctor. I'm sorry, but we can't tell you anything. He was obviously very good at hiding. We had no idea he was there."

The doctor stepped into the kitchen to phone for an ambulance.

"Right, I'll get dressed," said Lucy.

"What?"

"I'll go to the hospital with Charlie," said Lucy, firmly. "He has no-one else, does he? His mum's dead. He's going to need someone to watch over him, at least until he wakes up and knows where he is. Kenny, ask Sheila if she'll have the children if I'm not back by the morning, and you'll have to let Madge know there won't be any bread for the shop; her customers will have to have sliced bread tomorrow."

Kenny knew there was no point in arguing with Lucy when she was determined. He and Dan looked at each other and shrugged, as if to say, 'What can you do?' Ken was concerned because he knew how tired she was, but when she reappeared, dressed in jeans and a sweater, carrying a bag, she looked fresh and lovely. His heart swelled within him as he looked at her and thought again how lucky he was to have her as his wife.

The ambulance arrived and it wasn't long before the boy had been lifted into it. Lucy and the doctor also climbed in, and off it went, blue lights flashing silently.

"I'm going to have a police guard on the boy," said Dan to Kenny after the ambulance had left. "We don't want him trying to run away again, nor do we want our killer to reach him, if that's what he intends. I'll be off now to make the arrangements. Thank goodness we have him, that's one weight lifted, although we'll need to keep an eye on him. I'm grateful to you and Lucy, Ken. I'm always having to thank you two for something."

134

"I'm sure anyone finding the lad would have done the same. I'm just glad he decided to bunk down in our barn, and that Clarry led us to him. He's so sick that if he was somewhere else, chances are he might not have made it. So, I don't think we had much to do with it really, except he found our barn."

"Well, I'm glad he did. And Lucy will see him right when he wakes up. I'll be off now and I hope you'll manage tomorrow."

"Oh, don't you worry about that – that's one advantage in working for yourself, if you want time off, you can take it. I have good staff and I know things will carry on as if I was there. I won't foist our Rosemary onto my mother, poor woman." Kenny laughed.

"Handful, is she, your daughter?"

"Terrible two isn't in it, mate – and she isn't even two yet! It's no wonder my poor Lucy looks ragged at times. She's something of a shock after John, he was so easy. I often wonder if our Rosemary's namesake was anything like her."

For a moment, the two men pondered on Rosemary, the sister of Kenny's grandfather. She had been murdered when she was only sixteen.

"Poor lass," mused Dan. "Well, must go. Thanks a lot, Ken. I'll be seeing you."

They shook hands at the door.

"Remember me to Linda," said Kenny, to which Dan ruefully replied, "I will, but at the moment I'm not sure if she remembers who I am!"

"Been difficult, has it? Been working long hours?" Kenny was sympathetic.

"You wouldn't believe how this case has been – we think we're getting somewhere and then we hit yet another blank wall!"

"You'll do it – you've met blank walls before, as I recall."

"Humph. Glad you have faith in me, I'm not so sure myself," sighed Dan. "Right, I'm off. Goodnight, Ken."

Kenny watched Dan's car drive away and remembered that the door to the barn was still open so hastened across the garden and up the steps. He hesitated; was there anything in there belonging to the boy? Oh well, it didn't matter now, he'd look in the morning in the daylight. He shut the barn door and made his way back to the house.

Later, as he lay in bed, although tired, he kept thinking about Lucy and how she was faring in the hospital and also how the boy was. He hoped he'd get better. But his darling would be so tired and he knew she wouldn't leave the lad until she was happy he'd be alright. Sighing, he turned over. The bed seemed empty and huge without her beside him. Eventually though, he fell asleep.

Chapter 29

"Boss?"

Dan looked up. "Yes, Julie?"

"I've found a car hire place that has a black SUV in Ross-on-Wye. Most of the ones I've looked at all have silver ones, but this is the only one I've found with a black one. In fact, they have two."

"Right," said Dan, getting up. "We'll go out there now and have a word. You can drive, Julie."

The drive to Ross-on-Wye through the countryside was very pleasant and Dan couldn't help enjoying it. Julie drove competently, negotiating the bends and hills with skill. They found the care hire firm with no difficulty. It was a fine-looking place with cars also for sale.

They made their way through the glass door to be met with a pretty receptionist sitting behind a desk. She smiled pleasantly. "Can I help you?"

Dan showed his ID. "I certainly hope so. I am Detective Inspector Cooke and this is Detective Constable Coombs. We'd like to ask you about a car you might have hired out around the time of the August Bank Holiday. We're particularly interested in a black SUV."

"Oh, right. We have two of those." She reached for her computer. "The middle to end of August?" She tapped quickly. "Yes, both of them were out. One had been out all of August, I believe the family who hired it was going on a camping trip to Scotland. The other was hired on the Monday of the week before the Bank Holiday and returned on the Friday."

"I think that might be the one. Was it you who booked it out?"

"Yes, it would have been as I didn't have my holiday until after that. Hm, yes, come to think of it, I did. I remember it particularly because he was a very attractive man." Her eyes took on a dreamy look and her voice faded as she became lost in thought.

"Ahem!" Dan coughed to bring her back and she started.

"Oh, sorry!"

"Obviously he was memorable, Miss -erm?"

"Warner, Belinda Warner. Yes, he was very memorable. He had this way of looking at you that made you feel as though you were the only person who mattered to him. He had amazing eyes, the sort that melted you from the inside..."

"Erm, yes, I get your drift, Miss Warner. But do you think you could give us a more full description?"

"Sorry. He was quite tall, with dark hair and eyes and was very handsome! He had an attractive accent, English, yet with a sort of foreign twang, if that makes sense? He wore a dark suit and had expensive cufflinks and a posh watch."

"His name, credit card?"

"His name was Michael Soames and he paid with cash."

"Isn't that unusual? Did you see his driving licence?"

"Yes, of course. And yes, it's unusual to be paid in cash, but the customer is always right, you know. We don't mind, as long as they pay."

Dan gave a nod. "About the car, where is it now and when is it expected back?"

"As a matter of fact, it's not out just now. It has a fault, so it's in the repair shop."

"Is it now? May we see it, please?"

"We-ell, I'll call the boss, he'll probably take you over there. I can't leave my desk." She picked up the telephone and pressed a button. "Hello, Bob? Would you mind coming out here for a moment please?"

A door opened and in walked a man, who was obviously 'Bob'.

"What's up, Bel?"

"These two are police, Bob. They're interested in the SUV in the workshop."

"Oh? Why is that then?" The man's voice had the pleasant Herefordshire burr. He was of medium height, and had a receding hairline. However, his hair was still dark and his round face showed he was middle-aged. He frowned.

Dan turned to him and smiled pleasantly. "Are you the owner of this business, sir?"

"I am. Robert Brown at your service. What's this about my SUV?"

"We have reason to believe it might have been involved in a murder, Mr Brown."

Dan heard the receptionist Belinda give a rapid intake of breath. "Would it be possible to see the vehicle?"

"Y-yes, of course. A murder, you say? I hope no one used the car to run someone over. We never found any damage."

"No, not directly, sir, don't worry. But we have reason to believe, from witnesses, that the killer was using it."

"I'll take you over. Hold any calls I might have, would you, Bel?"

They followed Bob Brown through the door he'd entered from and along a corridor. At the end was another door leading to a back yard where there was a large workshop. They saw the car immediately.

"Hm, yes. What's wrong with the car?"

"We're waiting for a new gearbox. It shouldn't have gone wrong as the car is quite new, only a last year's model, but these things happen sometimes – perhaps it was a Friday afternoon model." The man laughed, but Dan could hear the strain in his voice.

"I'd like to have forensics go over it, Mr Brown. It seems to be the only lead we have to finding our killer. We can get a warrant, but it would be easier if you'd just give us your permission."

"May I ask who the victim was, Inspector?"

"Well, I see no harm in telling you. You may have seen it on the news. It was a young mother who was strangled in her bed. She was seen with a man driving a black SUV. We have every reason to think that he might have been a hired killer. But in killing her, he's made an innocent young lad an orphan."

Bob's face was ashen. "I did see it, yes. I can't believe he used one of my cars. Of course, you may take it, but I don't think you'll find anything as the car is always cleaned and valeted before going out again. Although it hasn't been out since then because of this gear problem."

"Right. You'll be surprised what forensics can do. We'll need the prints of your mechanic and anyone else who has touched or been in the car, for elimination purposes, you understand?"

"Yes. Yes, of course. Do whatever you need to. We are a respectable firm and if we can help catch a murderer, of course, we'll do so."

"That's very good of you, sir. Don't let anyone else touch it until we can take it away, please. I'll get the finger-printing sorted out. My constable will do that, won't you, DC Coombs?"

"Of course, sir."

They walked back to the reception. Belinda made no pretence of working. She was agog for news.

"Do you think that's the car, Mr. Cooke? Please don't tell me that gorgeous man got murdered!"

"No, Belinda, he hasn't been killed. We can't tell you more, I'm afraid. Someone will be in touch about the car, Mr Brown. We're grateful for your co-operation. It makes things so much easier. Obviously, if we find nothing, the car will be returned to you as soon as possible. Good day to you and to you, Miss Warner."

Dan shook hands with Bob, nodded at Belinda and went out, followed by Julie. As they got into the car, Dan noticed that Bob was leaning against the desk and both he and Belinda were watching them as they departed.

****

Charlie sensed he wasn't in his makeshift bed. Where was he? Scared to open his eyes, he had to because he needed to know where he was, even though he was fearful of the answer. It was very light the other side of his lids, which made opening them even harder. His arms hurt, but he was aware that his head didn't feel as bad as he remembered it had.

A cool hand touched his and a gentle voice said, "Charlie?"

He liked the voice; it made him feel brave enough to open one eye a little. He saw a young woman, dressed in a white gown with a white cap holding back her hair. But she had kind eyes and was smiling at him. She stroked his hand as she said his name again, "Charlie? Are you coming back to us? I'm Lucy."

Charlie opened his eyes more then, and looked at her properly. "Where...?" His voice came out in a croak and he realised his throat was sore. "Wa-er? Please?"

She held a kiddie-cup with a lip to his lips and he drank a mouthful, thankfully. Then he took another. He laid his head back on the pillows.

"Am I in hospital?" His voice sounded a little better now.

"You are indeed. You've been very poorly, we had to bring you here. You're having medication through the drip."

Charlie's eyes went to the line hanging beside him, leading into his wrist.

"How – how did I...?"

"How did we find you? It was our dog, Clarry. She knew you were poorly and brought my husband to the barn to find you."

He smiled a little. "Oh yes, Clarry. She's my friend."

"You saw her before?"

"Yes, she sat with me in the garden. She didn't tell on me until I got sick."

"That's right."

"Are you the lady with the two children?"

"Yes, I am."

"I'm sorry I stole the roll. I left some money on the step."

"Oh, that was you, was it? Well, you're welcome."

"What's going to happen to me now? Will they put me into care? I don't want to go into care, I'll run away again." He started up in the bed and pushed back the covers. Lucy put her hand on his shoulders and gently pressed him back.

"Now then, young man. I haven't sat here all night and half the day with you just to have you take off again."

"You've been here with me all the time?"

"Yes. I knew you didn't have anyone, so I came to be with you."

"Oh." Tears sprang up in Charlie's eyes. "Fank you."

"There now, I was happy to do it. We need to let the nurse know you've woken up. I'll ring this bell."

She pressed a bell and it wasn't long before a nurse came in. She smiled cheerfully. "Oh, hello there, young Charlie – you're back with us at last."

She took his pulse and his blood pressure and wrote on his chart. Then she checked the line.

"The doctor will be along to see you soon. But I can see you're on the mend. Are you hungry?"

The boy shook his head. "No fanks. I just want water."

"Well, you can have as much water as you want. Maybe you'll feel hungry later. I think some nice soup would be just the thing to begin with."

"Are you going to be here for a few minutes, nurse?" asked Lucy. "I'd just like to step outside for a moment."

"Yes, I'll stay here. You do what you need to do, Mrs Baxter."

"Don't go!"

"It's alright, Charlie, I'll come back. I just need to call my family to make sure my children are okay. You'll be alright with Nurse Evans."

"There now, lad, Mrs Baxter has been with you a long time and must be worried about her little ones."

He nodded as he remembered the two small children. They were so lucky to have a mother who cared about them. He thought he could remember a time when his mum had really cared about him. Charlie relaxed against the pillows and sank back into sleep.

Chapter 30

When Charlie opened his eyes again, Lucy was there, just as she said she would be. But there was someone else – a man, a stranger. He sat up but Lucy immediately stopped him gently.

"It's okay, Charlie, don't worry. This is a friend of mine, Detective Inspector Cook, and he would like to talk with you."

"Police?" Charlie's heart thumped in fear and his eyes opened wide.

The man came forward and stood by the bed. Although swathed in white like everyone else, the man had a pleasant face and kind eyes. When he spoke, his voice was soft.

"Hello there, Charlie. You've had us all worried. Half of Hereford has been looking for you. I'm glad we've found you at last but I'm sorry you're poorly."

"You won't put me in care, will you, sir?"

"Don't worry about that now, you have to get well first and you're safe here in hospital. But we do need to find out who killed your mum. Will you help me?"

Charlie instinctively felt that he could trust this man. Lucy had said he was her friend, so he must be nice. He nodded.

"But I don't know how I can help because I didn't see anything. I didn't see the man."

"So, it was a man?"

"Yes. Mum said she'd met someone special who was going to offer her a job and we would be able to live in a house. She said he had a posh house and needed a house-keeper and we could live there."

Dan and Lucy glanced at each other.

"Can you tell us what happened on that night before you found your mum in the morning?"

Charlie shrugged. "The usual. She went out and left me alone in the van. My bed is in the roof, it's very clever, it doesn't look like it's there. It's only a small space, made specially for me. Mum said my Uncle Simon made it for me so she could sleep underneath. They were very quiet when they came in but I weren't quite asleep. I couldn't see 'em but I heard 'em talkin'. But I can't tell yer any more cos I went ter sleep. I got used ter bein' able to go to sleep when she brought a man in and I'd put my fingers in my ears and my head under the covers..."

He felt unable to explain why he did that, but the policeman nodded understandingly. "And what happened in the morning?"

"When I woke up, I got out of the van right away cos usually mum's, erm, friends, were still there and sometimes they could be horrible. I've been clouted a few times, so it was always good to get away so as not ter give 'em the chance. I was surprised that 'e weren't in Mum's bed but I thought 'e might 'ave gone out ter relieve 'iself, yer know? But I went out an' 'is car weren't there. I allus used ter go ter the river an' sit there a while. I fought Mum was asleep, so I were goin' ter wait fer 'er ter wake up. But I waited an' waited an' she didn't call me, so in the end I went back ter the van and found that – that..." His tears welled up again and Lucy gave him a tissue.

"It's alright, son," said the detective gently.

Dabbing his eyes and sniffing loudly, Charlie continued, "When I knew she were dead, I was scared and ran away."

"After first getting a good breakfast from Mrs White," added the man and his eyes twinkled, making Charlie smile.

"Yeah," he said sheepishly.

"Well, I don't blame you for that. But you've certainly given us the run-around, young man. Not only have I been worrying about finding out who killed your mum but I've had to worry about you too."

Ashamed, Charlie put his head down. "Sorry."

The detective put his hand on the boy's shoulder. "It's okay, lad. I don't blame you for being afraid. But please promise me you won't run off again? You are safe here and I have an officer guarding you outside your room all the time, so no one can get at you, okay?"

"Yes, Sir." After the conversation, Charlie felt really tired again and he just wanted to sleep. Nurse Evans bustled in at that point.

"I think that's enough for now, Mr Cooke. This young fellow needs his rest."

"And so do I, I'm afraid," said Lucy. "Do you think you'll be okay if I go now, Charlie? I hope Dan has put your mind at rest and you know you're safe now?"

"Yeah. Fanks, Lucy, I do."

"I'll come and see you again, I promise. You just get well now, and don't worry about anything else. We won't let anything bad happen to you, we'll look after you."

He nodded as she stroked his cheek gently. As Lucy and Dan left the room, his eyes closed and he drifted off towards sleep. He vaguely sensed the nurse moving around, straightening his covers before he sank again into blissful oblivion.

****

"Grant, would you call Mrs Dale and let her know we've found Charlie, to put her mind at rest please? I'm going to call Clara Gleeson, in case Simon Denton has turned up there yet, although I'm sure he would have contacted us if he had."

"Of course, Boss."

Dan picked up his phone as Grant went to his to make the call.

Clara answered the call after two rings. As soon as she knew it was Dan, she said, "Oh, Mr Cooke, I've been so worried and I wanted to call you but didn't know if I should."

"Why, Clara?"

"I've been worrying about that detective you sent to get a picture of Simon."

"What detective? I've sent no-one."

146

Clara cursed in a way that would make a sailor blush and Dan put the phone away from his ear until she'd finished.

"Sorry, Mr Cooke. I had a nagging feeling about that bloke. There was something about him – I was almost sure he wasn't the fuzz."

"What did he want?"

"He wanted a picture of Simon, so I went around to his house – I have a key – and got a picture of him and he took a photo of it on his phone. He told me that you were worried about Simon and needed a photo to send out."

"You didn't take him into Simon's house?"

"No. He waited outside. Oh!" that last exclamation bothered Dan.

"What?"

"I left the key in the door. Do you think he might have taken a print of it or something?"

"He might well have," replied Dan, grimly. "Have you been in Simon's house since then?"

"No."

"Would you go there now, please, and see if you think anything has been disturbed? Don't touch anything, just call me back straight-away."

"Will do." Without another word, she put the phone down.

Grant came back from making his call. He was about to speak when he noticed the grim look on his boss's face. "What's up?"

Dan told him and Grant whistled. "I'm waiting for her to call me back. If he's been in there, he might have found out where Simon is. I hope he's not another target."

The phone rang and Dan snatched it up. "Cooke."

He listened. "Right. Call the police. Give them my contact and ask them to call me once they've had a look at things."

"I will. Oh, Mr Cooke, I can't believe I was so stupid. I was careful to leave him outside but I never thought about the damn key. You'd think being married to a con I'd have had more sense!"

147

"Don't worry, Clara, I don't blame you for it. If he had ID and everything, you weren't to know. Oh, I nearly forgot to tell you – Charlie's been found. He's in hospital but he's safe. I thought you'd like to know."

"Oh, I'm so glad he's been found, poor lamb. I'll get onto the police now."

"Keep in touch, Clara. And don't forget, if you hear of anything, phone me right away."

"Oh, I will."

Dan put the phone down, put his head in his hands and groaned. "Simon's house has been done over. Clara said it's in a right mess. Grant, find out which police force will be dealing with that and liaise with them. If they find any information on the whereabouts of Simon Denton, we have to know."

****

Simon opened one eye tentatively. He was clearly not dead because he had a massive headache. Sensing someone nearby, he opened the other eye and squinted to see a nurse about to check his blood pressure. She stopped, having noticed him looking at her.

"Och, Mr Denton, you're awake at last. That great. I'm going to take your blood pressure, just relax now."

He shut his eyes while she wrapped his arm and the machine pumped. He inwardly winced as it became too tight, but in a moment, it was released and let out gradually.

"Hmm, that's good."

He opened his eyes as she spoke and watched while she unwrapped his arm. His other arm was in a plaster and one of his legs felt heavy too.

"Got a hell of a headache," he croaked.

"You will have, that was a hefty blow on your head. I'd say you're lucky to be alive. Do you feel you could sit up a little?

It might help the head, although we'll give you something for that."

"Yeah, I think so, thanks."

The pillows under him gradually raised until he was in a semi-sitting position. The nurse rearranged the pillows to make him more comfortable.

"There, is that better?"

"Mm, thank you. Where am I?"

"Glasgow. You were airlifted here. Now, would you like a drink?"

Simon thought the small amount of water he managed was surely nectar from the gods. He laid back on his pillows, sighing in contentment and silently praying thanks that he'd been rescued. But he couldn't for the life of him understand why a complete stranger would attack him in such a way. He worried about his cottage – had it been robbed? But he had nothing, apart from his precious computer, his music system and collection of music DVDs. Was it someone who wanted to steal his latest book? No, it couldn't be. Anyway, he had it all backed up on an external drive, plus he sent it to himself, chapter by chapter through email. He'd be able to prove it was his book. Try as he might, he couldn't believe the theft of his latest manuscript was the reason behind the attack. No matter how he thought about the incident, all it achieved was a worse headache.

Closing his eyes, he tried not to think about it. He had to get well; it would do him no good to keep letting it go around and round. One thing for sure was he needed to talk to the police and contact Clara. He'd been away longer than usual and she may be worried. Fatigue overcame him and he let himself relax. It could all keep for now, there was no hurry...

****

Later that day, a police constable came to take his statement about his attack.

"The police were called at the same time as the ambulance, sir, and an appeal for witnesses was sent out. The walkers who rescued you reported seeing a car going past them several miles away from where they found you, much earlier in the day. Unfortunately, they weren't near enough to tell what the registration was, or even what sort of car it was as they were on a hill path and the road a long way beneath them. They noticed it because not many cars go that way. We have no way of knowing if it was the vehicle your attacker was using. Can you give me any description of the man?"

Simon told him what he knew, which wasn't much as the man had been well muffled up against the cold.

"And you didn't know him? Never seen him before?"

"No, never. If I'd known him, there wouldn't have been a need for him to ask me if I was Simon Denton."

"Fair point. And you don't know why you were attacked? You never argued about anything?"

"Not at all. He just asked me, was I Simon Denton? I said, 'Yes', then he hit me and I fell and must have banged my head on the ground. Then he attacked me when I'd fallen, and broke my arm and leg. It was a vicious attack, Constable. I keep racking my brains as to why the attack, but I can't come up with anything at all."

"Hm, does seem strange, Sir."

"Do you know anything about my cottage? Has it been robbed?"

The constable flicked through his notebook. "We've been told that the rescuers went in to find towels and things to splint your arm and leg, and a duvet to wrap you in because you were suffering from hyperthermia. They left the key with the landlord of the public house in Dalwhinnie so the local police went to examine the cottage. They reported that nothing seemed to be missing, but of course we can't know for sure until you see it, Sir. It had been disturbed; there were obvious signs of searching, there was mess left around, things out of drawers and cupboards, but your computer and music system were untouched."

"Well, I'm glad about that. It's strange though, for there would have been nothing to find, I have no secrets. I'm just completely mystified."

"Do you live in that cottage all the time? Or do you have another address?"

"No, I live in Plymouth." Simon gave his address and the constable shut his notebook. Simon's head was thumping; he was glad the interview seemed to be over.

"I think it's likely we'll liaise with the police down there, to see if we can find any clues. If we can't, it looks like it may well become one of those unsolvable crimes. We don't have much to go on."

"I appreciate that, Officer. You will keep me informed? I don't think I'll be going anywhere for a while."

"Of course. Try not to worry, we'll see what we can find out."

At that moment, the nurse bustled up. "I think Mr. Denton's had enough, Constable."

"I'm just going, Nurse. Thank you for seeing me, Mr Denton. We'll be in touch." With a nod to the nurse, the policeman left. The nurse fussed around Simon, helping him to get comfortable again. He closed his eyes and sank thankfully back into blessed sleep.

Chapter 31

The day after Lucy had spent most of the day in the hospital with Charlie, Kenny remembered there might be some of the lad's belongings still up in the upper barn. When he'd taken the children and Clarry over to his mum's house, so that Lucy could rest and recover from her long watch over the boy, he went back home to take a look around now there was daylight.

Once in the barn, he saw the makeshift bed that Charlie had constructed on the old mattress and the dirty blankets and cover sheets that had been draped over the old furniture. He followed the smell to the bucket that Charlie had used, and, wrinkling his nose, he carried it down to empty it, then went back up to collect the backpack he'd seen lying next to the bed.

After locking the barn door behind him, Kenny took the bag into the house and tipped the contents onto the settee. Although feeling guilty, because these were Charlie's private things, and didn't really know why he should look at them; but felt he should. There wasn't that much, a pack of three boys' pants with only one left, a scruffy pair of jogger bottoms and a few biscuits in a packet. Much to his surprise, he found a handful of notes, amounting to twenty-five pounds, a few lose coins and a photograph. He looked at the picture of a young man and woman, happily smiling at each other and frowned. He was sure he'd seen that man before...

That's it – how could he forget someone he'd grown up with, a playmate all through school? But why would Charlie have a photo of one of Kenny's best mates?

****

Later that day, Madge was surprised to see Kenny coming through the shop door, followed by DI Cooke and DS Grant.

"Hello Madge, sorry to barge in on you like this but could we have a word, please? Is your husband around?"

"Erm, yes, he's out the back, sorting stock. Len!" Madge called. "Can you come through, please?"

"Do you have somewhere more private where we can talk?" asked Dan.

Madge looked at him curiously, as Len appeared from the stock-room.

"What's up, love? Oh, hello, Kenny, Inspector, Sergeant. What's all this about?"

"Could we shut the shop for a short while, do you think?"

"Oh, erm – yes, I suppose. It's usually pretty quiet at this time." Madge was puzzled and not a little worried. What had happened?

Len locked the door and turned the sign around, then they followed Madge into the back where the stairs led up to the flat above the shop and into a large and pleasant room facing the road outside the shop. Dan glanced out, it had an enticing view of the centre of the village with the duck pond and green. Madge and Len had sat together on the sofa next to each other, and they both wore puzzled frowns.

"What's all this about, Inspector?" asked Len.

"Well, as you are aware, there's been a runaway boy, Charlie, that we've been looking for?"

"Why yes, he came into my shop and I gave him a meat pie. But what has that got to do with anything?"

"We have found Charlie, Madge. Kenny here found him two evenings ago in his upper barn."

"I heard he'd been found, Ken said that was the reason Lucy couldn't supply me with her bread for a couple of days. Is he alright?"

"He's poorly now, but he will be. Thing is, Kenny found a photograph amongst the boy's things, and he recognised it."

"A photograph?"

"Yes. Would you take a look at it, please?"

Grant handed the photo over. Madge gave a cry, hand to mouth. The colour in Len's face drained and he said in a strangled voice,

"Why did the boy have a picture of our son, Inspector?"

"I went to see Charlie this morning and he insisted that it was of his father and mother, said that he remembered his father's name was Stephen. Another witness who knew the boy and his mother years ago, told us the same thing."

"How can it be? His wife was called Pauline and she doesn't look anything like this girl."

"From the information we've gathered, it seems your son was having an affair with her."

Madge gave another gasp and gripped her husband's hand. "He looks so happy. He never looked that happy when he was with Pauline."

"We have been told he adored Mollie – that's our dead girl's real name – and apparently she was devastated when he never came again. That's when she took Charlie and went to live with her uncle."

"Poor girl. She didn't know he'd been – he'd been..." Madge broke off to sob into a handkerchief handed to her by Len.

"No, she probably didn't know who he really was. Ken here told me what happened to your son. I'm so sorry about that. We're still looking for her Uncle Simon, who we hope might be able to fill in some gaps."

Madge nodded into her hanky. Then she looked up, wide eyed, "Could that mean – that – that Charlie is our grandson?"

****

"I just can't believe it, Lucy," said Madge as she took a sip of her tea. "Fancy Charlie being our grandson." After hearing the news from Kenny and Dan, Madge had left the shop in the

154

care of Len and hurried to see Lucy, who dished out tea and cake, as she did to all, whether distressed or not.

"It's certainly incredible," remarked Lucy, as she took a bite of her piece of cake.

"When we heard of that poor girl being murdered and that little lad out there somewhere, I hadn't an inkling it would have anything to do with us. Mind you, with hindsight, there did seem something familiar about the boy when he came into my shop, but I couldn't put my finger on it. Now I realise he has my son's eyes." Madge's own eyes misted as she spoke, and Lucy reached out to squeeze the other woman's hand.

"It's wonderful, Madge. It means you still have something of your son's besides memories."

"That's so true. But I would never have thought he would have had an affair! Mind you, knowing Pauline, I'm not that surprised really. She must have been very difficult to live with – not that that excuses him. I brought him up to have good morals."

"I'm sure you did. You're not responsible for what happened. So, what will you do, now that you know who Charlie is?"

"Well, we have to look after him, of course!" Lucy laughed at Madge's fierce face. "Although we have to wait for the DNA results, we don't want to give him false hopes. As soon as we know for sure, we'll go and see him. We don't want to overwhelm the boy, especially as he's never seen Len and we thought that you could, well, explain to Charlie who we are and pave the way for us?"

"I'll be happy to do that, Madge. I'm so glad he won't have to go into care – he's so afraid of that. I think he must have been in care, or threatened with it at some stage, poor little thing. There's still so much to learn about him, but at least he'll be safe with you and well cared for. I know he'll be really happy about that."

"Well, I hope it'll work out, because I haven't looked after a child for a long time and the shop takes up so much of our time," sighed Madge.

"The village will rally round to help you. I'm sure that Charlie will find many friends here. He's a lucky boy to belong to our village; he couldn't be coming to a better place."

Chapter 32

The results came through the next day. Dan had pushed it through because it was important to know if Charlie was Madge and Len's grandson to put the boy's mind at rest. He immediately put a call through to Sutton's Old Village Shoppe.

Madge answered the phone and shrieked in joy, bringing Len rushing through from the stock-room. She apologised to Dan for blasting his ear drum, thanked him and put the phone down.

"Len, oh Len – Charlie is our grandson – he really is our Stephen's child! Isn't that wonderful?"

He held out his arms and as he cuddled her, he said, "Yes love, that really is wonderful. It's like a miracle."

"It *is* a miracle! Whoever would have thought it? I never imagined we had a grandson out there – why didn't our Stephen tell us? We've missed out on so much!"

"He was ashamed I expect. We've missed out, yes, but think what young Charlie's missed. And by all accounts, he's not had a terribly good life, from what Mr. Cooke has said. But we can make it up to him, help him get over the past and look to a better future."

"We can indeed." Madge drew away from him. "I must call Lucy; she said she'd come with us the first time we visit him – help break the ice, you know? He's only seen me once and he's not seen you at all."

Len nodded. "That's a good idea. You call her while I keep an eye on the shop."

****

The following day, Simon felt a bit brighter. It wasn't particularly easy to sleep with his leg suspended and his arm also heavy in plaster. However, he was used to sleeping in uncomfortable places, having travelled in many countries, and the

157

medication helped. His head hurt less and he'd managed to eat and drink.

In the afternoon, he was surprised to be visited by two detectives, who introduced themselves as Detective Inspector Fergus McInnes and Detective Constable Rory Campbell.

"Mr Denton, how are you?" D.I. McInnes was a brisk man, auburn haired and well-built, with brooding bushy eyebrows that fascinated Simon. D.C. Campbell was younger and slim with dark hair and dimples in his cheeks when he smiled.

"I'm improving, I think. I can only take it one day at a time. I'm surprised to see detectives visiting me though."

"Well, sir," said Fergus, as he drew up a chair to sit beside the bed and nodded to Rory to take another chair. "We've been in touch with the force at Plymouth and they've told us some interesting things." As he spoke, the eyebrows pulled together in a frown.

For a moment, Simon felt guilty but then he pulled himself up – he had nothing to be guilty about, did he? He hoped Mollie and the boy, Charlie weren't in some sort of trouble.

"Oh?" he said, in the hope he sounded calm, although he felt anything but!

"I'm afraid I have some items of bad news for you, sir. The first thing is, your home in Plymouth was broken into. Your neighbour, a Mrs – erm, what was it, Campbell?"

"Gleeson, Sir," remarked the other detective.

"Och, yes. Mrs Gleeson, reported it to the police. It seems someone impersonating a police detective turned up one day and said could he have a photo of you because the police in Hereford are concerned about your whereabouts."

"Hereford?" echoed Simon, "Why on earth are the Hereford police looking for me? I've never been there."

The eyebrows moved again into a position that showed the man's concern.

"Mr Denton, I'm very sorry to inform you that your niece, Mollie Denton, who was residing in Hereford, is dead."

Simon felt as though he'd been knocked on the head again. "Dead?" he whispered, "How?"

Fergus coughed uncomfortably. "It seemed she was murdered, air."

"Murdered?" repeated Simon, as he felt all the blood drain from his face. "How? Why?"

"Strangled, sir, in her bed. The Hereford police are searching for her killer. Mollie was living under an assumed name –"

"Mandy Smith."

"You knew then?"

"Oh yes, I knew. I gave her the van, so she could get away."

"Would you like to tell us about it?"

"Charlie!" Simon said, suddenly. "Where's Charlie? He'll have no one now."

"Her son is safe, that's all I know at the moment."

Simon gave a sigh of relief – thank goodness. "That poor lad has not had a good life. I've been worried about him for a long time. Worried about both of them."

"Tell us, Sir."

Simon told them all he knew about what had happened all that time ago.

"You say she was threatened? By whom?"

"I don't know, she wouldn't tell me. But she was very frightened and agitated. Giving her the van so she could go somewhere out of harm's way was the only thing I could think of to help her. I still own the van and I pay the road tax for it and the MOTs; at least, I always put money in her bank to cover the cost. I'd always kept it in good condition and I hoped she would do the same. I don't know if she ever had it maintained. Anyway, she lived all over the place, sometimes with travellers and sometimes on her own. She would write to me occasionally. I could sense a change in her though and worried in case Charlie wasn't being looked after properly."

"When was this – how long ago did she go away?"

159

"Oh, it has to be about seven years ago now. Charlie was only about five when they went."

"And you really have no idea why she felt she had to run away?"

"All I can think of is that it had something to do with Charlie's father. In fact, I asked her that and begged her to stay with me and fight, if he was trying to get Charlie. But she said it wasn't that at all."

"Did you believe her?"

"Yes, I did. She was always a truthful girl. I had no reason to doubt her. She said it was better that I didn't know anything, it was safer for me and she wouldn't have to worry about me."

"She said that, did she? Haven't you any idea what she meant?"

"Not a clue. I just couldn't imagine what it could be. I tried hard to get her to tell me but she just wouldn't. She was inclined to be stubborn so nothing I could say would make her change her mind. When she asked me if she could have the van, I admit I was reluctant because I loved it, it had always been my 'home from home' and I kept it immaculate. But I loved her and Charlie more and didn't want them to be in danger so I said she could have it but I would continue to own it and pay the tax on it. I also pay her a monthly allowance to help her and Charlie, which goes into her bank account automatically by direct debit."

"Haven't you been worried about her and the boy all this time?"

"Of course I have," Simon said heatedly and then winced at the pain in his head. More quietly, he went on, "I've tried to keep in touch and although her contact has been sparse at times, I knew they were alright. Although I have to admit I've been suspicious that she might be doing drugs."

"Hm. Do you have any idea why she might have been in Hereford?"

"Not really. Although..."

"Yes?"

"I seem to recall, now I've thought about it, that she once said something about Steve having relatives there – Steve was Charlie's father, you know."

"So, you think she may have gone there to look for them?"

"It's possible."

"Do you know who they are, Sir?"

"Not a clue. As far as I can recall, I never knew Steve's last name."

"Hmm."

"I suppose she could have been there in the natural course of her travels?" Simon mused out loud.

"Maybe, although it seems strange that the place where she might have found relatives is the place where she has met her end."

"Yes. And to think, I was leaving Scotland to try to persuade her to come back home, that surely the danger, whatever it was, is now passed. I was already too late," said Simon bitterly. "I should have done that much sooner, looked after her myself."

The gruff detective rose from his chair and, to Simon's surprise, he touched his hand and said, "You couldn't have known what would happen, Sir, and there's no proof that you could have kept her safe if you'd had her back before. Seems to me that the person, or persons, who were after your niece were pretty determined. By the way, we have a description of the man who came after your photo. Detective Constable?"

Rory hastily flicked through his notebook and read out the description given by Clara Gleeson.

"That sounds rather like the man who attacked me, although I couldn't see him all that well because of what he was wearing, but I remember thinking that he was a good-looking man."

"Seems the guy enjoys travelling!" remarked the Inspector. "I think you've had enough for today, sir. If we hear of anything else, we'll be in touch. It seems to me that the attack on you was designed to keep you out of the way for a while; probably not to kill you."

161

"Looks like it. Wish he hadn't done such a thorough job though. If I hadn't been found I'm sure I would be dead now, I'm very lucky."

"Lucky indeed. I'm sorry to have been the bearer of such bad news about your niece."

Simon nodded, hoping the threatening tears wouldn't show before the gruff detective and his constable had left. He felt the man's hand rest on his shoulder for a moment, and then they were gone.

A nurse bustled around the curtain a few moments later and wordlessly handed him some tissues and left him to his privacy. Ten minutes later, she was back with a cup of coffee. He managed a watery smile for her. This was a different nurse to the first one. She reminded him of his mother, although she would only have been in her forties but she had a homely, friendly face.

"If you need to talk, Simon, I have a few minutes," she said.

"Thank you. I've just been told that my niece was found murdered. It was a shock." He gave her a watery smile.

Her face showed what he'd felt at the news.

"My goodness, I'm so sorry – and on top of this too. Were you close?"

"Yes. I was like a father to her because my brother and his wife died. I brought her up. I think her death and my attack are linked somehow, although I'm not really sure how, or why."

"Goodness! I hope the police get to the bottom of it. I'm sorry about your niece. Drink your coffee now, hopefully it will help you feel better."

"Thank you, nurse. Thank you for your caring."

She patted his hand. "That's what I'm here for."

Chapter 33

Dan had no sooner arrived back at headquarters when his sergeant hailed him. "Boss!"

"What's up?" Dan walked over to the desk where Grant was sitting.

"Interesting developments. I've just taken a call from Glasgow."

"Glasgow?" Dan was startled. "Whatever for?"

"Simon Denton is in hospital there. Apparently, he has a cottage in a remote spot near a loch. He was attacked by someone. If some walkers hadn't happened to come by, he probably would have died, because he was left outside on the ground."

"My goodness – poor man! So, how did they know to contact us?"

"From the police at Plymouth. They contacted them after hearing where Mr Denton lives and learned about his house being broken into."

"Does he know who attacked him?"

"Not a clue. He says he was a complete stranger."

"Hmm. Very odd. Not a random attack, I think – what say you, Grant?"

"I say the same. It looks like whoever broke into Mr Denton's house found out about the cottage in Scotland."

"I agree that's what it looks like – but why? It's bizarre. Why didn't the bloke just kill him? But why would he want to kill him anyway; he's just a harmless author?"

"But related to Mollie Denton," stated Grant.

"Seems that was his crime. But I don't understand why either of them should be the object of a killer anyway."

Dan groaned. "I can't think! I need coffee and something to eat."

"I'll pop over to MacDonald's, shall I?"

"Yes, do that. Erm, before you go, let me have the contact for whoever you spoke to in Glasgow, would you?"

"Yes, it was D.I. Fergus MacInnes. Here's the number."

"Thanks."

Dan was dialling as Grant left the room.

****

"Rory!"

"Yes, Gov?"

"Get me the contact of one o' those walker witnesses of the Denton case, would ye?"

"Gov." Rory tapped on his desk computer, checked it and dialled a number. He spoke rapidly into the phone, then put his hand over it. "Gov? I have that doctor's wife, Mrs Renton. You want to speak with her?"

In answer, Fergus picked up his own phone and waited for the click as Rory transferred the call.

"Hello, Mrs Renton? I'm Detective Inspector MacInnes of Glasgow. You and your husband were involved in the rescue of one Simon Denton? Yes, he's beginning to recover now, although he'll be laid up for some time with his arm and leg. I was wondering if I might clarify something with you? Thank you. It's like this..."

****

Dan's phone rang as he and Grant were finishing their Big Macs. He snatched it up. "Cooke."

He listened for a few minutes, then said, "Thank you, I'm much obliged to you. Thank you for your help."

He put the phone down. "That's interesting, Grant."

"What's that, Boss?"

"The Scottish Detective Inspector just spoke to one of the walkers who rescued Simon Denton. They saw the same car twice

164

that day – the first time it was going towards the cottage, the second time going the opposite direction, and going a great deal faster the second time."

"So it was likely the attacker's car that they saw."

"Unfortunately not close enough to provide us with any details. But it does tell us something else, Grant."

Grant frowned. "What's that?"

"Well, if the walkers saw him, it's likely he saw them, especially as there was quite a group of them."

"I'm not with you, Boss. Oh – it means that he knew they were going in the direction of the cottage."

"Precisely, my dear Watson. He knew they were likely to go past the cottage on their route to Dalwhinnie. He didn't mean to kill Simon Denton at all – he simply meant to stop him going home. The big question is – why?"

****

Charlie's eyes widened when Lucy came into the hospital ward with Madge and Len. He smiled shyly at Madge.

"I know you. You're the kind lady in the shop who gave me a pie."

She came forward to stand next to his bed. "I am. You have a good memory, young man. How are you feeling today?"

"I'm a lot better, fank you." Then his face fell. "But I'm afraid of what'll happen to me when they say I can't stay here any longer."

Lucy took his hand. He looked at her and smiled.

"Now, Charlie. This is Madge and this is her husband, Len."

"Hello Charlie, I'm pleased to meet you," Len spoke softly and grinned at the boy. Charlie looked startled for a moment.

"What's up, lad?"

Charlie hung his head. "It's just me, I'm silly."

165

"No, you're not silly." Len perched on the bed and looked into his grandson's eyes. He felt his stomach turn over when he saw his son's eyes looking back at him. "Tell me, don't be afraid."

"You reminded me of my dad. You look a lot like him. But it's a long time since I saw him so I may be just imagining it."

"You're not imagining it, Charlie. I'm your dad's father."

Charlie looked at him and then at Lucy, frowning.

"Charlie, I've brought Madge and Len here to see you because we have found out that they are your dad's parents – your grandparents. We wanted to break it to you carefully as you've never seen Len before – but you have seen it for yourself."

"My grandparents? You're my dad's Mum and Dad? Gosh."

"We really are, and we'll tell you all about how we know. But it means you don't have to be afraid of going into care because you're going to live with us when you come out of hospital," said Len, gently.

He looked up at Madge, who nodded smilingly through her tears and took him into her arms to give him a bear hug. He looked over her shoulder at Lucy, who also smiled widely and nodded. Then he was hugged by Len and as he did so, he burst into tears and clung onto his grandfather, who rocked him while the two women looked on.

"I'll leave you two with Charlie now, so you can get to know each other," whispered Lucy to Madge and they hugged briefly.

"Thanks, Lucy, love. See you soon."

When Lucy looked back at the boy's bed, Madge was sitting on one side and Len the other and each was holding one of Charlie's hands. Three heads were bent together and they were completely engrossed with each other. Lucy smiled happily. She was glad that Charlie's story had a happy ending and he would now be cared for by his loving grandparents. She did so love happy endings.

Hastening down the corridors, she looked forward to telling Kenny all about it.

Chapter 34

While Charlie was receiving his good news, his Uncle Simon was lying in bed, mulling over everything that had happened. His writer's head was conjuring up all kinds of scenarios which was getting him nowhere. He tried to cast his mind back to when Mollie and Charlie were living with him and thinking through the events that led to her sudden departure.

"Uncle Simon, you have to help me. Charlie and me, we're in danger!"

"What danger? Is someone threatening you?"

"Yes. Someone is after me!"

"Why, what's going on? Why don't you go to the police instead of running away?"

"I can't! They'll get me if I go to the police. They might take Charlie. I have to go away or they'll kill me!"

Simon was startled – who would kill his niece? What could she possibly have done to warrant someone wanting to kill her?

"Please, please! I can't stay here anymore and I don't have anywhere to go. Would you, would you lend me Fred?"

"Lend you Fred?" he echoed, thinking about his precious camper-van. "How long for?"

"As long as it takes for us to be safe. I have a plan to put into operation to protect us, but I need to get away first, somewhere where they won't know where I've gone. If I had Fred, he would be a home for me and Charlie. It has that secret bed in the roof already made for him. He loves it and if we had Fred, it would be familiar for Charlie. Oh, please, Uncle, please let me take it. You wouldn't have to worry about us sleeping rough or anything if I had it."

He looked at her and then at Charlie, innocently playing with some little cars on the floor. His gaze went beyond her to the window, where he could see the back of his precious camper-van that he'd named Fred years ago, then back at Mollie's anxious, tear-stained face.

"Alright then, but you must promise me you'll look after Fred, keep it in good condition so that I don't have to worry about you driving around in him."

"I will." She threw her arms around his neck and he held her briefly, at the same time thinking how thin she had become over the almost year she'd been back with him. She'd never had a big appetite but she picked at her food and always seemed listless. Often, she seemed too tired to do much and he had watched over Charlie while she slept on the sofa or in a chair. He worried about the little boy – how would she cope with him on the road, especially on her own?

They had gone the next day, after he had stocked the van with everything he felt they'd need, especially food. And he'd not seen them since. What was it she had said? She had a plan to protect to put into operation? He hadn't thought much about it at the time, because he'd been so upset at their sudden departure and the loss of his precious van, his Fred, which had been his comfort on his many travels. Fred had been all over the world with him and had never let him down. It seemed his van was still going strong. He wondered if he would see it again – and what sort of condition would it be in?

Back to 'the plan', what could it have been? For the first time ever, Simon wondered if his niece had planned to do something illegal; was it the reason why she had finally been killed?

By the time the nurses came to settle him for the night, Simon had resolved that tomorrow he would ask if the detective with the fiercesome eyebrows would be willing to come and have a chat with him.

****

169

When Dan arrived at work on Thursday morning, a note asking him to call Farmer White was on his desk.

Graham Grant arrived in time to see his boss put the phone down. Dan rose from his desk.

"Don't take your coat off, Grant, we have to go over to Moreton-on-Lugg. Farmer White has reported that Mollie's van has been done over. Judy, call Forensics for me, would you?"

"Right, Boss, will do."

Tom White was waiting by the camper-van, where he could see the doors stood open. A feeling of deja-vu came over Dan as they stopped the car by him.

"Mr Cooke, I discovered this by accident, like. I check my grounds every so often, especially near harvest-time and I noticed the van doors were open. I knew they'd been left closed and I thought maybe some vagrant had decided to sleep in there. But when I looked – well, see for yourself."

The three men peered inside without going in.

"Oh my!" Grant whistled. "Someone's made a right mess of it."

"That's an understatement, Grant."

The contents of the drawers and cupboards were strewn on the floor, the drawers upside down on top, the cupboards hanging open. Mollie's bed had been lifted out and a knife had been taken to the mattress, or seat cushions as they were. The linings to the walls had been pulled off and the seats in the driver's cab had also been knifed and pulled apart. The compartment with Charlie's bed had been pulled down and that mattress and bedding pulled apart.

"Well, someone was desperate to find something," commented Dan. "Ah, here's the team. I'd better have a word. You didn't touch anything, did you, Tom?"

"No, I just peered inside, like, and then called you."

"I doubt you'll find anything, boys, but you never know. We'll leave you to it. I don't think we need to worry too much about it now, it's obvious whatever the person or persons were looking for, they've either found it or not. They won't be back."

"I'll be glad when it's off my property," remarked the farmer. "Well, if it's alright with you, Mr Cooke, I need to get back to my work."

"Of course. Thank you. Come on, Grant, there's nothing more we can do here. I'm going to call that Scottish detective when we get back. I don't envy him having to tell Simon Denton that his van has been destroyed."

****

Simon wasn't feeling so good. His headache seemed to be worse and his leg was painful too. Therefore, he'd done nothing about asking to see D.I. McInnes. However, just as he'd had the remains of his dinner taken away, Fergus McInnes and his sidekick Rory Campbell turned up.

"Hello, Detective Inspector, this is a surprise. I was thinking last night that I needed to see you."

"How are you today, sir?"

"Not that brilliant, if I'm honest. But I'm glad to see you, for I wanted to run something by you."

The two detectives pulled out chairs and Rory took out his faithful notebook.

"Is that so? What's that?"

"Well, last night I was thinking and thinking and I remember something Mollie said before she left my home. I didn't think anything of it at the time, I was more upset that she and young Charlie were going."

"Quite so. What was it she said?"

"I can't remember her exact words, but she said she had a plan that would help to protect her and Charlie."

"And that's it, Sir?"

"Yes. What, apart from running away from whoever threatened her, would help to protect her? Do you think she knew something about someone and was holding it over them?"

171

The fierce eyebrows folded themselves into a deep frown. "Are you suggesting that she was planning to blackmail someone?"

"Much as I hate to admit it, yes. I think she knew something and was trying to keep her and Charlie safe by blackmail. She might not have been getting money, only the assurance they wouldn't touch her and her boy."

The detective nodded slowly and drew in a deep breath. "I have some good news for you, Mr Denton, and I have some bad news. The good news is that the police in Hereford have found Charlie's grandparents. It happened quite by accident really, but nevertheless, the parents of the boy's father have been found. And they are willing to look after him from now on."

"That is good news. Perhaps when I'm better I can visit and hear all about it."

"I'd say that is something positive to look forward to, Sir."

"And the bad news?"

"The bad news is that someone has pretty much destroyed the interior of Mollie Denton's van. In the light of present conversation, it seems that your surmise might be right. I'd say, after your two houses and now the van has been thoroughly searched, someone is pretty desperate to get hold of something. The question is, have they found it, or will the search go on? And if it goes on, where will that person concentrate next?"

Chapter 35

Dan and his team had reached the same conclusion. And they had a good idea who the next target would be.

"If we work on the assumption that Mollie was blackmailing someone and was killed for it, the person concerned is looking for whatever she was holding against them. If we presume they haven't yet found whatever it was, the next obvious target is Charlie. We can keep watch over him in the hospital but it will be trickier when he goes to live with Madge and Len."

"Why don't I go undercover, Boss?" said Julie. "I could stay with Madge and Len, say I'm their daughter who's come to help look after Charlie."

"Good idea, Julie, although I don't like to put you in danger. You'd have to be armed."

Julie nodded.

"We need to bring Madge and Len in on this; they'd have to agree. Did you have arms training?"

"Yes. I almost requested to join the armed unit at one time but I decided to go for plain clothes instead. I'm actually quite a good shot, Boss."

"That's good to know. Charlie's not well enough to leave the hospital yet, so we've time to prepare the Harrisons. Now, the question is, if the evidence hasn't been found, what could it be and more to the point, what could Mollie have possibly known for someone to kill her?"

"Could be almost anything. She was into drugs and prostitution and has been on the road with all kinds of people. She could know something about one of her clients or just about anything. Where would we start?" Grant mused. "Although I have to say that I have the feeling it's not to do with anything she's found out along the way. Remember that she left her uncle's because she was afraid. No, it goes back to that time, I'm sure."

"I think you're right. But what could it have been?"

"Well..." began Julie, and then shook her head.

"Come on, Julie, out with it."

"No, it's a silly thought."

"Silly or not, let's have it."

"Well, what if it's something to do with Stephen Harrison? We know he was murdered, what if she knew something about it? And what if 'they' discovered that she knew and that was the reason she ran away? And she wouldn't tell her uncle because she wanted to protect him."

Dan looked at Julie's excited face and smiled. "Julie, you might have something there. But how could she know anything when she was living in Plymouth and he lived in Portsmouth? They're not exactly close by."

Julie's face fell. "No, you're right, Boss, the two places are a long way apart and she had a little one to look after. It can't be that, can it?"

Dan paced the room while the other two looked on anxiously.

"What was the name of the man accused of killing Stephen Harrison?"

"Dunno, Boss."

"Right. Grant, I'd like you to find that out, please, and what prison he's in. I want to ask him some questions. Julie, take your own car and visit Madge and Len. Tell them our plan. It would look more natural if I don't go with you, in case our killer is around; he might well know who I am. I'll call them to let them know you're coming. In fact, on second thoughts, the sooner you're installed in their house, the better. Go home and collect what you need and go straight there. I'm sure they'll be okay with it. Until Charlie comes home, act like you really are their daughter, help in the shop and visit Charlie with them. Get Madge and Len to discreetly let their regulars know that you are their daughter and if people there know the real daughter, they'll have to be let into the secret. I know you can rely on Lucy, Kenny, Sheila and Tom and I'm sure others. Madge and Len will know who knows their daughter and who doesn't. Keep your eyes peeled for anything you might find remotely suspicious. Oh, before you go, you'll have to be issued with a firearm. I'll get the authority for you from the Super."

By the end of the day, Julie was in her role as Madge and Len's daughter, accompanied by her firearm, and Dan had secured permission to visit David Ackroyd at Dovegate Prison in Staffordshire.

****

The following day saw Dan and Grant driving to Uttoxeter.

"So relieved that he's not long been moved from Pentonville, Grant, and he's now in Staffordshire. Wouldn't have been good to go to London, or miles up north."

"That's true. It's not a bad day for a run. Should take us around two and a half hours, provided there are no hold-ups on the motorways."

"We've allowed ourselves plenty of time and if we get there early enough, we'll eat somewhere before we go to the prison."

Fortunately, even though it was Friday, the roads remained reasonably clear. They reached Uttoxeter and ate at a pretty pub they found just outside the town. Then they drove on to the prison.

They were searched, then shown into a room with a large table with two chairs on one side and one on the other. Dan and Grant sat down, but stood up again when a door on the other side of the room opened and an officer entered, followed by a man, another officer behind him. He sat down and the two officers stood back, looking solid against the wall.

David Ackroyd was not what Dan expected. His dark hair was cut close to his head and his muscular arms had tattoos. He obviously worked out, for his body was slim but sinewy, although his face had 'prison pallor' showing that he didn't get outside much. Dan knew he was thirty-four years old and had once been a sailor.

"Mr Ackroyd, I'm Detective Inspector Cooke and this is Detective Sergeant Grant and we're from the West Mercia police in Hereford."

"Hereford? Why would the police in Hereford be interested in me? I've never bin there."

"No, we don't get many ships up the Wye," replied Dan.

"Oh, very good. What's all this about then?"

"We'd like to ask you some questions, about the murder of Stephen Harrison."

"I can't tell you much, only that I didn't do it. Not that anyone believes me," Ackroyd replied, bitterly.

"Well, it's possible your case might be reviewed, although I don't want to get your hopes up right now. It depends on what our investigations turn up."

"What investigations are they then? How do they involve me?"

"Obviously, I can't tell you that, but we have reason to believe it may have connection to the death of Stephen Harrison. So, with that in mind, would you answer our questions, please?"

"If I can, although I'm mystified."

"Hopefully, eventually, all will be revealed. Now, you don't deny that you did the other robberies in the area that you were accused of?"

"No, I've never denied that."

"Why did you turn to crime after having been in the Merchant Navy?"

"No job. It's hard to get work and I had a family to feed. My missus and me, we had a little 'un."

Dan nodded. "If you were in the Merchant Navy, did you know Stephen Harrison?"

"Oh yeah, we'd served on the same ship and we were mates. I was cut up when I heard he'd been done in – and even more cut up when they laid it on me. Why would I kill a mate?

176

He was about to start a new job – he'd just come out of the service – and he said he'd put in a good word for me."

"When did you leave the Navy?"

"About a year afore Steve. He knew I was hard up, couldn't get a job, so that's why he was going to help me."

"Did he know about the thieving?"

"Course not! D'you think I'm stupid? No one knew, not even my missus."

"When was the last time you saw Stephen?"

"A couple of days before he died. We had a drink together to talk about the job. He told me about his bit of stuff and that he was going to leave his wife and live with her and their kid. The job was in Devon, he said, although he'd let his wife think it was in Southsea. I already knew that and me and my missus had agreed we'd move that way if he managed to find me a job. I'd met Steve's missus a few times and I understood why he wanted to leave her."

"They found your finger-prints in the bedroom and the bathroom."

Ackroyd's head dropped. They sat waiting until he looked up again. "That was because I was in there a couple o' days before. I went round to see if I could talk ter Steve – about the job, you know? Well, he wasn't there, but she was and she, well, let's just say she offered it me on a plate."

"Are you telling me you had sex with your friend's wife?" Dan narrowed his eyes.

"It pains me to say it, but, yeah, I did. When she said Steve was away, I knew where he'd be, and I was going to leave, but she offered me a drink, said she'd be glad of the company. So, I stayed and we drank a bottle of cider. Actually, I had most of it, she didn't drink much but she said to enjoy it. I had to go up to the bathroom, and when I came out, she was there and was wearing a see-through nightie. She pulled me into the bedroom and practically raped me. I was pretty shocked, because she'd always seemed such a stuck-up cow in the past, but she must have fancied a bit o' rough; she was very insistent, and what red-

177

blooded man would resist an offer like that? I always was weak-willed. She made me go straight after and I admit I must have staggered around a bit, what with the drink and the action, I'd gone a bit weak in the knees. I must have left prints all over the place. But I was ashamed after. I tried telling myself why shouldn't she have some fun when her husband was off with another woman? But then if it was alright fer her, it weren't alright fer me, 'cos my missus didn't deserve it."

"And did this come out in court?"

"Yes. I didn't want to admit to it, because of the missus, because I love her and was ashamed."

"How did she take it?"

"Well, she wouldn't see me fer ages and didn't answer any of my letters. I admit I was frantic about losing my Liz and my daughter, Rosie. And every time I wrote to her, I apologised, told her I loved her and that I regretted having sex with Pauline. Eventually, she came to see me and we talked it through."

"Does she believe you killed Stephen Harrison?"

"No, she don't. She was angry with me for the sex and for nicking stuff off people but she don't believe I killed him because she knows we were good mates."

"It seems they found your DNA on the victim's clothes in the house. How do you account for that?"

Ackroyd shrugged. "I can't. And when they searched my house, they found one of the stolen necklaces in a jacket pocket. That seemed to clinch it for the jury, along with my story of the seduction, because Pauline denied it, said it was wishful thinking on my part, that I'd always fancied her and wished it had happened. Lying cow, I'd never fancied 'er."

"You don't know how the necklace got there?"

"No idea. I'll tell you sommat else. If I'd nicked it, I certainly wouldn't be daft enough to leave it in my pocket. I had a place where I kept my spoils until I could dispose of them. I never took nothin' to the house."

"Hmm. And you didn't have an alibi for the night of the murder?"

"No."

"So, where were you?"

"Where d'you think I was?" the man smiled fleetingly. "I never got nothin' though, the neighbours heard something and called the police. I had to get away quickly."

"Where was that?"

"Well, that's the thing, see? I was trying my luck a bit further afield. It was in Fareham."

"And what time did you go out there and how long were you there?"

"I went out about nine o'clock. I'd already staked my target house; the owners were away, see? But I needed to make sure the owners hadn't come back, so I watched from a distance to see if any lights went on and when I was sure no one was in, I sneaked round the back. I'd say I was away from home nearly four hours. It was a horrible night, I barely escaped and then had to drive and hide up in a place I know for a while until I thought the coast was clear. Then I went home"

"So, you got home, when?

"About one. I had to pretend to be drunk, my missus was dead mad."

"Didn't you tell the police all this?"

"I did, and they looked up to see if a complaint had been made in Fareham. But they still reckoned I could have gone straight from there to Steve's, killed him and robbed his house."

"And did you?"

Ackroyd looked Dan in the eyes. "No, Mr Cooke, straight up, I did not kill Steve and I wasn't in his house that night."

Chapter 36

"Did you believe him, Boss?" asked Grant as they sat stationary in a traffic-jam on the M-6.

"Yes. I believe that David Ackroyd is serving a sentence for a murder he didn't commit. If we ever get back, I want you to get hold of the records of the investigation and the court proceedings. We need to go through it with a fine-tooth comb."

"Okay. Oh, thank goodness, we're moving."

"It all sounded a bit weird to me, Grant. Ackroyd's story about the Harrison woman coming on to him like that, don't you think it was, well, rather strange? He called her a stuck-up cow. Is such a woman really likely to seduce a man like that?"

"Well, Boss, I have to say that women are a pretty hard species to understand. Even though I'm married and my Jenny is lovely, there's still things that apparently I don't get right."

Dan laughed. "Yes, I get that completely! But our wives are fairly normal, as far as woman are normal. I couldn't see either of our wives doing something like that, which makes me think that the Harrison woman isn't normal. Why would she seduce a man like Ackroyd? In fact, why would she seduce any man?"

"Perhaps she was secretly a sex-crazed woman?"

"Well, you read the letters that Stephen Harrison wrote to Mollie. That was sex-crazed. And they gave every indication it was something he wasn't getting from his wife."

"Perhaps she didn't fancy him any more?"

"I think it's possible that she couldn't cope with his kind of sex and it drove him away from her to another woman. Don't forget that his affair with Mollie was long-standing; he was around until Charlie was about three or four and obviously before Charlie came into being. Even if Mollie conceived early in the relationship, he must have been seeing her for almost five years at the least. I'd say it must have started quite early on in the marriage."

"That's sad."

"It is sad, Grant, and because of that, I feel we need to look more closely at Pauline Harrison."

"Do you think she killed him, Boss?"

"Well, it's often someone close to the victim in a murder case."

"But we know it was a man who killed Mollie."

"That's right. On the face of it, it's hard to see how the two murders are connected, apart from the obvious one that the two were lovers, but that very fact makes me suspicious. One thing we do know though."

"What's that, Boss?"

"Even if David Ackroyd killed Stephen Harrison, he certainly didn't kill Mollie Denton."

****

The following day, Dan studied and re-studied the investigation reports into the death of Stephen Harrison. There was also a list of the items stolen from the house. Pauline Harrison had been interviewed several times. Her friend, Sharon Keeble backed up her story. She hadn't actually seen Stephen when she called for them, but she'd heard his voice replying to Pauline's shout of 'Goodbye, love, see you later. Don't wait up.' Pauline had explained to her friend that Stephen was poorly so wasn't going out with them that night. He had a cold and she'd told him to go to bed but he was cat-napping on the sofa.

They'd left just after eight and returned around eleven thirty. That's when Pauline had discovered the body and screamed. Sharon heard it as she was getting into her car and she'd run back to the house. In fact, it was Sharon who called the police, because Pauline had become hysterical. Sharon had made her sit in the car to wait for them. When the body had finally been taken away, the police asked Pauline to check the house to see if anything was missing and that's when they had discovered that it had been a burglary.

181

Because the house was a crime scene, Pauline went to stay with Sharon and the search began for the killer. There had been other burglaries in the area and a man had been injured when he disturbed the thief in his house. From the man's description, and his prints all over the house, and when a missing necklace was found in David Ackroyd's house, they felt sure they'd found the murderer, although Ackroyd always strenuously denied it. A hair belonging to Ackroyd was on the victim's t-shirt, mingled with his blood, although the weapon was never found, nor any blood-stained clothes or shoes. But it was enough to convict David Ackroyd in the eyes of the jury, and he was found guilty of first-degree murder and given a life sentence, still protesting his innocence.

Leading the investigation was a DCI Harvey. In the report, DI Weaver, DS Johns and DC Thomas had been the ones to search Ackroyd's house and it had been DS Johns who had found the necklace stashed away in a jacket in the wardrobe.

Dan had told Grant to take the day off to be with Jenny while he went through the records.

"There's nothing you can do while I read, lad, go and make your pretty wife happy; she's not seen much of you since we started this. I'll call you if I need you. Otherwise, just relax for a day. I need to do some thinking."

"And what about your Linda, Boss?"

"I'll take her a pizza later."

"I'm sure it will make her very happy."

"Get off with you." Dan growled.

Having read all the information on the case, Dan sat back in his chair. It didn't ring true to him. Why didn't the jury believe David Ackroyd's story about how Pauline Harrison seduced him? Okay, so he was a thief and a bit rough round the edges, but why would he make up a story like that when it would put his marriage on the line? Dan was a pretty good judge of character and he felt that, whatever else the man did wrong, he'd been honest to them the previous day. So, if his story was to be believed, to what purpose did she seduce him – in his words, almost rape him? To get his finger-prints all over her bedroom? Seemed somewhat drastic, and she couldn't have known that Ackroyd was going round that night. Had it really been a sudden thirst for sex? Or had she suddenly seen an opportunity, an answer to a problem? What if she was planning to kill her husband and Ackroyd's presence in her house gave her an excuse to lay the blame on him? It would certainly account for her denial at the court hearing, or was that denial embarrassment on her part, that she didn't want the public to know about her sudden desire to have this man in her bed?

And then there was the necklace– he swore he never took it, so how did it get there? Could this DS Johns have planted it? If so, why? Had he been bribed, was he bent? To Dan's mind, if all the items on the list had been stolen, why was only the one necklace found? The other stuff could have already been sold, of course, but why not the necklace as well? By all accounts it was valuable, a gold choker inset with diamonds. Was it too distinctive to sell?

As he mulled over these questions, he knew he believed Ackroyd when he'd insisted he wouldn't have taken any of his stash to his house in case his wife found it. So, again, how come it was there?

The more he thought about it all, the more puzzled he became. As he stood up to fetch a coffee, his phone rang. It was Forensics. They had found hairs belonging to Mollie on the headrest of the hired SUV, also part of a finger-print of an unknown person in the car, and specks of dandruff with DNA that didn't belong to anyone tested. Dan thanked them and put the phone down. Almost immediately, it rang again and he picked it up.

"Cooke," he barked, then, "Hello, Mrs Dale, what can I do for you?"

"I've been thinking since I saw you, Mr Cooke and talking things over with Jim. He reminded me of one time when we had Charlie overnight for Mollie. It was quite odd really. She asked me a few days beforehand, because she was expecting Steve for a couple of days. When she brought him round, she was in a tearing hurry and dumped him and ran. When she came back the next day, she was changed."

"What do you mean?"

"She was tearful, but wouldn't tell me what was wrong. She kept hugging and hugging Charlie and I saw her looking at something on her phone. It was not long after that she went back to live with Simon and all her bubbliness was gone and she would cry at the drop of a hat."

"I don't suppose you can remember the date of that night?"

"I'm sorry, I can't. All I can remember is that it was in November, not long after Firework Night. We'd gone together to the park to see the firework display put on by the local council. There was a fair and everything there, although we didn't stay long because our children were only little – just long enough to see the display. It was the following Friday after that; not sure of the date."

"Thank you, that's interesting and I'm grateful to you for telling me."

Dan looked up the date of the night Stephen Harrison was murdered. Friday 9th November. He frowned. Could it be possible that Mollie Denton had been in Portsmouth that night? Had Mollie followed her lover back to his home and killed him?

Chapter 37

A minute later Dan dismissed that thought. He did not believe that Mollie would have killed Stephen, because by everyone's account she adored him – and he was planning on leaving his wife to live with his other little family. No, Mollie didn't kill him, but, if she had followed him to Portsmouth, she might have seen something. It seemed that Julie was on the right track in her earlier surmise that Mollie might have known something that put her in danger. Now he knew she could have been in Portsmouth, not Plymouth, the night of the murder, it was entirely possible. And she might have been trying to blackmail whoever was the guilty party – not that they had found any evidence of possible blackmail money. Nor had they found any evidence of – well – evidence.

Dan should have felt frustrated, but somehow, he wasn't. Now, he could see their way forward and there were things they could do. Certainly, a trip to Portsmouth was necessary; he wanted to talk with the investigating team and interview again some of the people involved in the case – Sharon Keeble, Janey Ackroyd and most certainly, Pauline Harrison, wherever she was now. Pauline Harrison – of course, Madge and Len might well know where she lived. He would talk with them, and take Linda, she might like to pay a visit to Lucy. He picked up the phone to dial his wife's number.

Linda was pleased at the prospect of seeing Lucy, and when Dan called Lucy, she immediately invited them to dinner. Dan didn't often mix business with pleasure, but he accepted right away and then called his wife to tell her. She was very happy about the invitation. Lucy's cooking was legendary and neither of them wanted to turn down the opportunity to partake of a dinner cooked by her. Not to mention the company, for the two couples were now good friends.

Linda dropped Dan at the village shop and went on to River View. He said he'd walk there after he'd seen the Harrisons.

"Best to get the business over with first, then I can enjoy the evening," he'd told her and she agreed.

Madge and Len were surprised to see Dan but took him up to the flat right away. Julie was there, looking comfortably at home. She looked different out of her usual working clothes, dressed casually in jeans and a jumper, her long coppery hair, usually tied up, loose around her shoulders. She stiffened when she saw him.

"Relax, Julie," he said. "How's it going?"

"Great. We've been able to convince most people I'm Madge and Len's daughter, haven't we?"

"Oh yes, love, except of course those who know you're not, like. But we trust our people and they know why you're here," replied Madge comfortably. "I must say I do like having another daughter."

"Yes, especially one who's so useful," remarked Len. "Are you sure you want to keep being a detective? We could do with you here to help us."

They laughed.

"I'm sorry – Dad – but I do love being a detective, so no, I can't be here for always. It's very pleasant though, I'm enjoying it enormously, it's a bit like being on holiday."

"Hmm, maybe I made a mistake sending you here, you're getting too comfortable," said Dan, smiling, glad to see that Julie fitted in so well.

"She might not be so comfortable soon, Mr Cooke. Charlie is coming out of hospital on Monday." said Madge.

"Is he indeed? Well, I'm glad he's better, but it also means we'll have to be extra watchful."

"Sit down, take the weight off your feet, Mr Cooke. Would you like a drink?" asked Len. "We were just about to have one."

"No, thanks, I'm joining my wife at River View. We've been invited to dinner there." Dan sat on the sofa next to Julie.

"Oh, you're lucky," said Madge. "You'll have a good meal with Lucy cooking."

Dan nodded. "I know. Julie, have you met Lucy yet?"

"Oh yes, a few times. She's very nice."

"She is indeed," he agreed solemnly. "Now, I came to ask you and Len if you can help me with something."

"Oh? What's that then?"

"Do you happen to know where your ex-daughter-in-law Pauline, lives now?"

Madge and Len looked at each other and then back at Dan.

"Why yes of course. She married again and lives not far from Windsor."

"Do you have her address, please?"

"Of course." Madge went to a drawer and came back with an address book. She found the place, then handed it to Dan, who copied into his notebook.

"Thank you."

"Why do you want that?" she asked him.

"Just following all possible lines of enquiry, Madge. She was your son's wife and Mollie was his mistress. It's natural to want to speak to her."

"Do you think she has something to do with Mollie's death?" Madge was wide-eyed at the thought.

"As yet I don't know," said Dan carefully. "She may be able to shed some light on a few issues. Obviously, I can't discuss it, I'm sorry. But I would like to know what sort of person she is – did you like her?"

"Oh, she was alright, Mr Cooke, a bit stand-offish, like," began Len. Madge looked at him with reproach.

"She was more than stand-offish. She was stuck up and unfriendly. I never liked her; I could never see what our Stephen saw in her but we had to make the best of it for his sake. She certainly looked down on us, we never felt good enough for her, did we, Len? Come on, love, be honest."

"No, we weren't good enough," admitted Len. "On the few times she stayed here, she treated Madge like a servant. She was beautiful, very particular over the way she looked. It was easy to see our son was besotted with her at first. They were married before we knew about it – it really hurt Madge that our son got wed without us there, like. They came to see us after."

"Do you have any pictures of her, by any chance?"

Madge went to the same drawer and drew out a photo. It was of Stephen and Pauline, obviously taken on their wedding day, for she was wearing a coronet of flowers in her hair. It was a good close-up and he could see that she was indeed, very beautiful.

"Could I have a copy of this?"

"Of course."

"I don't suppose you've seen her since she remarried?"

"We hadn't, until this year."

"What's that?"

"She came here this year, April time. We had a phone call out of the blue to say could she come to see us? I wasn't best pleased, was I, Len?"

"That's an understatement, love."

"Oh?"

"Yes, I was not happy, because hearing from her brought back the horror of what happened to our son. I know it was bad for her, finding him, like, but it was bad for us too. And she's done alright for herself; she's married to a very rich man and now has two daughters. We were left with nothing but our memories." Madge wiped a tear from her eye with the corner of her apron and Len perched on the arm of her chair to comfort her.

"We've got Charlie now, my dear," he said, gently.

She managed a watery smile and nodded. "Yes, thank the good Lord."

"So, what happened when she came?" Dan wanted to get back to the matter in hand.

"Well, that was the strange thing, like. She asked if she could stay the weekend, arrived much later than we expected on the Friday night – she said she'd been held up on the road. On the Saturday, because we're always so busy on a Saturday, she took herself out. Then, at tea-time, she rushed in, said she'd had a phone call from her husband and she was sorry but she had to go.

188

She gathered her things and left, just like that. No further explanation, just went. Not that we minded really, did we, Len?"

"Not at all – it meant we got to eat all of Lucy's Black Forest cake that she'd made for our guest." Len winked and Julie laughed.

Dan laughed too and said, "I'll bet you didn't mind that at all. I know Lucy's cakes."

"Especially as he ate most of it. He kept sneaking bits when he thought I wouldn.t know." Madge elbowed her husband and he clutched himself as if she'd really hurt him.

Glad to see Madge had cheered up, Dan stood up. "Well, I'll leave you good folks to your evening and I'd better get over to River View before I miss that dinner. Thank you for your help."

"I'll see you out," said Julie and the pair went down the stairs. They stood inside the shuttered shop door and talked quietly.

"Do you think the ex had something to do with Mollie's murder, Boss?"

"I do, although at the moment I haven't quite worked out how, because we know it was a man who killed her. But he could be a paid killer; we've just heard she's loaded now. Grant and I went to see the man convicted of killing Stephen Harrison and he was adamant he never killed him – apparently, they were mates and Mr. Harrison was supposed to be trying to get Ackroyd a job. Does it sound like he would kill a mate trying to help him?"

"On the face of it, it sounds unlikely, Boss. But criminals always say they never did it, don't they?"

"Well, he was up-front about the burglaries and the man he hit at one place. I looked him in the eyes when he said he didn't kill Stephen Harrison and I believed him – and so did Grant. I've spent the day studying the investigation notes and the court hearing and I think there are some quite suspect things about the case. Grant and I are going to go down to Portsmouth to see if we can talk to the investigating team and some of the witnesses involved. We could well be away a few days, so I want you to be especially vigilant over young Charlie until you know we are back. If you need help quickly, call the Super. I'll have a word with him before we leave."

"Yes, Boss. You be careful too on your travels."

"We will. Enjoy your last day of freedom tomorrow."

She grinned and saluted. "Sir! And you enjoy your dinner with the legendary Lucy and Kenny."

"No doubt there. Make sure you lock this door properly behind me."

He stood outside until he heard the lock click and the sound of bolts being slid into place, then he walked swiftly towards River View Lane.

Chapter 38

Dan kissed Linda farewell.

"I'm sorry, love, I don't know how long I'll be gone. I'll make it up to you when this case is over."

"Oh yeah. I hear you. Just you make sure you get back safely – and make sure you call me every evening!"

"I will."

"You promise? I know what you're like when you're getting close – and you are getting close, aren't you?"

"Yes, I feel we are. We just have some ends to put together. I'm pretty sure I know what's happened. Proving it is going to be difficult though."

"Well, if I know anything about you, if there's a way, you'll find it. Take care of that lad, I don't want an inconsolable young wife on my hands!"

"Linda, my darling, Grant is hardly a lad – he's been my sergeant for quite a few years now, I'd have thought he might be trying for Inspector soon, he's good enough. But I'll make the most of him while I have him. Must go. You take care yourself, my love. After this, we'll go away for a few days, I have some holiday due to me. Think about where you'd like to go."

"Where would you like to go?"

"Anywhere, as long as it's away from work. I'll even go to Skegness if I have to."

"I don't think it'll come to that." she laughed, and for a moment Dan thought how lovely she was and how lucky he was to have her. Then, he gave her another kiss and hurried away.

It was a long drive to Portsmouth, especially via Windsor. Dan decided they would go there first because they stood a better chance of Pauline Norton-Smythe being at home on a Sunday. It wasn't a very nice day, the wind howled around the car and the sky was dark, although as yet there was no rain. Not a good day for travelling, but there was no way Dan was going to let that stop them.

They were surprised at how much traffic was on the road, it being Sunday, but there were no hold-ups and they reached the area in the time promised by Google Maps of two and a half hours. It was ten forty-five when they pulled up outside some imposing wrought-iron gates, which were electronically locked. Dan, who was driving, reached out and pressed the button. Moments later, there was some crackling and a voice asked, 'Who is it?'

"Detective Inspector Cooke and Detective Sergeant Grant." He held his identification up to the small screen. The gates opened with only the slightest squeak and they drove through.

They stopped on the circular drive outside a very large, modern-built house, almost a mansion. A man stood in the doorway; he was slim with blonde wavy hair, blue eyes and was around six foot, maybe a bit more, dressed casually in faded blue jeans and a t-shirt, in spite of the chilly day, showing muscular arms.

Dan went up the step and held up his ID again. "Detective Inspector Cooke, sir. Are you Mr Norten-Smythe?"

"I am. How can I help you? You're a way out of your patch, if I may say so." Mark Norton-Smyth spoke with an English drawl, tinged with a slight London twang.

"Is your wife at home, sir?"

"She is. Come in."

He stood back to let the two detectives pass as a girl of about five came running up to him. "Hello, sweetness. Run and tell Mummy that someone's here to see her, will you?"

"Yes, Daddy," said the little one and ran off back the way she'd come. Moments later, a woman appeared and Dan immediately recognised her from the photograph, and although obviously older, it hardly showed.

"Mrs Norton-Smyth? I'm Detective Inspector Cooke from West Mercia police, and this is Detective Sergeant Grant."

The woman nodded slightly. "West Mercia police? What's all this about?"

192

"Is there somewhere we could talk?"

She sighed audibly. "I suppose so. Come this way. Would you like coffee?"

"That would be welcome, thank you."

"Darling, would you mind asking Mrs Bradbury if she'll bring coffee into the conservatory, please?"

"Of course, darling."

Dan and Grant followed the woman along the spacious hallway, aware that her husband hadn't moved. They went through an elegant lounge where double doors led into a large conservatory, gracefully furnished with soft-seated chairs and a glass-topped table. Large pot plants strategically placed added a feeling that one could be outside. Doors led outside, but were closed due to the cool weather. The room was pleasantly warm. The little girl was sitting on a child-sized chair exactly like the adult-sized ones, nursing a doll.

"Sophie, would you go and play with Mary while Mummy talks to these gentlemen?"

"Yes, Mummy. What do they want to talk about?" the child asked, eyeing Grant with a suspicion that Dan could see made him uncomfortable.

"I don't know yet, do I?" her mother said, somewhat impatiently. "Go along now."

The child ran off without another word. Pauline, already lounging on a two-seater sofa, waved an imperial hand at the chairs, which the two men took as invitations to sit down. As they did so, a middle-aged woman arrived, carrying a tray with a coffee pot, cups and saucers, a bowl of brown sugar lumps and a jug with cream, which she put on the table. Mark Norton-Smyth entered carrying a plate of biscuits, which he set near the coffee. Mrs Bradbury (at least, that was who Dan assumed it was) poured out coffees and handed them round, then offered the sugar and the cream. When she had finished, she said,

"Will there be anything else, Madam?"

"No, thank you, that's fine," Mark answered. The woman gave a small nod and quickly left.

"A very nice home you have here," Dan remarked.

"Thank you. Now, what's all this about?" Clearly, Pauline Norton-Smyth was not one for small talk.

"I'm sorry if this is going to upset you, bring back bad memories, but we are having to take another look at the murder of your first husband, Stephen Harrison and I'm hoping you will be able to help us."

He watched her carefully as her head went down for a moment, then she brought it back up, looked him in the eyes and said, "I will if I can, but I'm not sure why you're doing this, or what you are hoping to gain from me."

"I only want to check what you said in your statement to the police and in court. On the night in question, you were going out with a friend?"

"That's right. My friend Sharon Keeble. We were going to meet up with her boyfriend, and Steve was supposed to be coming too, only he had gone down with a cold or flu or something and wasn't well enough to go."

Dan nodded. "What time did you go out?"

"About eight."

"And was Stephen still alive when you went out?"

"Of course he was!" she snapped. "I called out to him when I left. Sharon will tell you."

Dan nodded again. "I read in the report that the accused man told the court that you had sex with him a couple of nights before the murder. Was he lying?"

"Of course he was lying! He'd always fancied me, kept trying to chat me up when he thought my husband wasn't around and putting his filthy hand on my leg or on my neck!" She shuddered.

"Why would he say that in court, do you think, when his wife would hear it?"

"I don't know. Desperate to get them to believe that his finger-prints were all over the place before the murder and robbery, I suppose. Better his wife should leave him than him be sent down for murder. She'd be better off without him anyway.

194

Anyway, didn't work, did it? Fortunately, the jury believed me, not him."

"Did you know your husband was having an affair, Mrs Norton-Smyth?"

"What?" She looked stunned.

"I said, did you know Stephen Harrison was having an affair? A very long-term affair, in fact, and he had a child."

"No. I had no idea." She put her head down and gave a sniff. Her husband went over to her and she buried her face in his chest.

"I think you'd better go," Mark Norton-Smyth said, coldly. "You've upset my wife. She's never got over her first husband's murder."

Dan stood up. "That's alright, Sir. That will do, I have all I need. I'm grateful to Mrs Norton-Smyth and I'm sorry she is upset. Thank you for your hospitality."

He left the room, followed by Grant, who'd hastily taken a sip of his coffee, only to find it too hot.

Mrs Bradbury was waiting in the hall to see them out. Before she shut the door, Dan asked,

"Mrs Bradbury, isn't it?"

"Yes Sir."

"How long have you worked here?"

"Six years, Sir. Me and Mary came at the same time. Mary looks after the girls, sir, Sophie and her sister Kathryn."

"What are they like to work for?"

"Well, he's alright, but she's – well, not so nice sometimes. Depends what mood she's in. He goes away quite a lot, working."

"Oh yes, what does he do?"

"Not sure really, Sir, but as you can see, they have plenty of money, so whatever it is, must pay well."

"Indeed. Well, good day."

"Good day, Sir. The gates will close behind you."

Grant had to drive on to turn around. There was a large building to the side that were obviously garages. Two of the doors were open.

"Look, Grant!"

Grant glanced to where his boss was pointing. In the open garage stood a red sports car.

Chapter 39

"My word, Grant, it was worth making this trip just to see that car. Thank goodness Mrs White remembered seeing it in the lane. Of course, we can't prove it's the same car, but we know that Pauline Norton-Smythe was in the area at the time, staying with the Harrisons. Too much of a coincidence, don't you think, Grant?"

"Absolutely, Boss. Anyway, you don't believe in coincidences."

"Too right I don't. We're closing in, Grant. The woman did know about Mollie and she also knew where she was staying."

"Are we going to arrest her, Boss?"

"Not yet. She thinks she's fooled us, let her think that for now. I hope we can get more information from the team in Portsmouth. Phew! That performance of hers was almost worthy of an Oscar. I didn't get to drink my coffee or have a biscuit, darn it."

"Nor me, Boss. The coffee was too hot to drink quickly, I only had a sip."

"Then I think we need to find some refreshment; we deserve it. Stop at the next place you find and it'll be my treat."

****

When they finally reached the police headquarters in Portsmouth, they were greeted, after waiting a few minutes in the reception, by a man who introduced himself as Detective Chief Inspector Harry Weaver.

"I'm pleased to meet you, Chief. I'm Detective Inspector Daniel Cooke and this is Detective Sergeant Graham Grant. We are grateful to you for sparing the time to see us."

"Not at all; I'm intrigued as to what this is all about. Come into my office and we'll have a chat there."

197

They followed him along a corridor and up some stairs and along another corridor until the came to a large space where people were working at desks. As they walked through, Dan was aware of the curious stares directed towards them. He had no time to worry about it, for they found themselves in a pleasant office with a large window that let in the light.

"How can I help you, Mr Cooke?"

"Please call me Dan."

"That's fine. As we're not working together, you may call me Harry," The eyes behind the glasses twinkled merrily. Dan liked this man and instinctively trusted him.

"Thank you, sir – erm, Harry. We have been looking at a murder investigation that took place here about eight years ago. I believe you were on the investigating team. It was the murder of Stephen Harrison."

"Ah yes, I remember it well."

"Is it possible that DCI Harvey is still here?"

"I'm afraid not. He retired seven years ago – right after the Harrison case had been heard, in fact. He died of a heart attack a couple of years ago. But, as you say, I was on the team; in fact, I was more involved with it than he was really. I'll be quite honest with you, Dan, I was never happy about it. But tell me why you are interested in it."

Dan gave him a quick run-down of what had happened and what they'd discovered. Harry gave a low whistle.

"You said you were never happy about the Harrison case. Why was that?"

"To tell you the truth, Dan, it was only my copper's nose – do you understand me?"

Dan and Grant both nodded vigorously.

Harry continued, "It seemed all the evidence was there – the finger-prints upstairs, the woman who heard Harrison's voice when she called for Pauline Harrison and of course, the necklace at Ackroyd's house. It seemed to fit, but I had to ask the question, why would an experienced burglar like Ackroyd leave his finger-prints all over the place in Harrison's house where he'd

198

committed a murder, when he left no prints anywhere else? He left no prints in any of the houses he robbed; we only caught him because the man he hit was able to identify him. The finding of the necklace was odd too."

"It was Detective Sergeant Johns who found it, wasn't it? No chance he could be bent?"

"Good grief no! If you knew him, you'd see the man is straight as a die. In fact, he's so straight he's hard to get on with in many ways because he never deviates from the letter of the law and he has no sense of humour at all."

Dan grunted, getting the picture.

"We went to see Ackroyd and I must say I believed him when he said he didn't kill Harrison. What did you think of his story that Mrs Harrison seduced him?"

"Knowing the woman, I'd have said it was highly unlikely, for she was, although I shouldn't say so, somewhat of a cold fish. I couldn't see her wanting to be with a man like Ackroyd, although why would he make up something like that? He was happily married, although his wife hadn't a clue about his thieving. Although sailors do have something of a reputation, don't they?"

"So they say. So, did it come out that Harrison was having an affair?"

"It did, but it was only hearsay. We couldn't trace her, and we had no evidence of it. There were no letters or anything like that amongst his personal things. There was nothing on his phone either."

"Hmm. But we have evidence that our dead girl was his mistress, and her son Charlie is Harrison's child. Interesting. Didn't you voice your doubts to your Chief?"

"Yes, of course. But he didn't want to know. As far as he was concerned, we had the evidence to convict Ackroyd. We shouldn't speak ill of the dead, but it's my own opinion he just wanted the case closed so he could retire with his reputation intact. To go out, having solved a murder case would have suited him well."

"So, in your opinion, Harry, who did kill Stephen Harrison?"

"Well, although we have no evidence, I'm convinced it was Pauline Harrison."

Chapter 40

DCI Weaver's statement did not surprise Dan. He was surprised, however, by the Chief's next remark.

"In fact, after DCI Harvey retired, I tried to look into the case again, privately. But I still wasn't able to come up with any answers to my own questions – and they were pretty much the same as yours. I've got nowhere with it though. Completely unable to find any proof whatsoever. I'll tell you, if you can come up with something else, something we can use, I'll be more than happy and I will do anything I can to help you."

"I'm very grateful to hear you say that. Some teams wouldn't like others coming onto their patch going over one of their investigations."

"Perhaps not, but you have evidence of the mistress, which I couldn't find, and it's tragic that the young woman has been murdered. A young boy's future is at stake and I can see that his life could be in danger. We can't have that. No, you tell me what you want and I'll do my best to provide it."

"That's good of you, Sir. If you know the whereabouts of Sharon Keeble and Liz Ackroyd, I'd like to talk with them."

"I can get that for you. In the meantime, would you like a coffee or tea while you wait?"

A young officer brought them coffee with a friendly smile and it wasn't long before they had the information they needed.

"Sharon Keeble is now Mrs. Payne and lives in Hayling Island. Mrs Ackroyd still lives where they were in Paulsgrove. I suggest that you try to see Sharon Payne today as driving to Hayling Island on a Monday morning is not something you really want to be doing. It should be fairly quiet today. Tell you what, why don't you go over to see her, then come and have food with me and my missus. If I tell her now, she'll be fine with that. Where are you staying?"

"We haven't thought about that yet."

"Stay with us, we have the room. This is our address and our number. Call us when you're done with Mrs Payne. I'm off home now, I wasn't on duty today really, I only came in to see you."

"Well, that's really good of you. Are you sure your wife won't mind?"

"Oh no, she loves having visitors! I'll see you later."

Dan and Grant looked at each other and smiled, then shook the DCI's hand gratefully.

"We'll see you later, Sir. Thank you."

"You're welcome. And it's Harry."

****

They easily found the address in Hayling Island. Harry was right, it was fairly quiet on the roads, being Sunday. Their knock was opened by a man of around Dan's age, stocky, about five feet ten, receding hairline and a homely, but pleasant face. He was wearing jeans and a sweater, his feet in socks.

"Yes?"

Dan held up his ID. "Are you Mr Clive Payne?"

"Yes. What have I done?"

"As far as we know, nothing, Sir. We were hoping to have a quick word with Mrs Sharon Payne. Is she in?"

"She is. Shaz, someone wants to see you."

"Who is it?" they heard a woman's voice call.

"Police."

"What?"

The question was followed by the woman herself, who peered over her husband's shoulder.

Dan held up his ID again. "Mrs Sharon Payne? I'm Detective Inspector Cooke from Hereford and this is my Sergeant. Would you be good enough to talk with us for a few minutes please? It's about the murder of Stephen Harrison."

"Really? Oh well, then, come on in."

They followed the couple through the hall and into the lounge where they were invited to sit. The room was not large, but careful furnishing made the most of the space. A cream corner sofa was inviting and it faced a large television in the opposite corner. A three-tiered, cream coloured 'wotnot' in the other corner held a pot-plant on each tier and the bay window let in lots of light. Altogether a pleasant room, mused Dan.

"Would you like a drink?" the woman asked.

"No thank you, we don't intend to keep you long. We don't want to spoil your Sunday afternoon too much."

Sharon, had brown, shoulder-length hair and a well made-up face. Her nails were immaculate and varnished in pink. She also wore blue jeans and a jumper in pink, the same colour as her nail varnish. On her feet were a pair of pink fluffy slippers.

"Why do police from Hereford want to know about Stephen's murder? And so long after it?"

"I'm afraid we can't answer that at this time, except to say that certain events in Hereford has led us towards this case. I'm sorry to be so mysterious, but hopefully all will come to light eventually."

"Hmm, right. So, what do you want to know?"

"Firstly, how long had you and Pauline Harrison been friends?"

"Oh, only a few months, hard to say. It was when I met Clive that I got to know Steve and Pauline and became part of the group."

"So, it was more that Clive and Stephen were friends then? So, why didn't you go to meet them on that night, Mr. Payne?"

"I'd been delayed on the road. I'm a lorry driver and there'd been an accident somewhere and I couldn't make it back in time, but the girls decided they'd go ahead anyway and I'd join them when I could."

"I see. And did you join them?"

"As a matter of fact, I did. I was only about fifteen minutes late, as it happened."

203

"Were you surprised that Stephen wasn't there?"

"Yes, of course, until I heard he was ill."

"But you weren't with Sharon and Pauline when they went to Pauline's house after your evening out?"

"No, I was in my own car and Sharon had hers. We weren't living together then. So Shaz took Pauline home and I went to my home."

"I see. So, Sharon, can you tell me what happened when you went to pick Pauline up?"

"I told all this to the police at the time!"

"Please indulge me. Just tell me again."

"Well, as Clive said, we intended all going together, but as he wasn't back, I went to fetch Pauline and Steve in my own car. I arrived just before eight and Pauline opened the door and told me Steve wasn't coming because he was poorly and was having a drink of hot chocolate on the sofa. She shouted, 'Goodbye love, see you later' and he answered. She shut the door and we left."

"Right. Um... when she shouted to him, was she standing outside the door, or was she still inside?"

Sharon went to the door of the room, opened it at a thirty-five to forty degree angle and positioned her body so she was looking out to the hallway and part of her still behind the door.

"She was like this. Then, when he answered, she came out properly and shut the door."

"Do you see that, Grant?"

"I do, Boss," came the reply.

Sharon sat down.

"Thank you, that was helpful. Now, when you heard his reply, did you hear it clearly?"

"No, it was not clear, it was very quiet, like he just mumbled."

"So you didn't hear him say actual words?"

"No. But I never thought anything of it. If he was ill and maybe nodding off, that's what he would have sounded like, perhaps."

204

"But she shouted quite loud?"

"Yeah. I remember thinking at the time that it was loud when he was only sitting close by, although perhaps he was asleep and she wanted him to know she was going."

"He was in the room?"

"Yes. Their house wasn't like this with a hallway. Their front door opened straight into their lounge."

"I see. Do you remember if she had a mobile phone with her?"

"Yes, she had it in her hand when she came out and I saw her put it in her bag."

"And you weren't asked any of this in court?"

"No."

Dan stood up. "Well, thank you. I think that's all we need."

"You don't want to know what happened when we got back?"

"Not really. I've read the report. It must have been bad for you."

"It was. He looked terrible, all that blood everywhere and the expression on his face..." She gave a shudder. "Poor Pauline, she took it so badly, I had a terrible time trying to calm her. I had to deal with everything, call the police and ambulance and so on. I still have nightmares about it now."

"I can understand that. Just for a matter of interest, did you know David Ackroyd?"

"We did." It was Clive who answered. "We all served on the same ship together so we all knew each other quite well. Steve and I left the Navy at the same time. I'd not long met Shaz then, had I Shaz? And Dave, well, he was in a fix because he and his wife had a child and he'd struggled to find work. Steve was trying to help him, see? We were so shocked when we found out about him, weren't we, Shaz?"

Sharon nodded vigorously. "Could have knocked us down with a feather, love."

"Yeah, he was a bit rough and ready but I never believed he would kill a mate, especially one trying to help him. It just didn't ring true, Mr Cooke, d'you know what I mean?"

"I do, Mr Payne. One other thing, what did you think of Pauline Harrison?"

"To be honest, we didn't really like her, did we Clive? We put up with her because she was Steve's wife."

"That's right, I didn't like her at all. I could never see what Steve saw in her. She was a right stuck up cow," said Clive, unconsciously echoing David Ackroyd's opinion. "We felt sorry for her though, and did what we could to help her when Steve was killed. But we were really glad when she met that rich playboy of hers and moved away, weren't we?"

"Too right we were, love. Not that we ever got a word of thanks for how we helped her, nor have we heard anything from her since she went. Good riddance, I say. We've got a good life now and we're happier without her, aren't we love?"

Clive put his arm around her. "Too right, love. If we ever hear from her again, it'll be too soon."

Chapter 41

"Are you thinking what I'm thinking, Grant?" Dan asked as they drove away.

"Depends what you're thinking, Boss. I'm thinking that Pauline Harrison could have faked Stephen Harrison's voice on her phone."

"Exactly. Oldest trick in the book, that. She only had to record his voice on her phone at some point and then play it behind the door on her way out that night. She was careful to keep the door only partly open so Sharon wouldn't see anything."

"I'm liking it, Boss."

"So am I, Grant."

"Are we going to tell DCI Weaver?"

"Probably, but we'll ask him not to do anything until we've found out more. In any case, we still don't have any proof."

"That's true."

"There's no doubt he'll be interested to know that his instinct about Pauline Harrison, or Norton-Smyth seems to be spot-on. I'd love to know what Mollie Denton knew or saw or whatever."

"Indeed. Whatever it was, it ultimately signed her death warrant."

****

Mrs Weaver turned out to be a lovely lady with a friendly face. Her white hair was short and she wore glasses.

"It's so good of you to have us here, Mrs Weaver, but we really don't expect you to put us up, we can easily book into a Bed and Breakfast place."

"Nonsense. I wouldn't dream of you doing that. We've plenty of room and I enjoy having guests, I assure you it's no trouble at all. Harry can show you your rooms, and then you can have a little natter in his study until the dinner is ready."

The rooms were very pleasant. Dan found himself almost wishing they were staying for longer, but they had already made great progress, and should be able to return home tomorrow, after visiting Liz Ackroyd.

In Harry's study there were comfortable leather armchairs and a large mahogany desk, just the sort that Dan himself would have loved.

"Beautiful desk, Sir, is it antique?"

"Yes, it is – been in my family for four generations. And it's Harry, remember? Would you both like a little appetizer?" He went to a cabinet on the wall and took out some glasses and looked at them questioningly. Dan and Grant looked at each other and then each said, 'Yes please.'

As he poured out the brandy, he said, "I don't often indulge, but I do like a small glass of port at the end of the day if I know I'm not on call. Although of course, one can never really guarantee that won't happen, as no doubt you both well know. Make yourselves comfortable, lads, and tell me how you got on with Sharon Payne."

He listened intently to their account of the interview with Sharon and her husband. At the end, he grunted, "I should have thought of asking her about the door. That puts a whole new light on events. Interesting that not many people seem to like Pauline Harrison, isn't it?"

"It is indeed. Do we know anything about her? Where she came from, how they met, what she did as a job?"

"Unsurprisingly, they met in a bar. Apparently, she was some kind of entertainer, a singer or something, and also served behind the bar."

"A barmaid?" Grant nearly choked. "With her airs and graces? Hard to imagine!"

Harry grinned. "It is indeed, Graham, but that's what she was doing when they met. After that, she got a job as a receptionist in a big hotel; no doubt they thought her looks would help business. I hope she wasn't as frosty with their customers."

They laughed and just as they did so, Emily put her head around the door to say dinner was ready.

It was a happy meal and evening. The food had been good, a roast chicken and vegetables, followed by apple crumble and custard.

"Plain food," said Emily.

"It's wonderful," said Grant. "I love a dinner like this – and your apple crumble was wonderful." He sighed in contentment.

Harry smiled. "I have a wonderful wife. She has to be, to put up with me and all the hours I've left everything to her while I'm busy chasing criminals. I love Sundays like this, they're fairly rare so we make the most of it while we can."

"My poor wife is the same," said Dan, ruefully. "She's hardly seen me since we started this investigation. She can't cook like this though; I'm hoping Lucy will give her lessons – she's an amazing cook!"

"Who is Lucy?" Emily asked. "You don't have another woman on the side, I hope?"

Dan and Grant both laughed and told their hosts about Lucy and Ken and the village of Sutton-on-Wye. The evening passed very pleasantly as the four sat together chatting about all sorts of things, trying to be careful not to 'talk shop' too much, for Emily's sake.

****

The next day, after a hearty breakfast cooked by Emily, Dan and Grant put their overnight bags in the car ready to set off. They hugged Emily, who said they would be welcome to stay any time and bring their wives. Shaking hands with Harry, Dan thanked him for his help.

"I'll keep you informed, Sir, erm, Harry, and I'll be happy to let you have Pauline Norton-Smyth on a plate when we have the proof we need. We do need to discover the identity of the man who killed poor Mollie and beat up Simon Denton, for I feel it was the same man. I want them both in the bag."

"Absolutely, lads, do your utmost. It'll give me great pleasure to get her banged up. And Ackroyd will be relieved, I'm sure."

"Yes, I'm sorry we can't get him out right now, for he's served his sentence for the robberies, but we'll have to leave him until we have what we need. If he's going to be exonerated, we must have proof of his innocence."

"I agree. At least he's not still in Pentonville."

Fortunately, the satnav helped them find the Ackroyd's house easily. The door was opened by a woman holding a lit cigarette. She was quite tall, well-built and her dark hair with blonde streaks was tied back in a neat pony-tail. She wore black trousers and a green nylon overall with a motive that said 'Cathy's Homecare Services'.

"Hello," she said with a frown. "I don't talk to Jehovah's Witnesses."

Grant hid a smirk while Dan held up his ID. "We're not Jehovah's Witnesses. I'm Detective Inspector Dan Cooke and this is Detective Sergeant Grant. We're from West Mercia police in Hereford. Are you Mrs Elizabeth Ackroyd?"

"Yes. What do Hereford police want with me?"

"May we come in? It's better than talking on the doorstep. We won't keep you long."

She reluctantly opened the door but looked around anxiously outside before she shut it. She waved a hand at a doorway.

"Go in there. I don't have long, I need to get to work, see?"

The room was sparsely furnished but spotlessly clean. They sat on a sofa that sucked them in and she sat on another two-seater.

"Certain events in our area has led us towards the murder of Stephen Harrison that your husband was found guilty of."

"He didn't do it –"

Dan held up his hand. "We don't think he did. But we need evidence to prove it. We are talking to all the people involved in it. We already saw David, we visited him at Dovegate."

She sat up straight. "You did?"

"Yes. Do you mind telling us what you can remember of that time?"

She leaned back and stubbed out her cigarette in an ash-tray on a small table. "I'm trying to give it up," she remarked, "But my job is so stressful and I've had all the worry of bringing up our daughter on my own. She's a good kid though, and fortunately she's doing well at school and has some nice friends. I'm trying really hard to save up so we can move when Dave comes out – you know, start again somewhere else – but it's very hard on my crap wages. We were all set to move to Plymouth, or that way, because Steve Harrison was going to speak up for Dave, then Dave got nicked, the idiot. Fancy him nicking all that stuff an' me having no idea." She fumbled with her packet of cigarettes, with shaking hands. She didn't light up, but held it between her fingers as she moved her hands around.

"The silly sod. We could have worked things out together if he'd told me, but he made out he was working evenings – well, I suppose he was." She gave a humourless laugh. Dan let her talk on, realising she needed it. When she finally dried up, he asked,

"What did you think of his story about how Mrs Harrison seduced him?"

She started pacing the small room. She lit her cigarette and took in a deep drag. Blowing out the smoke, she said; "I didn't want to believe it at first – I couldn't believe it, knowing her – she was so stuck up, I couldn't picture it. It was because of what she was like that Steve went and found himself another woman."

"So, you knew about the other woman?"

"Yes – well, only that there was one and she had his little boy. He showed me a picture of them and she looked lovely and

211

obviously adored Steve. And the little one was so cute. I didn't know anything else, where she lived or anything. But he told Dave he was going to leave Pauline and live with his girl in Plymouth and of course he told me. I was happy for 'im and excited that we might go there too. Then we heard about Steve..."

She sat down again and put her face in her hands, her elbows resting on her knees. The ash from the cigarette fell to the carpet unheeded. When she looked up again, she had tears running down her cheeks.

"When they arrested Dave, it was for the burglaries and the assault on that man, the stupid ****. That was bad enough, but when they searched this place and found that necklace and then said 'is finger-prints was all over their upstairs, I couldn't believe it. And then, in court, Dave told that story about her – about her..." Liz took a tissue out of her pocket, wiped her nose, put the cigarette in the ash-tray, and looked at Dan, helplessly.

"You didn't know what to believe?" he finished for her and she nodded, sniffing into the tissue again.

"I walked out of the court. I couldn't bear it. The thought of him being with that – that woman, was too much to bear. How could he *do* that with a woman he couldn't stand? He'd told me often enough what he thought of her and how he thought Steve was doing the right thing going off. I wouldn't talk to 'im fer ages, even though he kept writing letters to me apologising over and over for everything. After nearly a year, I went to see 'im and we talked about it all. I love the silly sod, don't I? We're alright now, but it's so hard doing without him, Mr Cooke."

Dan nodded. He liked this woman and completely understood what she was saying. What a lucky man David Ackroyd was.

"Now, Mrs Ackroyd, I wonder if you can think back to that time, to the days between Stephen Harrison's death and when they searched your house and found the necklace. Did anyone come here in between?"

She stared hard at him for a moment. "I can't think."

"Please try, it's important."

212

"Hang on a minute, I'll be right back." She left the room and a few minutes later, returned, holding a book.

"My mum told me I should keep a diary when we had Rosie so I could always remember all the little things she did and how she developed. I'm not quite so good at keeping it now, because I'm always so busy, but I wrote in it every day then. Let me look."

She turned the pages. "Firework night," she murmured, then put her finger on an entry. "That was when we heard about Steve. Clive Payne called Dave. We were both so shocked." She turned the pages slowly, scanning the writing as she did so. Then she stopped and pointed at her writing.

"The only visitor here before the search was Rosie's health visitor, on Wednesday, fourteenth November. Oh, I remember now, it wasn't the usual health visitor, but a much older woman. She said that my usual one was off sick and she was covering her work until she recovered. But just after she examined the baby, she asked if she could use my bathroom as she'd been on the road since just after nine and hadn't had a chance to 'go'. To be honest with you, I was worried, because she looked pale and she must have not felt very good because she was up there quite a while. When she came down, she said I was the last visit for that day and she was thankful because she wasn't feeling too well."

"Can you give us a description of the woman?"

"Um…short grey hair, sort of curly, and glasses. She was wearing a tweedy sort of coat, which she never even undid, and clumpy lace-up shoes. She reminded me of Miss Marple, you know, in the television series? Only not as chirpy as Geraldine McEwan or that other one. There was one thing that I remember thinking was a bit odd though."

"Go on?"

"Well, she had false nails and glittery nail polish. I remember remarking on them – because I thought they didn't go at all well with the rest of her – although I didn't say that, I just said I liked them. She said it was one of her fetishes, she had to

213

have posh nails. But she said Rosie was doing just fine and she left and I never thought any more about her until now."

"And you never told the police any of this?"

"No, they never asked. And anyway, I'd forgotten about her with the stress of my Dave being arrested. I never gave it a thought that a little elderly lady would have done anything."

"Well, no, most of us wouldn't, so I don't blame you. But I have to say, it seems suspicious."

Dan stood up, "Well, we won't keep you any longer, Mrs Ackroyd. Thank you for talking to us, but I would ask you to not mention this to anyone, not even your husband or daughter. I don't want to raise your hopes or theirs, but we'll do our best to get this sorted out. And especially don't mention it to anyone that it might somehow get back to Pauline Harrison. Are you okay with that?"

"Oh yes," she said fervently. "I'm ever so grateful to you. If you can get that murder charge off my Dave, it will mean the world to all of us."

"We'll do our very best. Is that your daughter?" Dan nodded at a photograph on the mantle-piece.

"Yes, that's Rosie, she's almost ten but that was taken last year."

"She's pretty. Dave Ackroyd is a lucky man to have such a lovely daughter and a caring wife."

"Thank you."

"Can we give you a lift to work?"

"No, it's only just around the corner – one of the reasons why I work there – no travelling!" she laughed.

As they drove off, they saw Liz hurrying in the opposite direction.

"I think she's feeling better now than when we arrived, Boss," remarked Grant.

"Yes indeed. We've given her hope, and I pray we can fulfil it. Now, let's get home."

Chapter 42

It was late afternoon by the time they returned to headquarters.

"I want to check if young Charlie has been released from hospital yet." Dan reached for the phone. "Can you find us something to eat and drink?"

"Sure, will do."

When Grant returned, bearing coffee and sandwiches, Dan told him that Charlie was indeed out of hospital and happily settling into his grandparents' home. Julie had assured him that all was well.

"Glad about that. Boss, you were very quiet on the journey home. I got the idea you were thinking things through."

"I was. We are both convinced that Pauline Norton-Smyth murdered Stephen Harrison and framed David Ackroyd. But we still have no proof. We can't prove that she seduced him in order to get his finger-prints in the bedroom and we can't prove that she was Liz Ackroyd's 'health visitor'. But it fits, doesn't it?"

"It does, Boss."

Dan paced the room. "We've got to get her, Grant. I'm certain she is behind Mollie's murder, the sighting of her car in the road near the entrance to the field that time makes me even more certain. I'm sure she's hired a professional killer; she has the money to do it. Or at least she's paid someone to do it – and to find whatever it is she thinks Mollie had to blackmail her with."

"The trouble is, we don't know if they found it, do we? They tore the van apart and thoroughly searched Simon Denton's two houses. I don't understand why he had to attack Denton though."

"Maybe because he was there. Perhaps the bloke hoped Denton would be out and he'd be able to search the house. It's a long way up there, perhaps he needed to get on with it, come what may."

Grant nodded; that was logical, given the location of Denton's cottage.

"Or," Dan continued with his train of thought, "It's possible he injured Denton to stop him going home to find out what happened to Mollie, because Clara would tell him, and then he'd try to find Charlie. He'd want to take him home with him, I'm sure of it."

"I think you're right, he would. Why would they not want him to do that, I wonder?"

"Perhaps because they needed to isolate the boy to try to find out if he has anything? They'd already searched Denton's house and knew whatever it is wasn't there. So, who else would Mollie trust, other than her uncle? She seemed to be pretty much a loner, never staying anywhere for long and there's no evidence of her corresponding with anyone, either in letters or on her phone. The only other person would be Charlie, her son."

"But would she really expect him to look after something so dangerous?"

"No, but she might hide it in his things."

"He only has his back-pack and a few bits and pieces."

"I want that back-pack examined. Hmm, I don't want to draw attention to the fact that Charlie is being guarded by Julie. I know, I'll get Kenny Baxter to pop in and ask Charlie for his bag. I think that will be safer, and we'll get it sent to Forensics."

Dan's phone rang and he snatched it up. "Cooke. Who? Ah, right. I'll be right down."

He put the phone down. "It's Eddie from Leominster. He wants to see us. Come on."

When he came into the outer office, Dan eyed the figure in the hoodie, who was hunched up on a chair, no doubt wishing he wasn't there.

"Eddie, good to see you, lad." Dan could sense the desk sergeant's surprised gawp as he led the boy into the 'soft' interview room. Eddie's body language clearly showed he was uncomfortable as he slouched into the room and flopped into the proffered chair. Dan shut the door.

216

"Would you like a coffee, Eddie?" he asked.

"No, I ain't stoppin'. This place creeps me out, man. Never thought I'd walk into a cop-shop o' me own accord, like."

Dan sat in the chair opposite. "I get that, Eddie. Does this mean you've remembered something else?"

"Yeah, I've bin thinkin' about Mandy and everythin'. Like I said, we was mates, like, more than -well, you know..."

"Yes, I know."

"Well, like I said, I've bin thinkin, an' so I've brought you this." Eddie reached into his pocket, brought out a mobile phone and laid it on the desk between them. Dan didn't touch it.

"What is it?"

"Well, it's a phone, like," began the boy.

"I can see that," said Dan, patiently. "Why are you giving it to me?"

"It was Mandy's. One day when I was alone wiv 'er at the van and the boy was down by the river, she gi' it me. She said she needed me to look after it fer 'er. When she gi' it me, she looked really serious an' she didn't often look like that. She said she needed someone she could trust ter look after it fer her because it was worth a lot to 'er and it weren't safe to keep it in the van. She said, she said..." his voice cracked and he stared hard at the table. "She said that I was the only friend she had, like, and she couldn't keep the phone in the van no more. She was afraid, Mr Cooke, and I feel really bad for not telling you before. And, and I should've brought it to you before but I was really tempted, you know? I could have sold it, cos I needed the money, you know, like?"

Dan nodded gravely. "Did she say anything else?"

"Just that, if anything ha-happened to her, I was to give it to the police." Now the young man had tears rolling down his face. "I'm sorry, Mr Cooke, I should have come before. But, well, me and the police..." His voice faded out and he looked down at the table again, trying to dab at his face with the sleeve of his hoodie wrapped around his hand. Grant silently handed him a wad of tissues and he took them and blew his nose.

217

"It's okay, Eddie, don't worry. You did the right thing in the end. Mandy would be proud of you. And you should be proud of yourself, you were her friend when she had no one else. It's good that she trusted you, so she must have seen something in you, mustn't she?"

"Yeah, I suppose so." The lad sat up straighter. "She told me that she'd come to Hereford to try to find Charlie's grandparents, even though she didn't know who they were. She knew they 'ad a shop in a village and although she loved Charlie, she hoped when she found them that they would 'ave 'im cos she didn't think she was a good enough mother anymore."

"I see. That's very interesting. Anything else?"

"You'll think I'm making this up, like, after what happened, but she also said she was afraid because someone was after her, which is why she kept moving around, like, and she'd soon have to move again. She'd thought it would be easy to find the kid's grandparents because she'd been told Hereford was a small place, but when she got 'ere, she realised it were much bigger than she expected and she hadn't a clue where to look for those people. She said she liked it here though, an' she especially liked me, cos I was 'er friend, she could talk to me, like, and she didn't really want to leave, because she didn't usually have anyone to talk to."

Eddie's voice faded out and Dan could see another tear begin to trickle down the lad's cheek, which he brushed away swiftly.

'No, and I bet you don't either,' thought Dan, giving the lad a moment to compose himself.

"Eddie, I'm grateful to you for coming here today. It's made things much clearer. I'm going to tell you something that you must not tell anyone just yet, will you promise me?"

Eddie looked surprised. "Yeah, I promise."

"Completely by accident, we've found Charlie's grandparents. Charlie's been poorly in hospital but now he's better and has gone to live with them. So, you needn't worry about him any more."

218

Eddie's eyes widened. "Cor, Mr Cooke, that's amazin' like! I'm really glad the little critter has got somebody ter tek care o' 'im now. Mandy would 'ave bin pleased." Then his head drooped again.

"What's up, lad?"

"I can't 'elp blamin' meself, Mr Cooke. If we hadn't bin such good mates, she would 'ave moved and wouldn't be dead now. It's my fault."

This was something Dan hadn't expected. You just wouldn't credit that a 'hard boy' like Eddie would blame himself for such a thing. Perhaps he wasn't so far gone as one would expect...

"You are not to blame, Eddie." Dan spoke firmly, and the boy looked up in surprise. "You can get that out of your head right now. We have good reason to believe that this would have happened eventually anyway, wherever she was. Someone was out to get her, and had gone to great lengths to make sure they did. If it hadn't happened here, it would soon have been somewhere else. And at least the good thing is, it happened where Charlie's grandparents have been found. I want you to never think you were to blame for Mandy's death. Just be glad that in you she found a friend, because I feel she'd been friendless for a long time."

Eddie looked into Dan's eyes for the first time then.

"Thank you, Mr Cooke."

"Just one thing I'd like to ask you. Did she give you the phone at the same time as she told you about how she'd hoped to find the grandparents?"

"Nah, she give it me afore then, around April time. I was surprised because I hadn't known her all that long. But she kept checkin' that I still had it. Every time I saw her when we were alone, I had to show it 'er. It was later that she told me the other stuff."

Dan stood up. "Well, thank you, Eddie. It must have been a great temptation to sell the phone, especially after Mandy died. But you came through. Do you have a contact number? We can

219

let you know how Charlie gets on and you may even be able to see him at some point. Not now, because we don't want too many people to know where he is, but we hope, when we've managed to find the killer, that he will be able to live without fear that something will happen to him."

"Yeah, I'd like ter see 'im again." He gave his number to Grant, who made a note of it.

"Can we give you a lift back to Leominster?"

"What, me in a cop car? Nah, I don't think so! Thanks for the offer, like, but I'll get the bus."

Dan gave the phone to Grant. "Take that down to our experts, Grant. I'll see Eddie out."

Chapter 43

The experts found some interesting things on Mollie's phone. Dan and Grant peered over Roy Berrington's shoulder as he brought up a picture on the screen. It wasn't very clear, obviously taken at night and appeared to be of a woman near a wooden fence, shedding dark clothing. They could clearly see her bare feet and legs and the bottom of a dress; impossible to tell what colour it was. Another picture showed a woman with a black bag in her hand by the back end of a car. The next one showed the back end of the car as it was driven away.

They gaped at the last picture of a man on a sofa, his face contorted with shock, but obviously dead, with blood all over his front. Grant drew in a sharp breath and then looked surprised as he heard his boss swear. Dan rarely swore.

"You recognise that, Grant?"

"I do. It's like the photo of Stephen Harrison taken by the team in Portsmouth."

"Why would Mollie Denton have that picture on her phone?"

"Take a look at the date, Sir," said Roy. "But especially look at the time on the clock behind the body."

Roy clicked and the computer focused on the clock on the wall and enlarged it. Although pixilated, the time was clear.

"Look at that, Grant. It says 19:26 on the clock and the photo is dated 9.11.2010."

Grant whistled. "My word, Boss, that's amazing. If Pauline Harrison didn't go out until eight, this is proof that Stephen was dead before she went."

"Exactly. Ron, can you get a close-up of the woman's face in that second photograph?"

"It won't be clear, sir, but let's see..."

They watched the screen intently as the figure in the photo became larger.

"As you can see, it's not great because the closer you get, the more pixilated it becomes."

"It's good enough. What do you think, Grant, is that Pauline Harrison?"

"I think so."

"So do I. Is there anything else of interest, Roy?"

"I'll say – look at this."

Moments later, a face appeared that they immediately recognised as a younger Mollie Denton, on a film, and they listened carefully to what she had to say.

'I saw a programme on the television how someone left a video film to be played to their family after their death and so I decided to try to do something like that in case anything happens to me. I've had a terrible experience, so this is my live diary. The date is the eleventh of November, two thousand and ten. My friend has taken Charlie round the park to play, so I thought I'd do this now while I'm alone in the flat.

On Friday, the ninth, I followed Steve when he left me to go home. I wanted to know where he lived, because he wouldn't tell me, and I also wanted to try to make sure he was really going to leave his wife this time. I didn't know how I'd do it, but I had to try. So, I left Charlie with my friend and hurried to catch the same train as Steve. I made sure he didn't see me. When we got off at Portsmouth, I followed him home. He caught a bus and so did I. I'd brought a hooded rain coat with me that I knew he'd never seen before, so I could put the hood up to hide my face from him. But he wasn't expecting to see me so he didn't look anyway. I followed him to his house and saw him go in just before seven.

I didn't know what to do and I didn't want to be seen, so I walked up the road on one side, then back on the other side and I found that there was a service road that ran behind his house, so I followed it and found the back of his house. It was dark, but as his house is at the end, a street light shone a little light into the garden. There was a light on in the back of the house and there were no curtains or blinds. The gate was already open, so I crept in to try to peep through the window, but suddenly the back door opened and I bobbed down against the wheelie-bin. Terrified, I watched as a figure emerged, dressed all in black from head to foot but then the light went out. The figure stepped outside but I could still make her out as she took off the black clothing, starting with the feet because even they had black things over them. She put on shoes and took the other things off. I saw a blond woman in a dress but I couldn't tell what colour it was. I watched her put the black clothes in a bag, then she went out of the gate to a car. I managed to take a picture of her by the car as the angle was just right from where I was crouching. Then, I crept out of the gate, bent low, and took a picture of the back of her car with the number plate.

When I looked back at the house, the door was still wide open, so I went right up to the door-step, took off my shoes – and to this day, I don't know why I took off my shoes – and tip-toed into the house. I thought I might be able to speak with Steve while she was gone. The television was on and so I called, quietly, 'Steve, Steve, where's she gone?' There was no answer, but I could see the top of his head on the sofa, and thought he must be asleep, so I crept around to poke him but when I saw him, I almost screamed, but stopped myself in time. He was covered in blood and had a horrible surprised expression on his face. His eyes were open and I thought he was looking at me, so I said 'Steve, has she gone to get help?' He didn't answer, didn't move. I was going to touch his neck like I've seen them do on the telly but something stopped me. I took the picture, then afraid she'd come back, I left by the back door, picked up my shoes and ran down the service road. When I was about halfway down, I heard a car and turned to see it stop outside their back gate and the woman get out and go in the garden. She didn't see me because I'd pressed myself against a hedge at the back of one of the houses.

In shock, I walked around until I didn't know where I was and found a bed and breakfast place. Luckily, the owner lived there and opened the door to me. I told her I'd missed my train and she gave me a room where I stayed the night. I paid for it there and then, left before breakfast and came home. My whole life was wrecked and I couldn't stop thinking about how my Steve had looked. It had to be his wife that killed him because there was no one else there. I didn't know what to do. I was afraid, that if the police knew I'd been in the house that night, they'd think I'd done it.

The film stopped abruptly. Dan and Grant looked at each other. "Wow."

Dan stretched his back. "Now we know, but I wish she'd gone to the police instead of running away."

Grant grunted. "Yes, it would have saved David Ackroyd, and that woman would be behind bars."

"And Mollie herself would still be alive," commented Dan. The three men stood in silence for a couple of minutes until Grant muttered,

"Poor girl."

"Yes, she lost everything, or rather, Charlie lost everything when she made that decision. Not right away, of course, but eventually."

"Thank goodness he has the Harrisons."

"Indeed."

"Do you think she knew about Ackroyd?"

"She may have done. If she did, she obviously decided it was better him than her in trouble. And she eventually decided to put as much distance as she could between herself and Pauline Harrison."

"But somehow Harrison must have found out that she had evidence."

"Yes. Thanks, Roy. If you find anything else on the phone, call me."

"I will, Sir."

As they walked back to Dan's office, he said, "Right. We have what they were after, which means we know they will keep looking. Charlie will be their next target, which means we have to have a plan."

"Do you have a plan, Boss?"

"I do indeed."

"Thought you might," Grant smirked.

"You know me too well, Grant. This is what I have in mind..."

Chapter 44
Tuesday Morning

The following day, at a television news presentation, Dan put his plan into action and this was the last step. The interview took place outside Police Headquarters. Grant stood beside him in silent solidarity as Dan read out his statement:

"Hereford police are happy to report that the lost boy, Charlie, the son of our murdered woman, who we now know was Mollie Denton, is now out of hospital and has gone to live with his grandparents. We would like to thank all those who played a part in helping trace the boy, who ran away when he discovered his mother was dead.

However, we need the public's help as we are still seeking Ms Denton's killer. We have traced the vehicle he used to a car hire firm. From there, we have reached a dead end. He is described as being tall, with dark hair, designer stubble and a handsome face. (An artist's impression of 'Des' appeared on the screen) He wears expensive clothes, last seen wearing a dark suit and a light pink shirt. He uses various aliases; we know of Michael Soames and Mollie knew him as Desmond. If anyone knows who might have had a grudge against Ms Denton, also known as Mandy Jones, please get in touch with us, the number is at the bottom of your screens, or your local police station. This man is dangerous; we believe he is also responsible for administering serious injuries to another man. Do not try anything yourselves if you think you know him. Thank you."

"Detective Inspector Cooke," called out a woman reporter, "where do Charlie's grandparents live?"

"For Charlie's protection, we will not be disclosing his whereabouts."

"Do you know why his mother was killed?"

"We are currently pursuing several lines of enquiry. Thank you for your interest."

With that, Dan turned away from the cameras and went inside the building, followed by Grant.

Once inside, they went straight up to Dan's office to put the next part of the plan into action.

"Right," he said to those assembled. "We don't know where our man is staying, whether he's nearby, or even in the county. Maybe he's further away, awaiting his instructions. Everyone involved is already in place. Now, all we can do is wait and keep our fingers crossed – and I'm sure a prayer if you're that way inclined. Now, Julie Coombs is our key person. Johnson, as our communications liaison in this operation, you need to be alert at all times. Although Julie is our main contact, if an emergency does occur and she can't contact you, our other officers can all do so. Now, the trap is set. We must all hope that our killer will take the bait."

Monday Evening

The Super had given permission and preparations had begun. Of course, they needed Madge and Len's cooperation, so Dan went to see them.

"It'll mean going tonight," he explained, "because the statement will be broadcast in the morning. Our man could then turn up at any time."

"But what about the shop?" asked Madge, her brow creased in a worried frown.

"I can manage it for a couple of days, Madge," said Julie. "I've been paying close attention to what you do, and there will be a couple here, pretending to be you and Len and they can help. In fact, they'll have to because they are supposed to be you. I know what Len does in the stock-room. I'm sure the shop will tick over just fine until we get this over with."

"But are you certain he'll come, Mr Cooke? What if he isn't interested in Charlie?"

"I am sure, because he's been after something Mollie had and they haven't found it yet. They will be convinced Charlie has it as he's the only one left who Mollie would have trusted. He has to find it, it's very incriminating evidence. What he doesn't know is that we already have it."

"Oh really? How come?"

"It was delivered to us by a friend of Mollie's. I'll tell you about it when this is over. For now, I want you to pack a few things, and get ready to go. Ah, here are your replacements now, and our make-up artist."

"This is Sergeant Ann Chambers and Sergeant Derek Walker, who are to become you two. This is PC Adam Hill who will also stay here to help, although he won't be seen unless necessary."

While Dan was speaking, the make-up artist was deftly transforming Ann into Madge. Eventually, with the help of a grey curly wig and spectacles, she looked remarkably like her. Adding padding in various places, and wearing a pair of trousers and a blouse belonging to Madge, with a shop overall over the top, she could easily be mistaken for the shopkeeper. Next, it was Derek's turn to be made into Len. This was more straightforward as they were of similar build and Derek's hair was thinning, just like Len's.

"I never thought my lack of hair would come in so useful," he remarked ruefully and they laughed. A pair of Len's trousers and a jumper easily made the transformation.

Looking at the two pairs side by side, Dan thought it was remarkable, and Charlie could hardly believe his eyes.

"That's great. Now, Grant here is going to take you three to a safe place. You will love it there and the people – and Charlie, you will enjoy what they have there, it's a special place. Look upon it as a holiday, and we'll be in touch when all is safe again."

"Oh well, I suppose it'll be alright," remarked Madge. "What do you think, Charlie?"

"I want the man who killed my mum to be caught, Grandma. Mr Dan is a good man and we should do what 'e ses."

Len put his hand on his grandson's shoulder. "You're quite right, my boy. Let's go, Sergeant Grant."

After Grant had driven away with them in a car with darkened windows, Dan heaved a sigh of relief. Thank goodness they were safe. They were going out to Castle Farm, where Dave and his wife would look after them splendidly and Ron would love showing Charlie all the vintage cars that Dave had in his colossal barn. Now, it was back to business.

"Right, Julie, Ann, Derek and Adam, you all have devices that you only have to press to alert for help. Julie is our prime contact, but if anything happens and she can't contact, you all can, okay? I suspect that our man is a master of disguise. I don't, for one moment, think he is really as described but that he used the same persona, if a different name, for the hired car firm, in order, obviously, to mislead us. So, be on your guard. Julie, you've been here a few days now and know pretty much all the regular customers who come into the shop. You know who you can trust to give a nod to and let Ann or Derek get closer to; do your best to keep other customers at distance. So, if anyone comes into the shop who you don't recognise, be on your guard immediately. Press the number for 'alert', and press it again for 'okay'. If it's not okay, press the number for 'danger' and we'll send in the troops. If you press the alert button but don't press it again for okay, we'll come anyway. Is that clear to you all?"

The four in front of him nodded.

"Good. You can relax this evening, I'm sure. The statement goes out tomorrow so be in role and on your guard. You're all intelligent and clever people and I don't need to teach you to suck eggs. But this man is clever. The woman behind him is wily. We don't take chances. Above all, be careful, we don't want any casualties."

Dan felt wound up. He worried about them all but what else could be done? The problem was that Sutton-on-Wye was a twenty-minute drive from the city so he needed to have armed officers in situ to deal with the situation should their killer arrive there. He'd toyed with the idea of staying in the village himself but realised that he needed to be in the city to do the broadcast and also the killer may well know his face as he'd been on the television before. The man would not know any of the officers now in the Harrison's flat.

When he arrived home, Linda had a nice meal ready for him and afterwards they sat together quietly and she rubbed his shoulders, knowing he was tense.

"It's coming to a close, Linda," he said. "I know Pauline Norton-Smyth is behind it. We have incriminating evidence against her. This is the last piece of the puzzle – if we can get him, we'll have everything we need to present the case against her and exonerate the man who was falsely found guilty for her crime. I just hope he takes the bait that we've set."

"I hope so too, because you can't carry on with this kind of stress for much longer. Promise me we'll go away for a while when this is over."

"We will, my love. Have you found somewhere you'd like to go?"

"Not yet. But I will when we know when we can go. Now, would you like a nightcap or something else?"

"Not a night-cap, much as I'd like it, just in case. I must keep my head clear until this is over. I'd like a Horlicks. In fact, I'll make it."

"I'll do it, love."

"No, you relax, you made us a nice meal. I'll be right back, then perhaps we can have a reasonably early night."

"Oooh, promises," giggled Linda, as she settled further into the cushions. Dan smiled as he went into the kitchen.

Chapter 45

He sat, relaxed, in a recliner chair in front of the television. The flame-effect fire bobbed and danced as he glanced at it. The picture of that Detective Inspector spouting on the television aroused emotion in him and his hand gripped his glass tighter. Realising that he could damage the delicate expensive crystal glass, he made himself release the grip and instead he held it up and looked at the flame through the amber liquid.

So, the kid was out of hospital. He'd realised he couldn't get at him in there and so he'd gone home. She hadn't been pleased; she had wanted him to get at the boy in the hospital but when he'd pointed out that there had been a police guard, plus the boy didn't have his things with him there, she had realised he was right. He'd tried to find out where the boy's things were to no avail – but maybe the lad didn't have it anyway? But where else it could be? None of the girl's companions at the Black Swan were trustworthy enough. That only left her son – he had to have it. How brilliant that he was at the grandparents. He could easily get at him there.

He turned the news off and found a film on another channel. As he watched the cops trying to work out what was going on, he laughed at the irony. Tomorrow, he would head back to Herefordshire. He switched off the television; he needed to get a good night's sleep as he had a good drive in the morning and hopefully he would soon be back, mission accomplished. He would be glad when it was all done and his life could go back to normal.

****

It was late when Madge, Len and Charlie arrived at Castle Farm. The warm welcome they received from Dave and Margaret lifted Madge's spirits. They had already seen each other at the

Sutton-on-Wye Summer Fair so weren't complete strangers. Except for Charlie, of course. The Blackwoods had been filled in regarding him by Dan when he called them. They greeted Grant like an old friend, which of course he was.

"You will stay and have supper with us, won't you, Sergeant Grant?"

"I should be getting back really..." began Grant, then he remembered that his wife Jenny was on a late shift and would not be at home. "Actually, I'd like that very much, thank you. It will keep me going on the drive home."

"That's settled then. Let's eat now so this young man can get to bed, he looks like he's nearly asleep now."

Charlie looked at the adults surrounding him at the large kitchen table. A simple meal of ham, eggs chips and peas had been set out for them and he thought it was a feast from Heaven. He'd eaten well at his grandparents' place and loved the shop and the village already. This place was different again, very big and spacious and this lady had lots of nice things, but again, he liked it. He felt comfortable with these people, even the detective sergeant that laughed with them. The farmer, Dave Blackwood, was well-built as you'd expect but he was jolly and friendly. His wife was a lovely lady with a kind face and curly white hair. If only his mum could be here with him and could have known Madge and Len, his dad's mum and dad, and that he had always known them, so that his bedroom in their flat above the shop wouldn't feel strange to him, which it did, as he hadn't slept in it one night yet.

"It's so good of you to have us like this," his grandmother said as she picked at the food. "And I know we have to keep Charlie safe, but I do worry about my shop."

The lady called Margaret, sitting next to her, put her hand on hers. "Try not to worry, Madge. Dan and his people know what they're doing. We have to trust them and hope this will soon be over so you can go home. But I hope you'll like staying with us."

"Oh, I'm sure we will. But I'm used to being busy, you know, like, so please give me things to do, for I don't expect to be idle while we're here."

"Don't worry, there's always loads to do here. And young Charlie will love Dave's collection and will have a wonderful time with Ron."

"Ah yes, your resident Lord," said Len. "I'd forgotten about him. Won't it be too much for him to have a young boy around?"

"Good gracious nom he'll love it. He really enjoyed having young Harry here. And Charlie will like being around the collection and the farm."

"That's right. I tell you, Charlie, I wish I could stay here for a while instead of having to catch criminals," laughed Grant.

"Go on with you. You love your job." Margaret nudged him.

Charlie enjoyed the talk and the food, but he could barely keep his eyes open. He felt strong arms lift him, half asleep, up the stairs and lay him on a bed and his shoes removed. A cover was pulled across him and he was away to dreamland.

****

Downstairs, Grant finished the last of his dessert, a light mousse, with regret. Time to leave.

"Madge and Len, try not to worry about your shop. Julie's a great young woman and detective; she won't let anything go wrong. She's seen how you run things and will do her best for you. Let's hope our man won't take too long to show up."

He stood up. "Dave and Margaret, I can't tell you how grateful Dan and I are to you for doing this for us yet again – it's becoming a habit, using you as a safe house."

Dave clapped him on the shoulder. "It's no trouble at all, lad. We're happy to help, aren't we, my dear? We love having folks to stay, and Ron will be overjoyed with young Charlie there. My, he was tired, wasn't he?"

"Yes. He only came out of hospital today. I think he was ill through sheer exhaustion and stress, poor little boy. And he's been in so many strange places lately and now he's in another strange place." Madge's eyes were sad, as she thought about her grandson's plight. Len put his arm around her.

"He'll be alright. He has safety and love and will be just fine, you'll see."

"Absolutely right. Well, I must be off. We all have to be on high alert from now on."

Grant shook hands with Dave and Margaret gave him a hug, then he shook hands with Len and Madge.

"I'll see you out, Graham," said Dave, and the two men left the room.

Once outside, he said, "What happens if the man doesn't come?"

"I don't know. We'll cross that bridge if we come to it. Frankly, he's been so desperate to find the evidence he thinks Mollie had, I'm convinced he'll turn up, although quite when, I've no idea."

Grant got into the car. Dave held the door ready to shut it. "Just take care, Graham, and the rest of you. It sounds to me like this man will stop at nothing to get what he wants."

"Too right, Dave. But we're as prepared as we can be. This time we'll get him, I can feel it in my bones."

234

Chapter 46

Julie and her group had two quiet days in Sutton-on-Wye, managing the shop. There wasn't enough work for four people. Adam in particular became somewhat bored as he had to stay out of sight in the flat. He cleaned and polished until everywhere was shining, watched television and prepared everyone's meals.

"You're a great cook, Adam," Julie complimented him as she watched his chopping vegetables for their dinner that evening. "You'd make someone a wonderful wife."

Derek put his arm around Adam's neck. "Will you marry me, Adam?"

"Oooh, I thought you'd never ask!" Adam pretended to flutter his eyelashes. "Can I think about it?"

The three laughed.

"We'd better get down to the shop, Derek, if you can bear to leave your intended. Ann's down there on her own. It's almost closing time and we often have a rush of people dashing in because they've just remembered something they must have."

"Yeah, I remember from last evening."

The shop doorbell rang as they entered the shop. A couple of villagers wandered around, looking at the shelves. Derek scooted into the back room as Julie went into the shop.

"I'm glad you've come, love," said Ann in a passable Madge voice. "I need the lav, can you take over, like?"

"Of course, Mum. Oh, hello Sue, did you suddenly need something?"

"Yes, I realised I was low on nappies for my little lad. I hope you've got them in the right size. Is Madge alright?"

"I think so, she's just nipped to the loo. It's easier for her to do that while I'm here."

"It's been nice for her to have you here. How long are you staying?"

235

"I'm not sure. It depends on how things go – you know how it is. I'm between jobs just now," replied Julie, ad libbing quickly. "Have you found what you need? We'll be closing shortly."

"Oh yes, I have them."

Julie rang up the packet of nappies and Julie heaved a sigh of relief when Sue left. It had proven tricky keeping Ann out of the way of the people who knew her well. It wasn't a problem with Lucy, she knew why they were there, as did Sheila, Lucy's mother-in-law.

The other villager, who Julie knew by sight, bought her loaf of bread and also left. As Julie was about to shut the shop, a man rushed to stop her. He looked quite old and had a greying beard and a mop of hair that was similar.

"Sorry, are you closing?" he said, out of breath.

"Well, I was but if you need something quickly, I'll serve you, but I'll put the 'CLOSED' sign up."

"Thank you. I just need..."

"Have you closed up yet, dear?" Ann came through from the back. "Oh, can we help you, deary? Have you forgotten something?"

"Yes, I...are you Mrs Harrison?"

"Why yes."

"Is your husband here?"

"Why do you want my husband?"

Julie secretly pressed the 'alert' button. The man looked harmless, but ...

"I need to see him about something. He called me about financial advice."

"Oh? He never told me about that. He's out the back. Len!"

Derek came through and the minute he was in the shop, the man whipped out a gun.

"I want the boy! Where is he?"

"What boy?"

"The kid of the girl who died of course. He's got something I want. Where is he?"

"He's not here," answered Derek. "He's around a friend's house, playing."

"I don't believe you! Get upstairs – all of you – now!"

'Please let help come quickly,' prayed Julie as she pressed the red button. It bleeped, and she drew in a breath, just as he turned around and fired a shot at her. Pain seared through her thigh and fell as Ann screamed.

Julie heard shouts and noises and more shots. She was helpless. The darkness closed in on her.

****

Dan and Grant and two other armed men ran up to the shop door. It was locked, but was soon broken open by one of the men. They rushed inside, to find Julie in a pool of blood in the back room.

"Julie!" Dan felt for the pulse on her neck. "She's alive – call an ambulance!"

He raced up the stairs, to find a man lying on the floor, obviously shot, and Ann tending to Adam, who had also been shot in the shoulder.

"I've already called for an ambulance, Sir," said Derek.

"Is he alive?" asked Dan, nodding at the man on the floor.

"Yes, although he's badly hurt. Adam shot him when he shot at Julie."

"Well done, all of you. I'm worried about Julie, she's already lost a lot of blood. I didn't think he'd be using a gun. Oh, I hope the ambulance hurries up."

Although it seemed an age, the paramedics arrived, followed a few minutes afterwards by three ambulances.

"Grant, you go with Julie, please. I'll go with our gunman."

"I'll stay with Adam, if that's alright, Sir," said Derek.

"Indeed, I'd be grateful. Ann, will you be okay here? These guys will help you make the place secure."

"Of course, Sir," Ann replied.

"Thank you. Let's go!"

Dan sat beside the prisoner, who remained unconsciousness in the ambulance, his thoughts with Julie. He blamed himself; he should never have left her there, she was only a detective constable after all. If she died... He shook away the thought – no, she wouldn't die, she couldn't die. If only the ambulance would go faster, for he needed to get to the hospital and find out.

When they arrived at the hospital the ambulance entrance was full of blue flashing lights. His man was quickly lifted out of the vehicle and Dan followed into the Accident and Emergency Department. While the gunman was rushed straight into an operation theatre, Dan went to find out about Julie. He found Grant pacing a corridor.

"She's being operated on, Boss. I'm really worried. All we can do is wait."

Dan nodded, and his feelings of guilt went deeper. "Do you know how Adam is?"

"He'll be okay, they think. The bullet skimmed his shoulder. He'll be out of action for a while but at least he didn't take a bullet."

"Thank goodness. It's bad enough having Julie in a bad way. I feel so responsible, Grant, I should never have left her in there."

Grant put his hand on his shoulder. "She wanted to do it, Boss. And there were three other armed officers there and we were waiting outside. It shouldn't have happened that way. Goodness only knows what made him shoot at her. Do we know how he is?"

"He's in theatre, but I think he'll be lucky if he survives."

"Are you going to let the Harrisons know tonight?"

238

"No, the morning will do. We have a long night ahead and it's better if we leave them in blissful ignorance for now."

Grant nodded. "I'd like to call Jenny, if that's okay? Let her know where I am and so on, so she doesn't worry."

"Of course, Grant. I'll be calling Linda shortly. First, I must let Julie's parents know what's happened."

"Where do they live?"

"Worcester, I think. No time to go there. Much as I hate to give bad news over the phone, I think they'll want to know as soon as possible."

Two hours later, the doctor came to see Dan, who was dozing fitfully in a chair.

"Inspector, the patient is out of surgery. He's very poorly and probably won't make it, I'm afraid. But you need to see something."

Dan followed the white-coated man into Intensive Care. After donning a white cap and gown, he entered the room that was being guarded by a police constable. Going over to the still figure in the bed, Dan looked at the man. Instead of what he expected – an older man with a beard, he found, to his astonishment, that before his startled eyes was the haggardly pale but still handsome face of the blond-haired Mark Norton-Smyth.

Chapter 47

Pauline Norton-Smythe's head jerked up from the book she was reading at the sound of the imperious sound of the intercom and hurried to answer it. Her housekeeper had gone home and the children were in bed, with their nanny Mary in the room next to them. On her way, she glanced at the large grandmother clock on the wall of the hallway. It was almost nine-thirty – who could be calling at this hour? She wasn't sure about opening the door this late when her husband was away on business.

She pressed the button. "Yes, who is it?"

A disembodied voice, distorted by the crackle of the intercom said:

"Mrs Norton-Smyth? I'm Sergeant Neil Thompson and this is Police Constable Dickson. May we come in for a moment please?"

"I suppose so."

She pressed the button that would open the gate, but for a crazy moment thought about locking it and running out the back way. But why? She had no reason to run, had she? She opened the door to admit the two policemen.

"What's all this about, officers?"

"I'm afraid we've some bad news for you, Mrs Norton-Smyth. It's your husband –"

"Mark?" Her hand went to her face as she gasped. "Has he? Is he?"

"I'm afraid there's been an accident, ma'am. He's in hospital and we've been asked to take you there right away because he's in a bad way."

"Oh! Oh, yes. Of course."

She looked around, not knowing what to do. Sergeant Thompson took her gently by the arm and sat her on a chair in the hall.

"Sit down, ma'am. You've had a shock. Get the lady some water, would you, Constable?"

The constable returned with a cup of water which Pauline took with shaking hands and sipped, thinking rapidly. What could have happened? He should be in his London flat where he stayed when he was there on business.

"When did this happen?" she asked, putting her cup on the hall table beside her.

"I believe around six, ma'am. They didn't know who he was at first. I believe he's been operated on. Our station was contacted and we were assigned to take you to him. Can I respectfully suggest that you pack some overnight essentials?"

Pauline made a great effort to pull herself together. "Of course. I must let my nanny know what's happening."

"Do what you have to do, ma'am, but please be as quick as you can. We've been given to believe that time is of the essence. You need to be there for him."

Nodding, she headed towards the stairs on legs that felt like jelly. She had lost one husband, was she about to lose another? She had really loved Steve until she found out about the affair – and especially the boy he fathered. It had taken her a while to fall for Mark, although she'd married him fairly soon after she'd left Portsmouth, enticed by his money. But she knew she did love him, and the thought that he might die horrified her.

All the time aware of the two pairs of eyes watching at her, she tried to push herself to go faster up the stairs. Thankful for the bend in the staircase which took her away from their sight, she tapped on Mary's door. She could hear the television and wondered if the young woman had heard her knock. However, a few moments later, the door was opened by Mary wearing her pyjamas and dressing gown.

"Ma'am?"

"Mary, are the girls both asleep?"

"Yes, they are."

Pauline hesitated – should she go in to the girls? A little voice in her head seemed to be pushing her to see them. She gave in to the impulse.

"I'd like to pop in and see them."

241

She noticed the astonished look on Mary's face, but she didn't care. First, she went to her sleeping step-daughter and kissed her forehead, then went to Sophie and spent a moment gazing at her sweet daughter. She smoothed a strand of hair from the child's face and then kissed her. Neither of the girls stirred. She envied their carefree sleep.

"I have to go away for a while, Mary. Two policemen have come to tell me that my husband has had an accident and I need to go to him."

The girl gasped, "Oh madam, I'm so sorry. Will he be alright?"

"I don't know. They say he's seriously hurt and I need to go without delay."

"When will you be back?"

"I don't know that either. I'll contact you when I know more."

"What shall I tell the girls?"

"You'll have to tell them the truth, that their daddy has been hurt and I've gone to be with him. That's about all you can say at this point. Take care of them, Mary."

"I will, ma'am, don't worry."

"I'll just fetch my things then I'll be off. Lock the door and put the chain on when I've gone, would you?"

"Of course I will. I'll go downstairs, ready."

Pauline grabbed a bag and stuffed in a few things she might need. Knowing it was cold outside, she put on a cardigan and a coat and a sensible pair of shoes and went downstairs to the waiting policemen.

As she went out, Mary said, "Goodbye, ma'am, please give Mr Norton-Smyth my best wishes for a quick recovery."

"I will. Lock that door now."

Pauline heard the sound of the lock behind her as she went down the two shallow steps and then settled into the back of the police car with the sergeant beside her. The young constable got into the driver's seat and switched the engine on.

"If you go a little further along, there's a place where you can turn," she said and saw the driver nod.

As the car speed along the straight country road lined with trees, Pauline tried to make herself relax but found her mind was unable to. What would she find when they reached the hospital? How badly was Mark injured? She closed her eyes and tried not to think. Eventually, she became aware that they were travelling at great speed, the blue light silently flashing and she looked out of the window but could only see dark countryside. Where were they going? Surely, they should be near London now? She would have expected to see lots of street lights and houses.

"Where are we going? We're not in London!"

"I didn't say he was in London, Mrs Norton-Smyth."

"So, where are we going?"

"Hereford."

"Hereford!" she exclaimed, sitting up straight. "What on earth is he doing in Hereford?"

"We really couldn't say, ma'am."

Pauline's thoughts raced – what was Mark doing in Hereford? Why hadn't he told her he was going there? What an idiot – that was the one place they shouldn't be going – didn't he realise? Until she got her hands on that evidence that – that – woman had, she wasn't safe. She felt that detective knew more than he'd let on about what happened to Steve. Did these policemen know anything? Or were they just the messengers? She groaned inwardly and risked a glance at the sergeant next to her. He caught her look and patted her hand.

"Don't worry, Ma'am, we're doing our best to get you to him quickly. I'm sure the sight of you will help him recover."

She let out a quiet breath of relief – so he didn't know anything. She fumbled in her bag for a tissue and dabbed at her eyes. "I can't help being worried, Sergeant."

"That's understandable in the circumstances, Mrs Norton-Smyth."

"Oh, do please call me Pauline. Mrs Norton-Smyth is such a mouthful. And I fear that I might not be Mrs Norton-Smyth for much longer."

"There now, we're doing our best."

"I know, and I'm very grateful to you both," she sniffed.

"Pity Hereford isn't a direct route, those country roads take longer. But we can't help it."

"No, it's a very inconvenient place as far as roads are concerned."

"You know it?"

"Strangely, I do. My first husband's parents lived in a village there so we used to visit them quite often."

"You were married before?"

"Yes. He died."

"I'm sorry to hear that, particularly in the present situation."

She gave a strangled sort of laugh. "Seems I'm a dangerous person to be married to."

"Oh, I'm sure it's not you. Just a strange turn of fate. Let's hope your husband pulls through," he said, kindly.

Not trusting herself to say anything else, she nodded, and wiped her eyes again.

She knew when they finally turned off the motorway because the travelling wasn't so comfortable. Although the constable was an expert driver, he couldn't do anything about the way the roads twisted and turned and went up hill and down. Pauline started to feel queasy. She travelled better when she was driving and she thought of her beautiful red sports car with a pang. If only she was driving it now, although she wished she wasn't heading towards a hospital where her husband was lying ill, possibly dying.

Constable Dickson managed to shave a lot of time off the two and a half hours it normally took to Hereford, being able to drive well over the speed limit on the motorway, lights flashing their warning. It was just after eleven thirty when she stepped from their car into the hospital.

They were met by a policeman at the main entrance.

"Mrs Norton-Smyth? I'm Constable Riley. I've been sent to bring you to your husband."

"Would you like us to come with you, Pauline?" The sergeant asked her.

"Oh, would you please? I'm – I'm afraid."

"Of course. Constable, you stay here and relax. Get yourself a drink?"

"Thanks, Serge, I think I will."

"Course not, lad, you deserve one, getting us here so quickly. I'll meet you back here later, okay?"

They walked the corridors until Pauline was completely confused, although Constable Riley seemed to know exactly where they were going. Eventually, they came to the Intensive Care Unit and she was shown into a room where a nurse was checking the lines of the drips and a monitor bleeped quietly beside the bed. Mark lay, still and silent, in the bed.

The nurse gave her a friendly smile and indicated to her to come to his side. She kept her eyes on him as she walked towards him.

"Can I touch him?" she asked the nurse.

"Yes. Talk to him, he can hear you."

Pauline put her hand on his, lying inert on the bed covers.

"Darling, I'm here." She kissed his forehead and examined his face with her eyes; he was so handsome with his blonde hair and perfect features. She always got so much pleasure looking at him. Now, his face was pale as if he were already dead. But at the sound of her voice, his eyes flickered open.

"Polly." His voice was barely a croak as he spoke his pet name for her. "I'm sorry, Polly, I cocked it up."

"What did you do?"

"I did it because I love you. And I've let you down. Tell the girls I love them."

His eyes closed and the monitor gave a long, continuous bleep.

"No! Mark, don't leave me! You can't die, you can't!"

A team of doctors and nurses rushed in, alerted by the monitor and she was kindly but firmly pushed out of the room while they tried desperately to restart his heart but the monitor continued its mournful sound. A doctor came out and pulled his mask down.

"I'm sorry. We did all we could."

Pauline buried her face in the solid chest of Sergeant Thompson. She didn't see the two other men who followed the team from the room until one of them spoke.

"Pauline Norton-Smyth, I arrest you for the murder of Stephen Harrison and conspiracy to murder Mollie Denton."

She started back from the sergeant and spun round to see the speaker – that flaming detective who had come to her house. He continued to speak, cautioning her as he put on the cuffs. She looked at the sergeant, who was obviously surprised and then back at Dan. "What are you talking about?" she spat. "David Ackroyd murdered Stephen and I don't even know who Mollie Denton is."

"Don't bother to argue, we have all the evidence we need. Your husband gave us a statement earlier, confessing to the murder of Mollie Denton and the assault on Simon Denton."

"What has that to do with me? I don't know those people."

"Oh, but you do. We have the evidence that you hired a hit-man to kill Mollie Denton. Except the hit-man was really your husband, Mark Norton-Smyth."

Pauline felt as though she had been punched in the solar plexus. *'Oh Mark, you fool!'* she thought. Now she understood his last words to her. All the fight went out of her.

"Can I say goodbye to my husband?"

Dan nodded, and took her into the room, where only a very short time before she'd been talking to her beloved Mark. His face looked like he was peacefully sleeping. She bent over and kissed his forehead as she had done earlier. "Goodbye, my love. Thank you for trying. I love you."

When they led her out of the hospital and into a waiting police car, she saw the detective who had arrested her stop to talk

246

with the two policemen who had brought her here while his sergeant continued her towards the car. He climbed in next to her and the constable who had waited for her arrival at the hospital got into the driver's seat.

It was but a few minutes' drive to the police headquarters, it being close to the hospital. She was checked in, her things examined and labelled for safe-keeping and she was taken to a cell.

The heavy door clanged shut. She sat on the unforgiving bed and put her head in her hands. A few hours ago, she had everything in life she wanted. Now, she knew, that through her insane jealousy, she had lost it all.

Chapter 48

Alan Taylor stood in his back-bedroom window, surveying his garden. He was supposed to be decorating the bedroom ready for the new baby, due to put in an appearance in a few months' time.

He and his wife, Fiona, had been thrilled to buy this place. Houses here were expensive because of the fact that Portsmouth is an island, albeit permanently connected to the mainland. They'd struck lucky because it was cheaper than normal, due to the fact it had been the scene of a grisly murder a few years before. The woman whose husband had been killed had left soon after his death and the house was sold. However, the wife of the couple who had bought it found she couldn't live there knowing what had happened, and so they'd moved away, leaving the house empty for a year or so.

As a Detective Sergeant, this hadn't particularly bothered him, nor Fiona. They had simply been thrilled to find a house they could afford and indeed, they'd lived here very happily for over a year. Fiona was a beauty therapist and worked for a salon in town, until she took maternity leave. His mother-in-law was on standby to help once she returned to work.

They had both worked hard on the house, installed a sparkling new bathroom and a shiny new kitchen and decorated throughout. This room was the last to be done and then they could install the baby furniture that was currently in storage at Fiona's parents' house. Alan had taken a day he was owed to finish painting the room.

However, he was distracted by the garden, as he had been several times lately. Okay, so they'd done their best to tame the shrubs that were there and keep the grass cut, but that was all. An area that had been a vegetable plot had been allowed to grow wild; Alan didn't have time to grow vegetables, his job was too demanding. Any time he did have at home he devoted to Fiona because being a detective's wife was hard, he often had to work long hours or run off out again after being at home a short time.

He was so lucky to have found her, she was not only beautiful but was patient and understanding about his job. She knew what she was taking on, for they had been seeing each other seriously for quite some time. If he was honest, he would have lived with her long before, but she was an old-fashioned girl who wanted to be married properly and wouldn't live with him until then. He admired her for her values and respected her and her parents, and they were very happy.

Not for the first time, as he looked at the garden, he frowned. Something was not right out there and now he knew it was that shed. It was not in the right place. Having been there for two summers now, they'd remarked often that it was a shame that the shed was in the sunniest spot, but other than mentioning it, neither of them had thought any more about it. Perhaps it was having a child on the way that made Alan feel that he needed to pay serious attention to the garden. It had to be a safe place for their child and any subsequent children they might have, for they both agreed that they didn't want only one. They were lucky to have this garden, their house being an end terrace with the extra space that an end house has. A gate at the side front ensured that the road was safely out of harm's way and that extra side bit made their garden wider than their neighbours' gardens.

The garden would be his next project, and the first to get his attention was that shed. Having made that decision, he picked up his roller and resumed his painting.

****

Madge and Len were glad to be home. Charlie, however, was sad to be leaving Castle Farm. He'd had such a great time with the elderly Lord Ron and the vintage car collection and had enjoyed helping on the farm, feeding the chickens that were allowed to roam and going out on a tractor with a farm hand.

"Never mind, love," said Madge comfortably. "You'll find plenty to do around the village now that you're safe from harm. You can enjoy the garden centre, maybe Kenny will let you help him sometimes, or even Lucy, with their huge garden. And maybe Harry will bring you with him when he comes here to help Ron."

Charlie now knew all about Harry and what had happened with his family, and that he came here sometimes to help. He looked forward to meeting Harry and all the other people that Madge and Len talked about.

Dan had come himself to the farm to tell them what had happened and also that he'd arranged for specialist cleaning of their premises.

"I'm sorry that Mollie's killer has died, because he deserved to go to prison, but at least we now have the person behind it all. We're grateful to you, Madge and Len, that you allowed us to lay a trap for Norton-Smyth – not that we knew it was him at the time – and we're grateful to you, Dave and Margaret for once again helping us out by looking after this precious boy and his grandparents."

"We're always happy to help, you know that. What about the two officers who were shot?"

Dan's gave them a sobering look. "I'm afraid Julie Coombs is going to be out of action for some time. She had a pretty similar wound to the one George had, remember? She lost a lot of blood and has been very poorly, but she's in a more stable condition now. When she comes out of hospital, she'll go home to her parents in Worcester to complete her recovery. Thankfully, the other officer only had a flesh wound in his shoulder, the bullet only grazed him. He's being cared for by his parents too."

"Will there be an enquiry as to why he shot Norton-Smyth?" asked Dave.

"I'm afraid so, but as there were witnesses in the form of Ann and Derek, the officers who were impersonating Madge and Len, and Norton-Smyth shot at him first, hopefully it will be okay. He's pretty shaken that he's actually killed a man, by all accounts."

"And what about Pauline Norton-Smyth?"

"Ah well, as yet, I can't tell you until she comes to trial. But there's no doubt she will be found guilty and Dave Ackroyd will be pardoned for that crime. Whether he'll come out of prison straight away, I don't know, because he still committed robbery with assault."

"All something of a mess really, isn't it?" remarked Margaret.

"Yes, but it's being sorted. The important thing is, that young Charlie is safe now and he has found his grandparents. And I'm sure that once his great-uncle Simon has recovered from his injuries, he'll be given a chance to get to know him too. After years of only having his mother as family, and putting up with her associating with all kinds of undesirables, Charlie will now have a secure life with a family who loves him, and that's going to mean a lot to him, I'm sure, although he'll always miss his mother."

Chapter 49

The opportunity to move the shed came sooner than Alan had expected when Fiona's dad had offered to help him after hearing about their plans to improve the garden. Their next-door neighbour, Fred Barratt, offered to help as well. Because of Alan's work commitments, Fred and Fiona's dad, Peter, got together to lay a stand for the shed in its new place. Now, the time had come to actually move it. Fred's son, Fred junior, was also been roped in to help.

"You know, I said to my wife when that shed was put there that it was a strange place to put it – in fact, I even said so to that woman," said Fred senior. "She gave me a right mouthful, she did, and told me to mind my own business. But it seemed strange to me that she put the shed there and then put the house up for sale. Why erect a brand-new shed in a place that you're just about to sell? Wouldn't add to the price, it seemed dead money to me – and in the oddest place. Anyroad, it'll be grand in the new position."

They heaved the shed across the small garden to its new stand and secured it in place.

"Hey, what's that?" Young Fred was staring at the ground where the shed had been. He kicked some earth that had been under the shed and a piece of black plastic surfaced.

"Just a piece of plastic," said Peter and he pulled at it. It didn't come out, so he cleared more earth with his hands. The earth and plastic seemed to be in a round hole and they could now see the top edge of it.

"Could it be an old well or something?"

Fred senior scratched his head. "Now I come to think of it, I believe there is an old well there. Should have a cover on it though."

Alan made a decision. "Let's clear it and it fill it in properly. I don't want any child of mine to have an accident here. Perhaps that's why she put the shed over it."

"Aye, that would actually make sense," said Fred. "You can go home now, lad, we don't need you any more now, thanks for your help." Fred nodded at his son.

"Nah, I want to see if there's anything in that there hole."

So young Fred stayed to watch the men as they cleared out the hole. It soon became clear that the earth on the top was in fact only surface covering. Underneath was a large black plastic bag. At last, they managed to get it out, surprised to find it wasn't that heavy. Peter undid the knot in the top, fearing it might be a dead cat or something. Instead, he lifted out a large, black garment covered with a stain, brown with age.

"Don't touch it!" Alan said. "Don't take anything else out of the bag. Leave it, I'm going to call my boss."

"What do you think it is?" asked Peter.

"I'm not sure, but that looks like blood to me," replied Alan. "And bearing in mind what happened here a few years ago, it could be connected."

An hour later, the bag and its contents had been taken away by Forensics and Alan explained to DCI Weaver how they'd found it. The DCI frowned.

"We made a thorough search of this place at the time of the investigation. It wasn't here then, I'm sure of it."

"Perhaps it's not connected then? Perhaps it's just a bunch of old rags that she used to fill the hole."

"Well, the hole was full of earth when we looked at it and in fact, underneath the bag it's still full of earth."

"Fred, my neighbour here, said he asked her why she put the shed there and told him to mind his own business – isn't that right, Fred?"

"That's right, lad, I did and she did. She wasn't a nice woman, I have to say. We tried to be friendly, me and the missus, but she wouldn't have anything to do with us. A right stuck up madam, she was."

Weaver wondered how many times he'd heard that in the investigation of Harrison's death. Now it seemed, it wouldn't lie down and die. The woman had been arrested with the evidence on Mollie Denton's phone and had been remanded for trial. Could this bag, unearthed from her property, be another piece of evidence?

****

Once back at the headquarters, Weaver received a phone-call from Forensics.

"We've unloaded the bag and it contained an all-enveloping garment that would have covered from head to foot, including the face, and pieces that obviously covered the shoes. But guess what else we've found."

"I'm not into making guesses, Morley, what was in the bag?

"Jewellery. In fact, all the items, except the necklace found at Ackroyd's that were on the list of missing items from the Harrison house."

Weaver whistled. "Oh my, so she staged the robbery and just threw it all away. What does that say about the woman? Do you think it's Harrison's blood on the clothes?"

"Well, of course, that will take a while, but I'm ninety-nine-point-nine percent sure it will be. We will send you a report. And, to answer your question about what does it say about the woman – I'd say it shows she was one very determined person."

"I agree with that verdict. Thanks."

After that call, he picked up the phone and dialled Dan's number. He would find this piece of information very interesting indeed.

A few days later he received the report of the tests on the black garments. It was indeed Stephen Harrison's blood and they'd also identified Pauline Harrison's DNA on the cloth. There was no doubt whatsoever that this was what she'd worn when she had so callously, deliberately and so accurately stuck the knife in her husband's heart.

254

Chapter 50

Simon Denton was spending Christmas in Sutton-on-Wye. In fact, he was living in the village, at Sutton Court.

After the devastating events at the village shop and everything had settled down, Kenny and Len had taken Charlie to visit his uncle in the hospital in Glasgow. Simon had been thrilled to see them and especially that Charlie had recognised him and had shyly hugged him. Although no longer ill, Simon was incapacitated because his shattered leg would take a while to heal and he couldn't use crutches because of his broken arm. He was reliant on being pushed around in a wheel chair.

"They want me to convalesce at a place in Glasgow, but I'd rather be near familiar people," he'd told them.

Kenny had gone to see Cessy and Neil at Sutton Court to see if they had a place there so Simon could convalesce near his great-nephew. The arrangements were made, and two of the carers took the Court's own special vehicle and fetched Simon from Glasgow.

"I'm so grateful to you all," he said. "They were very kind to me in hospital but I'm glad to be out."

"We're happy to have you, Simon," said Cessy. "And young Charlie is welcome here any time he wants."

"That's really kind, thank you. This is a lovely place."

"Thank you. We like it. Now, let me show you to your room."

So, now it was Christmas and Simon was much better. He knew that soon he'd have to return to his home in Plymouth. He was strangely reluctant to do so. Over the few weeks he'd been here, he'd got to know so many people – Lucy, Kenny, Sheila and Tom, Cessy and Neil and all the residents of Sutton Court, Harry and his family and of course Charlie, Madge and Len. Charlie's grandparents felt like family, although they weren't related. Like Charlie, he had immediately seen the likeness to Steve in Len's face. They treated him like family too, coming often to see him. Never in his life had he experienced this, he'd been a loner with pretty much only Clara as any kind of companion since Mollie and Charlie had left. Even before that, he'd never mixed that much, always wrapped up in the stories he wrote. He travelled alone too, and foreigners he'd met held pretty much the same view as his Scottish neighbours, except for the odd one or two people he'd become fairly friendly with. But once he'd left their country, he didn't tend to keep in touch. In fact, he was awful at communication and rarely checked his emails, except for those from his publishing company.

The way of life in such a friendly village really appealed to him and for the first time in his life he considered selling up in Plymouth and moving here. Clara wouldn't be happy about it, but perhaps she could consider moving too? However, she'd lived there all her life and was getting on a bit so it wasn't likely. But he couldn't help following the train of thought he'd begun in the cottage. Now, he didn't want to continue to live his solitary life. Still fairly young, not quite forty, he didn't want to miss out on something better. He had money but apart from his van and his Scottish cottage he'd just stashed it away. But what good was it having money to not use it?

His train of thought was broken by the arrival of Charlie, Madge and Len, followed by Lucy and Ken and their two children. People were arriving ready for the usual Christmas Carol Singing that took place at Sutton Court every Christmas Day. So many villagers gathered here for this annual event. Simon had heard all about it from the residents. It was the high-light of a time that was special for everyone. He'd also heard how the villagers gathered around a huge Christmas tree on the village green on Christmas Eve night to welcome the arrival of the big day. He loved the sound of it and realised that he wanted to be part of it next year.

Christmas had always been a quiet affair for Simon. Clara would cook a chicken and roasties and they would eat it together and then watch television. When Mollie had been with them it had been better but after she'd gone, he lost incentive and didn't even bother to decorate, it was just another day to get through. But here, amongst these elderly people he found joy in the celebrations. The old carols, familiar from his childhood, reminded him of happier times when he and his brother were boys at home with their parents. His mother had made sure that it was a special time for her family. But his parents had gone, as was his brother, and he'd been left with only Mollie as family. He was only ten years older than Mollie, and looking after a young girl was a complete venture in the dark, he'd learned as they went along. She had been the sunshine in his life until she'd left with Charlie. When she came back, she wasn't the same, the light had gone out and he had to deal with it the best he could, while not knowing what had caused the change.

Charlie pressed to his side and he put his arm around the boy. They were already close, and he couldn't bear the thought of being away from him again. His eyes met Len's over the boy's head and a look of mutual understanding passed between them. Charlie was the comfort that both of them had in the loss of their loved ones.

As he listened to the singing and joined in where he could remember the words, Simon knew he'd turned a corner and had to move forward to a new life. He looked at the smiling faces of Lucy, Kenny and the other singers, and smiled back. Along from Lucy there was a young woman with shining red-gold hair. With her was a little boy of about five. When the singing was done, the boy came over to Charlie.

"Hello, Archie," said Charlie. "This is my Uncle Simon."

"Hello," said the little boy, shyly. The woman with the glorious hair came to join them.

"Hello there, Charlie," she said, but her eyes looked at Simon with interest.

"Hi, Flora. This is my Uncle Simon," he repeated. She smiled and Simon's heart did a funny sort of leap.

"Hello, Simon. I'm Archie's mum. He and Charlie are good friends, aren't you?"

257

Simon's throat suddenly felt closed up but he managed a strangled "Pleased to meet you and Archie. Is his dad here too?"

"No, thank goodness. 'Es dead, I'm happy ter say."

"Oh." Then he smiled, "Good – that is, I'm glad it's okay with you that he's dead."

"Believe me, it is. 'E were a bad lot. Glad ter get shot o' 'im, I can tell yer."

"You come from London?"

"Yeah. 'Ow did yer guess?" she grinned. "But we live in the village now. We love it, don't we, Archie?"

The little boy nodded.

"Where d'yer live?"

"Plymouth," he said, and was gratified to see that her shoulders slumped and she looked down.

"Tha's a long way from 'ere."

"It is, but I'm thinking of selling up and moving this way – to be closer to Charlie, you know?" He glanced at his nephew, who returned his look steadily for a moment and then hugged him. Flora smiled at him as he hugged Charlie and he felt his heart do that funny flip again.

"Oh, please come and live here, Uncle Simon. It's lovely, everyone's so nice, and I've got friends here. Oh look – there's Harry and – oh!"

"What's up?" Simon asked him.

"I know that girl."

"Which one?"

"She's with Harry's sister. Oh look, they're coming over!"

The three young people came over to them.

"My friend here wanted to say hello to you, Charlie," said Rowena. The girl beside her smiled at him.

"Hello again. I'm Gloria."

Charlie beamed at her. "Fanks for helping me. I like your name, it's like your hair."

"I met Charlie when he was on his travels. I stopped some kids bullying him," she explained to those around her. "I didn't know who he was then, of course. But I'm glad he's okay now." She ruffled the boy's hair. "See you around, kid."

The two girls wandered off but Harry stopped to chat for a while. Lucy and Kenny came over to chat too, in fact, most of the singers stopped to at least say 'hello'. Flora and Archie slipped away to talk to others. Although he enjoyed the attention, Simon's eyes often lifted to locate Flora elsewhere in the room. It seems she felt it, for her eyes and his often met and she would smile shyly.

Drinks and cakes were handed around and it was a very happy scene. Flora didn't come back to him, because Archie had found a friend he wanted to be with, so she stayed with him. But it was obvious they were aware of each other.

Later, when all was quiet, he allowed himself to think about her and wondered how it would feel to run his fingers through her lustrous hair, to hold her...

Surprised at himself, for he'd met many women on his travels, many dark-skinned beauties that enticed men. He'd been attracted, yes, but had never felt the all-encompassing desire that a few minutes, in fact, just once glance at Flora had produced. And it seemed she was interested in him, too. He thought he wasn't too bad looking, but would he turn out to be too dull for her? She was so lovely that she could have had any man she wanted, he was sure. Would she settle for a dull old writer? That was another thing, she was only about Mollie's age, maybe even younger, and he was in his late thirties and she would think that too old, surely?

His thoughts swirled round and round about Flora. Did he, could he, have a chance with her? He knew nothing about her and yet he wanted her as he'd never wanted any other woman. What on earth was happening to him? For a moment, he envied the quiet, uneventful and completely dull life he'd had, with nothing to complicate things. The attack on him had changed his whole life, the outlook he'd always had. Because of that, he'd come here, and found a family and this wonderful community that he was now burning to remain in. And because of that, all his desires

259

as a man had awakened as if from a hundred years' sleep and in a few short moments he knew he'd move heaven and earth to get himself closer to his heart's desire.

One woman's insane jealousy had robbed him of his beloved Mollie, but, in the strange way that Fate works, it had led to him finding a possible path to a whole new life. And Simon was determined to go all out to get it. After all, didn't he and Charlie both deserve a happy ending?

Chapter 51

The trial of Pauline Norton-Smyth finally took place in April the following year. She was found guilty on the charges of murder, conspiracy to murder and perverting the course of justice, in the case of framing David Ackroyd. Her sentence was heavy, two life sentences for the murders and five years for framing Ackroyd. She would be in prison for about thirty years, maybe a few years less for good behaviour if she was lucky.

She had traced Molly through a private detective and it had been her that had frightened Molly Denton so much by threatening to kill Charlie that the young mother had taken off in the van.

It also transpired that she hadn't known it was her own husband who she'd contracted to kill Molly and find the evidence that Molly had told her she had, thinking it would protect her and her boy, when she'd found her on that visit to Hereford. Charlie hadn't seen the woman because he'd been helping Farmer White at the time, but Molly had seen her.

"I can't understand why she didn't move on then, knowing that she'd been found by Pauline," remarked Kenny, when Dan was telling them about the trial.

"Yes, I've wondered that myself and I guess we'll never know the answer to it. It could be that Eddie's friendship held her here, or she still hoped to find Charlie's grandparents. She told Eddie that she wanted him to stay with them as she didn't think she was a good mother to him. And we know that she did in fact leave him alone a great deal. She'd become an addict and they can become difficult to understand as their thought processes aren't the same as ours," replied Dan. "Mark Norton-Smyth wasn't really a contract killer, but, using a phone not known to his wife, he'd pretended, because he'd known of his wife's intentions. Police found that phone he was using and seen her messages on it. Before he'd died, Mark had given me a statement, confessing all. With all the evidence presented, the jury couldn't help but find the woman guilty of all charges."

"I feel sorry for their two children," said kind hearted Lucy, "What will happen to them?"

"Norton-Smyth's parents have taken charge of them and packed them off to an expensive boarding school," replied Dan.

"Poor kids."

"Yes, it's awful, particularly as none of this needed to happen. It was all because Pauline Norton-Smyth couldn't get over the insane jealousy and hatred of her first husband's lover and child, and even when she'd married a rich man and had a child of her own, it still ate at her. In a way, I feel sorry for Mark Norton-Smyth because he only did what he did because he loved her and wanted her to be able to put it all in the past and feel safe, if only he could have got hold of that phone with the damming evidence. He could easily have had sex with Mollie if he'd wanted and he could have killed her in a much worse way but he drugged her so she wouldn't know. He could have killed Simon Denton but he wasn't by nature a killer and was certainly not a crack shot, or Julie Coombs would certainly be dead. All he wanted was to able live life with a contented wife but by her very nature it wasn't possible. It took a cold and calculated person to stick a knife into exactly the right spot while that person was looking into her eyes, and someone who she was supposed to have loved and still couldn't get over long after, even when she'd achieved everything she wanted. Frankly, I don't know how Mark Norton-Smyth could have loved her as much as he obviously did, but there you are, no accounting for taste."

"Obviously a very dangerous love," commented Lucy.

Kenny put his arm around her. "Yes, I'm glad I have a boring, home-loving wife, whose most excitement comes from cooking dinner for me."

"Boring? Are you saying I'm boring? Where's that knife...?"

He held up his hands to ward her off, with fake alarm in his eyes, grabbed her hand and pulled her to him and kissed her lovingly. "You'll never be boring, my love. You're wonderful, just the way you are."

They all laughed together and Lucy picked up the knife again. "Cake, anyone?"

****

It was Christmas Eve and Simon put his arm around Flora's shoulder and hugged her. Their breath puffed out in mini clouds. A smattering of snow had fallen and enhanced the scene on the village green. A huge Christmas tree, decked with thousands of lights stood tall and proud and around it were gathered many people. They had just attended the Christmas Eve Torchlight service in the village church, led by the Reverend Trevithick and then had filed out of the church and across to the village green to join in with a tradition that was unique to Sutton-on-Wye. When everyone was gathered, they sang 'O Come, All Ye Faithful' and when they'd finished, the vicar put his hands in the air and said "Thank you, Father, for the gift of Your Son." Everyone said "Amen", then he said, "I hope you all have a wonderful Christmas". Everyone clapped and gradually started to leave, shaking hands with the Reverend on their way and wishing him a happy Christmas.

Simon picked up Archie on his shoulders. "Come on, lad, it's time you were in bed, or Santa won't come." Charlie grinned up at his uncle. He'd filled out over the past twelve months and had grown taller. Simon looked at him with pride and gave him a light punch on the shoulder. "Time you were in bed too, Charlie, you look like you're sleep walking."

"It's great, isn't it, Uncle? Mum and me, we never did anything like this."

"Nor did I," answered Simon.

"And nor had we until we came here," added Flora.

"Merry Christmas to you all." Lucy and Kenny had come up to them. On Boxing Day, they were going to Lucy's house for

263

the afternoon. They had all become firm friends over the past twelve months. In fact, Simon didn't know what he would have done without their help.

It had taken three more months after last Christmas for Simon to be fit enough to be able to drive home. Kenny had taken time off and driven Simon up to Dalwhinnie to fetch the caravanette. They'd spent a jolly few hours in the pub with the landlord, filling him in on all that had happened. He was amazed, and waved away Simon's offer of payment for taking care of his vehicle. Simon took Kenny to see his cottage. It had been left in an awful mess, but it didn't take long for Simon to tidy everything back into place.

"This is a wonderful spot, Simon," Kenny stood outside, breathing in the cool spring air.

"It is. I love it here, but it started to get lonely, you know? After Molly left, I bought this place and came here every summer to write but this last time I was here – somehow, it didn't feel quite the same."

"What will you do with it?"

"I'm not sure as yet."

"You should bring Flora here and see what she thinks." Kenny knew that Simon was seeing Flora and was serious about her.

"I will. But I have to sort things out in Plymouth first. Clara isn't going to be happy with me for leaving."

Lucy loaned Simon the bungalow that had belonged to Sam Williams until he and Flora sorted out what they wanted to do. He was grateful to be given that option; he still wasn't sure if Flora would want to be with him.

Having recovered the van and sorted the Scottish cottage, Simon went to Plymouth. He was horrified at the mess there, but as he had to sort everything out ready to move, in some ways it made it easier. Instead of putting everything away in the drawers and cupboards, much went straight into black bags. He decided to keep only a few favourite pieces of furniture, things that had come from his parents' house. The rest he disposed of.

Clara was, as he predicted, unhappy about losing her neighbour but at that time didn't want to move. Instead, she would visit him in Herefordshire at some point.

"It'll be nice to have a holiday, I ain't had one in donkey's years," she said. He had to leave it like that, but decided to keep in close touch. He really was going through a huge life change – and changing his ways – it was about time.

By May, he was living in the bungalow, and his courting of Flora was at full rate. He was delighted that she loved him back and she was warm and loving towards him.

One evening, early in their relationship, she had become serious and said she needed to tell him something. Worried at this, his heart did a tumble. What if she didn't want him? Was she letting him down gently? He couldn't bear it.

He made himself sit quietly and listen to what she had to say, bracing himself for the worst. But instead, she told him about herself and her former life, the things she'd had to do and the dreadful man who had been her husband. Then she hung her head and said "I 'ad ter tell yer about me, cos I've been really bad, done bad things and I've been a pro. Yer won't want me now."

Simon's heart swelled within him. He actually already knew most of it, having asked Kenny about her quite some time ago. He lifted her chin with his finger and said simply, "I already knew."

"You did?"

"Yes. I asked Kenny about you after I saw you at Sutton Court. Now I'm going to tell you something."

Her eyes widened in question.

"I love you. I've loved you since I first saw you Christmas Day and I've not been able to think about anything else except how I can get back to you. You couldn't help what you had to do, you were a slave to that dreadful man, Lucian Avery, and your horrible husband, Jake. We've both had pasts, my love. I had all that dreadful business with Molly and I've lived a life entirely self-contained and selfish, since then. Then I saw you, and everything changed. We are not our pasts; we can put them behind

265

us where they belong and go forward into a new life. We have to get to know each other better and we have time to do that. I have things I must sort out first, like selling my house in Plymouth. Lucy told me that I can live here until things are sorted properly. But I'm hoping our future will be together, Flora. I don't think I can live without you now."

He kissed her tenderly and her arms went around him and the kiss deepened. Simon felt his heart would surely burst, he was so happy. When they surfaced again, Flora's face was flushed, eyes big with love and desire. Simon had never seen any woman look at him that way before.

"What about Archie?" she finally managed to ask. "He's another man's kid."

"He can't help that, can he? He's great, and he needs a dad. Perhaps I can become his dad legally. Actually, I was thinking of adopting Charlie. What would you feel about that?"

"I think that would be great, if that's what he wants. He and Archie are already friends. What would Madge and Len say, do you think?"

"I don't know. I do know that they don't find it easy to have Charlie there as they are always so busy with the shop. If he lived with us, they could be grandparents instead, having him on Sundays when they're free to enjoy him. We'd have to discuss it with them of course. In any case, when I'm living here full time, I'll be transporting him to school for them and helping in other ways. Madge and Len are great but there's a limit to what they can do."

"Yes, it's a lot for them. I sometimes have Charlie round at my place after school and sometimes he goes to Netta's because the girls help him with his homework. Rowena's friend Gloria is particularly good with him."

"Yes, there is a lot to sort out. But we have so much to look forward to."

In the summer, he'd taken Flora, Archie and Charlie to the cottage in Scotland. It was a squash, more like camping out because the boys had to sleep in sleeping bags on the floor. They loved it so Simon applied for planning permission to extend the cottage to make room for them all. It was to become the family's favourite place for a holiday and Simon would also let it out to others that they knew.

Simon received a good price for his house in Plymouth and was able to buy a four bedroomed house in the village, on the new estate, in fact, next door to Stephanie and Alex's house. They were married in September, as Simon couldn't wait to make sure Flora was his for always. The village gave them a wonderful reception in true Sutton-on-Wye style. Clara came to the wedding and also fell in love with the village. Finally seeing no point in staying in Plymouth, and being offered Lucy's bungalow on a permanent basis, she left her old home with barely a backward glance.

****

Now, as Simon, Flora, and Charlie turned to leave their spot by the huge Christmas tree, Clara approached them, holding onto the arm of a tall and sprightly gentleman with a fine head of white hair and bright blue eyes.

"Merry Christmas, you four," she called. "Have you met Paul? He's going to take me home in his car, I'm frozen to the marrow. But it was lovely, wasn't it? I'm glad you persuaded me to come, Simon. See you tomorrow – or rather, later today, if I can bring myself to leave my warm bed. Come on, Paul, I can hear it calling me. Cheerio."

They followed the couple to the road where their own car was parked.

"Who was that with Clara?" he asked Flora.

"Oh, that's Paul Clements, 'e's a solicitor. 'E's a lovely man, he 'elped me a lot when I 'ad me trouble."

"A solicitor, eh? That's a big leap from a master criminal," laughed Simon.

"Yep. From what Lucy told me, he was a great friend of her Aunt Bea and was really upset when she died and has been lonely since."

"Well, looks like he might have found an end to that!" Simon laughed.

"Good luck to 'em, that's all I can say. If she makes him 'appy, what more can they want?"

Simon stood up from depositing Archie in the car and caught hold of Flora, standing beside him.

"Well my love, if they find half the happiness you've brought to me, they will do just fine." He kissed her tenderly, hugging her as close to him as he could. "Happy first Christmas together, my darling."

"Happy first Christmas," she replied, as she nuzzled his lips. "And may we have many more."

"Are you two at it again?" came a disgusted voice from the car. "Put her down, Uncle Simon, we need to get home so we can do Christmas."

Simon let her go with a last quick kiss, helped her into the car and hurried around to the driver's side. He started it up and drove the relatively short distance back to their new home.

When he pulled into the drive, he sat for a moment to look at it. It represented his new life, a life in which was everything he held dear. Through one woman's insane jealously, he had found all that he never dreamed he'd have. Hateful woman she might be and was now having an uncomfortable life in prison, but in that moment, he was thankful to her – or rather, to the tireless investigations of Dan Cooke.

His shiny camper-van was parked on the hard-standing beside the house. Simon thought briefly of 'Fred', which was now being lovingly renovated by Dave Blackwood and would become part of the Castle Farm Collection, with the proviso that Simon could use it, should he ever want to. Dave was thrilled to have the 1970s vintage VW to add to his collection. Much as he loved the camper-van, Simon doubted he'd use it again, for he wanted the past to stay where it belonged.

He opened the door of the house and they all crowded in, glad to be out of the cold.

"Right, last one in bed does tomorrow's washing up!" he called. Both boys screeched and ran for the stairs.

Simon and Flora laughed at them. Then, after they'd hung up their coats and scarves, they joined hands and slowly climbed the stairs together.

I hope you enjoyed this story. If you would like to help me, please leave a review on Amazon. It doesn't need to be a book – a few words will do. Every review counts. Oh, and please tell your friends! Thank you.

Other Books by Jeanette Taylor Ford:

Rosa, a ghostly psychological thriller. Elizabeth (Izzy) has to run from an all-consuming affair and comes to manage her grandfather's estate in Norfolk. But all is not well at Longdene Hall, and Izzy soon finds herself in a terrifying situation. Who can she trust?

Bell of Warning, a haunting historical novella. Jeanie loves her hometown of Cromer. She also has the 'Gift' and begins to 'see' the mysterious Kendra, who once lived in the village of Shipden, now sunk into the sea off Cromer's coast and to hear the legendary warning bell of Shipden's church, which rings out when there is danger. Can Jeanie find out what it all means and can she save her neighbours from impending doom?

The Sixpenny Tiger, a touching story of a boy brought up in a children's home and the young woman who loves him. Together they discover the true meaning and power of forgiveness.

The Castle Glas Trilogy:
The Hiraeth – how Shelly, abandoned as a baby, finds her family, aided by two modern-day witches, a ghost and a wonderful Welsh castle.
Bronwen's Revenge – continuing the story of Shelly and her family's fight against her Aunt Bronwen, now a vengeful ghost
Yr Aberth, (The Sacrifice) More adventures with Shelly, including the final banishment of Bronwen.

The River View Series: (Cosy Crime)

Aunt Bea's Legacy – Introducing Lucy, her beautiful house, River View, and the village of Sutton-on-Wye. Under the strange conditions of Aunt Bea's will, Lucy comes to live at River View. But ghostly footsteps and other weird happenings disturb the peaceful atmosphere. Is the house haunted, or is something else behind them?

By the Gate – D.I. Cooke and D.S. Grant investigate a seventy-year-old murder when human remains are found in one of Lucy's fields.

Fear Has Long Fingers – a new family comes to Sutton-on-Wye which brings great danger for another resident. Can our two detectives find the kidnapped teenagers and save the woman snatched by a ruthless underworld criminal and his gang?

For Children:

Robin's Ring – Robin finds a magic ring, but can he and his cousin Oliver find the other Items of Power?

Robin's Dragon – further adventures with Robin and Oliver. The wicked Bowen the Black has kidnapped Edric's daughter, Princess Adriana. Can the boys, with an exciting helper, find her and bring her home safely?

Robin...Who? (Due to be published in 2020). Robin and Oliver, helped by Oliver's sister Marion, seek to obtain a magic bowl needed to save the Princess Adriana

Jeanette Taylor Ford is a retired teaching assistant. She grew up in Cromer, Norfolk and moved to Hereford with her parents when she was seventeen. Her love of writing began when she was a child of only nine or ten. When young, her ambition was to be a journalist but life took her in another direction and her life's work has been with children – firstly as a nursery assistant in a children's home, and later in education. In between, she raised her own six children and she now has eight grandchildren and two beautiful great-grandchildren.

Jeanette took up writing again in 2010; she reasoned that she would need something to do with retirement looming, although as a member of the Church of Jesus Christ of Latter Day Saints she is kept busy. She lives with her husband Tony, a retired teacher and headmaster, and two annoying cats, Mindy and Suzie, in Derbyshire, England.

Printed in Great Britain
by Amazon

43465265R00155